Did you wonder where I was
when you looked up at the stars?
I was there beside you, listening to you sing.
Never forget that dreams are real, my love,
a beginning for our new life,
our destined awakening in the sun!

DREAMER

ON THE

MOUNTAIN

PROLOGUE

Candelaria rose early in the morning before dawn, before the narrow slice of sunlight peeked above the hills to the south. Dressing in her husband's clothes, she was reminded of him as she tucked in his old shirt and fastened his old leather belt. He was gone, up there in heaven with her son and her parents, her sister, and all her grandparents. She was not alone, though she felt the quiet at times. Her younger cousin, Aurelia, had slept elsewhere the night before, about which Candelaria tried not to think. Even so, the creaking of the floorboards underfoot crept into her thoughts and she became annoyed.

The room was cold. Her breath blew out in fog as she struck a match to light the oven. It soon ignited and began heating the kitchen. Taking a moment to warm herself, she sighed and smiled in contentment. Putting aside her frustrations, she made a pot of coffee, scrambled an egg or two, and turned off the oven. That was all she needed to do before she left for work in the orchards.

Walking in the early morning mist, she spotted a coyote crossing the road ahead of her. "One day," she mused aloud, though only in a whisper, "I will have grandchildren and I will tell them a story about this coyote, just like my grandmother used to tell me stories." Further musing as she walked along, scanning the tall, dry weeds and grasses along the road, she ventured, "Maybe I will become one of the Grandmothers, a Dreamer, a Storyteller."

She continued whispering, delighting in the mystery, speaking its secrets aloud as though telling a story to some unknown, yet known, other person. "Years from now," she said, "after I am gone, you may come to Pine Valley. Walk the old roads where the old ways yet live. Listen to the wind. A feeling may come over you, a sense of awareness as your heart opens to receive the wisdom being offered. When that happens, you will know, because you will be filled with love and peace. You will know the essence of Pine Valley, just a place in the mountains, but it is a very special place. It is a dream, carried in the heart and nurtured in the soul. It is where I live, the home of my ancestors."

CHAPTER ONE

Robert Cadwallader stood on the outside of life as if he were a ghost. The pants and collared shirts he wore were frayed at the cuffs and had holes in them, visibly tattered, not unlike his self-esteem. His very mind was frayed and tattered, full of holes he tried to fill with whiskey, of which there was never enough. The holes in his mind, and in his soul deep down, were an abyss and, therefore, bottomless.

Sitting at his favorite table at the soon-to-be-abandoned old roadhouse, he held a glass in one hand and a bottle in the other. While sipping his drink, he peeled away the bottle's label. Its bright, golden hope slowly became as tattered and torn as his broken soul.

Klucky stood at his post behind the bar, looking toward the quiet man, concerned. It was too early for a bottle of Scotch. He knew Robert and he knew what the war had done to a lot of men. Klucky figured, since Robert was there at his place, there was no need to intervene.

"He's safe," Klucky whispered to himself. "He's among friends."

Robert was a good-looking man when he was young, like a rugged Jack London, energetic, with dark brown, curly hair. He had dark eyes and thick eyebrows. He thrilled at the prospect of waking up each morning. Heading out the door, he looked to see what others were doing, maybe working on a car, fixing a tractor, or scavenging old junk from the dump. He loved working with his hands, to hold on to something and examine it, then know how it worked and how to fix it.

Within himself were years of living amongst a people who all lived for the now. Steeped in their souls and the blood in their veins dwelled a history, a heritage back across the water to a land called Wales. He dreamed of it, like he was a fantastic bird that could fly over those cold northern seas and live to tell about it. The rockiness, the green, the waves crashing upon the steep and craggy shoreline in a thunderous leap, and women bundled in heavy sweaters, woolen scarves, and high woolen socks—leastways, that was how he dreamed it, though never knew it for himself, except within his dreams.

His great-grandfather, Cedric Cadwallader, had immigrated to America from Wales. Cedric brought across the water with him, the rich, musical tradition within which Robert had grown. Continuing until late at night, the songs would be sung. The eyes of their listeners were enlivened as if seeing through fog across memory and time to the land of their ancestors. The music filled Robert's life. The fiddle and the songs faded over the years, but, for Robert, the words still needed to be honored. He sang them softly under his breath while in Klucky's, but they came out in broken whispers, like his thoughts, too faint and raspy. One song was a long ballad about warriors and kings and a bloody battle.

He sang, "Alone, he strode across the land in sadness and in grief. And though he died so long ago, he yet may still be seen."

Robert thought of himself as such a man, one who could be seen, but who had died long ago.

•   •   •

In the semi-darkness, Robert gradually succumbed to his final hour, for he would soon be driven to his trailer home, never to reach the door. He peered toward the plate-glass window across the room. Sounds grew distant...a car door slamming shut, gritty dirt kicking up as tires peeled away in a hurry...and voices fading. The square of glass revealed a land of green instead of the sunlit, wan sort of day outdoors. His youth called to him, a friend in need beckoned, and he gave himself to it. The joy of saints, smiled upon by the grace of God, shining His light on them in their dismal, barren cell, became a reality. It was in Pine Way and he was walking to a friend's house.

The year was 1926. He was at the McGrew's, neighbors of the Cadwallader's, with the Walker's house between the two. Smiling, Clarence McGrew stepped out of his family's garage, wearing a greasy undershirt and tan pants that hung low on his skinny body. His blond hair was a thick shock of curls in sweaty disarray.

"Bobby! Good to see you!" he said. He wiped his hands with a rag and shook Robert's hand.

Robert returned his friend's smile and said, "Hi, Clancy! Heard you were having some car trouble."

Clarence went back into the garage and, placing his hands on the fender of his Model T, peered into the engine. Robert remained where he was, not moving. Everywhere he looked, he saw green, green trees, green grass, green bushes. A faintness came over him and he reeled, then fell to the ground, asleep. He dreamed of a glaring, piercing light and a pretty girl's smiling face, Charity Walker's, the girl next door.

Clarence could bring Robert out of his spells, but the war that befell the nation in the early 1940s would not be so accommodating. Doctors gave him something that caused other problems. The nightmarish experience of the battlefield grew more surreal. Thankfully, someone bought him a ticket home, another way of saying he received a medical discharge. Arriving home in Edenville, he was supposed to follow up with a visit to a doctor over at the vet's office, which he did, but what they gave him was worse. He was unable to work. His wife needed him, his daughter needed him, and he needed a way out, something to relieve him of his troubles.

Robert's brother-in-law, Prosperous "Russ" Walker, never liked him. Well, Robert never liked Russ, either. However, it was one of Russ's friends who showed Robert the way out. They were making their own whiskey back in the hills, near a town called Laketon. Clarence strongly advised Robert to stay away from them, but Robert refused to listen. He went to Laketon regularly, getting drunk at their make-do tavern. It was a corrugated tin outbuilding with a heavy plank laid across a couple of tall rounds of wood. Customers sat across from their self-appointed bartender. They welcomed Robert but soon began to call him Caddie, like Russ did.

Lucy Shoseegan, a native woman, was living in Laketon. Not long after Robert first appeared, she heard about his sudden bouts of sleepiness. She knew him and his family from her time living in Pine Way. Everyone in Laketon witnessed their friend falling down asleep, but it was Lucy who told them to bring him to her house whenever it happened. Her house was a plywood shack of sorts, scraps pieced together in front of a log cabin. She used the dirt floor cabin to house her goats and chickens while she lived in the shed-like structure out front. Cobwebs, fallen branches, and leaves decorated the ramshackle dwelling as it disintegrated into the rest of the forest. When friends brought Robert over, they dumped him on the floor, which was a carpet remnant thrown on top of a sheet of plywood. She watched him and sang over him, wondering, to what purpose could The Man Upstairs have for a person like Robert Cadwallader? She soon learned when he awoke and told her what he saw.

"A golden chariot up in the clouds, driven by a white-haired man in a fury, determined to send an important message to the gods of Man lost in their struggle merely to exist," was what he said.

From that time on, Robert was welcome and visited often. Laketon, with its irregular inhabitants, was the only place where no one looked down on him, maybe because they knew what that felt like. Lucy told everyone what Robert's real name was in her native language, which meant, "Dreaming Man." She said he was like the condor, once spotted soaring high above and gathered on the ground, feasting on the carcasses of elk. Her people believed the condor flew between worlds, drawing along with it knowledge that connected the two worlds and made them One, to those who knew how to listen.

She said, "This man has a gift."

So, whenever an episode struck, someone would ask their ragged-soul oracle, "What did you see, Dreaming Man?"

Everyone would gather around to listen as Robert told them something like, "I dreamed of a valley where all the People returned to live. They came to live in houses, just like the townsfolk. And they grew plants all around that had healing powers for the sick and for the weary. They sang their songs once again, the smoke of the sacred plants mingling in cleansing and healing, and in a celebration of renewal."

•   •   •

Robert returned to the present as the remembrance faded. He wanted to go home but was too drunk.

Klucky wished he could turn back the clock. He wiped down the bar, wondering why he bothered. The roadhouse was condemned. He tried to keep it going, getting away with it as long as he could. He needed the money, so much so, he considered burning the place down to collect on the insurance. It was too late for that. The notice came, the sign tacked out front. "Killed my business," he told everyone who still showed up and were asked to come around to the back door.

"Well," he spoke to the unconscious man, "we better get you home."

Klucky telephoned someone to come get his friend. After a while, a man came walking up from town and, together, they carried Robert out to the car. They laid him on the back seat and the man sat behind the wheel to drive Robert home. After the car departed down the highway, Klucky experienced a sense of finality regarding the situation. He returned inside and flipped the "open" sign around, so it would read, "closed." Accepting defeat, he gathered what few items of value he kept around the place, loaded them into the trunk of his Pontiac, locked up the roadhouse, and drove homeward.

"I guess I'm retired now," he said.

•   •   •

Left in his car to sleep it off, Robert soon awoke. The car was so hot, he could barely breathe. He sat up and opened the door. Once the spinning settled down, he stepped outside and vomited in front of his trailer. Staggering, he tried to climb the steps, when the hunters descended, his stalkers, the gunmen for his blood and the money in his pockets, he assumed. However, they were not after his money, only his silence, for Robert Cadwallader talked too much and knew even more. The man who wanted him dead had warned him. Robert told the man something so eerie, yet so true, that the man ordered him killed, as if that would change the man's ill fate.

What Robert had said was, "I dreamed of you. I saw you in prison and the guard was a woman you knew. She said, 'I'm on the outside, remember? I can tell anyone anything I want to and you can't do a damned thing about it.' That's what I dreamed."

No one saw the men come for him and put him in their car. They drove him around town before shooting him point blank, executing him in an alley, then leaving him where he dropped. Dreaming Man, as Lucy Shoseegan had called him, flew like the condor to the land of his dreams, where he awoke, at last, for good.

CHAPTER TWO

Lucy Shoseegan's mother said, when the gold strike happened, people came from everywhere. It was as if someone got a stick and dug up an ant's nest. People were crawling out of the earth like a swarm, furiously scrambling and biting. Such was the unthinking swarm that came digging some more, even blasting the mountainsides with torrents of water and tearing down the bare earth. The ants had done it to themselves, Lucy's mother said. They had destroyed their own nest and blamed everyone else for it when the flooding happened and the earth began to run. No trees were left to capture the water and protect the land from washing away. The fires came when their ramshackle mining camps caught ablaze and burned everything to the ground. The military came and drove out the native people who were there long before the newcomers. Native children were kidnapped into slavery. Villages were burned. Anyone who dared to fight the onslaught were shot or hung. Eventually, outright massacre of native peoples ruled the day, driving any survivors into hiding. It was incomprehensible, the level of hatred, greed, and destructiveness to which the newcomers rose, justifying their actions by the value of the land they claimed as their own and the treasured prize they sought.

Lucy had heard about her mother from a relative who told her the stories. That woman became more like a mother as the stories of Lucy's real mother became a dream. After several years, it was all a dream. Hearing the women talk about Pine Valley, sharing what they remembered and envisioning the day they would walk upon the valley floor once more, taught Lucy a great lesson. She was impressed by their joy at the prospect of returning home. To her, it was a vision of peace, a place where there was plenty to eat and all were welcome, where they would stay and grow old, watching their grandchildren play. So often did they talk about it, that it seemed as if their very words went up to the sky, carried aloft on the wind, traveling to all those who sought such a place in which to live.

Lucy was only a girl, but she was taught everything she needed to know about plants, how to use them and how to propagate each one for a later harvest or a healthier crop. She learned the songs that spoke to the earth as she carefully sowed the seeds for the coming year. While singing, she collected plants for medicine and gave offerings to the sun, the moon, and the stars. She was taught songs for opening the sacred doorway to the land of the ancestors when someone died. Singing would protect and guide their spirit to the land and life beyond, she was told.

Her life in the mountains was preparing her for her people's return to Pine Valley. Their first task: collecting the dead from the massacre that drove them from their beloved homeland.

Entering the valley, Lucy heard the massacre taking place, believing it was the memory of when she had experienced it as a small child. What she was hearing, were the disembodied screams of those who were chased down and murdered years before. She could see flashes of fleeing images, people running pell mell between the trees. Her task of guiding spirits home would not be an easy one, she realized, for many of the dead were caught between the land of the living and that of the departed. Dwelling in shadowy forms, they suffered in a dark place of trauma and horror.

Everyone took turns recounting what happened during the massacre as they slowly made their way across the valley floor. Walking beside her teacher, Lucy no longer knew past from present, or present from future. It was one story she was experiencing, seeing herself as the small child she was when the massacre had taken place, and as the old woman she would become one day.

Her teacher took her hand and, referring to the ghost-like images all around, asked, "Can you see them, Lucy?"

Looking up at the woman's solemn, haunted visage, Lucy replied, "I am there with them now."

Crossing the valley floor, the people combed the area for any sign of their loved ones' remains upon which the great bears and the wolves had surely grown fat. Much wailing and grieving took place, especially when one woman found her husband's deerskin pouch she had made for him. The bones they found, she knew were his. Once all the dead they could find were gathered, the remains were taken to a special place to honor them in ceremony.

Afterward, mention was made that settlers were seen passing through their valley, which necessitated the use of spiritual protectors. Lucy's people had a small village in a secluded place away from any trails, especially the well-traveled Emigrant Trail. The burial and cremation ground was to the south. It was unmarked to avoid detection by strangers. The people called upon spirits to guard the site from intrusion and to protect their new village, to keep it secret.

When Berto Mendoza and Joaquin Muscio first arrived, Lucy told her father that strangers had come to Pine Valley. Investigating the matter, he discovered the two cowboy miners with their mining pans. They were dipping them in the water, which was swirled around in the pans. Lucy's father, Hector Shoseegan, feared that he and his people might have to leave again, most likely for good. He approached the two men, the other brown-skinned people like those he had met on the ranchos, at the missions, and in the pueblos, and spoke to them in Spanish with what few words he knew.

"Hola!" Hector called out to them.

He stepped carefully down the embankment, sliding in the soft, powdery dirt, trying not to lose his balance on loosened rocks. He had an injury from the massacre that left one leg weak, which the other men noticed.

"Hola!" they replied. Setting their pans aside, each of them stood and smiled broadly.

Hector wore a double-holstered gun belt with two revolvers. He scanned the area to find one lone rifle propped against a boulder. His fellow tribesmen would have thought him careless to approach strangers and begin a conversation with them. But Hector believed they were harmless, seeing them behaving in a friendly manner instead of reaching for the rifle.

Berto asked, "Cómo estás?"

Hector merely shrugged and said, "Hmph. Bien."

Hector was a much stronger man before the massacre. Although still in his thirties, he had seen enough death to last him many lifetimes. Letting his guard down, he sat on a rock and rubbed his leg, trying to recall more words in Spanish.

Pointing to himself, he said, "Nombre, Hector."

Still grinning, Berto pointed to himself and said, "Behr-to," then pointed to his companion, saying, "Kee-no."

Hector nodded, greeting each one again. "Hola, Berto. Hola, Quino," he said.

He motioned to them to follow him. Joaquin was unsure of what to do and looked at Berto. His friend left with Hector without question. Joaquin wondered what the Indian could want with them. Hastily stowing away their belongings beneath some bushes by the creek, he picked up his rifle and went with them.

"Berto!" Joaquin called to his friend in a loud whisper. "Berto!" He was struggling to climb up the embankment. "Estás loco?" he asked.

Hector knew what Joaquin had said and answered, "Sí, mi amigo!" Together, Hector and Berto laughed at their worried and upset friend. Hector added in his own language, "Don't worry. I won't eat you." He laughed some more.

Joaquin asked Berto what Hector had said, but Berto only shrugged, shaking his head at Joaquin's needless worry. Berto had understood Hector's true intentions, that he only wanted their friendship.

Hector took them to his village, which so alarmed some of his people that they, soon thereafter, retreated to their mountain refuge. Joaquin spotted Lucy and was instantly in love with her. Berto showed interest in the shelters Hector's family had made and the plants they had collected and were drying, especially the food being prepared.

After visiting the village, Hector took them to the burial and cremation site, which was unusual. The two men stood by and watched Hector pick up a branch from the ground, plant it upright in the small clearing, and look up toward the sky, closing his eyes.

Joaquin asked Berto, "What do you think he's doing?"

Berto answered by going up to Hector, placing a hand on his back to console him and bowing his head in prayer. Joaquin followed suit. It was as Hector hoped it would be, because he liked the two men, his new friends, and wanted to remain in the valley.

The two Mexican men were around eighteen years of age. They also saw in the older man a good friend. Joaquin visited Hector every day and Berto built their mining shack in much the same fashion as the tribe's bark plank huts, but with his own added touches. When the cabin was finished, it had one room, one door, and one window overlooking the valley and their mining claim. However, Berto continued to embellish upon his humble creation, much to his friend's annoyance.

Joaquin criticized Berto one day. "You are like an old woman," he said, "always fussing about the camp and singing, singing, singing! I can hardly stand it anymore!"

Berto and Joaquin were getting on each other's nerves, especially since Berto paid special attention to Lucy and recited poetry to her. On their last day together, Joaquin sat by the campfire cleaning his rifle and became disgusted. Berto was singing while arranging various cuttings of plants on a large, flat rock. Joaquin was incredulous, wondering what Berto would do next.

He yelled, "That's it! I'm not going to witness this any longer! You are becoming a woman! Next, you'll be wearing a dress and telling me to bathe!"

He picked up his rifle and his few belongings, his bedroll and jacket, and prepared to leave. Everything was tucked away in his saddle bags, with his bedroll and jacket strapped behind his saddle, his rifle in the scabbard alongside. Mounting his horse, he flung out one last comment to his disappointing friend.

"You can sing yourself to death, for all I care! I'm going hunting, my friend!" he said.

Berto knew what that meant. Joaquin would be gone, possibly for good. The days of sharing their quiet campsite were over. Berto grew lonely and, as more settlers came to live in the peaceful valley of pines, he retreated to his rustic life on the mountain. He spent less time mining and more time with Lucy. Eventually, they were married and she came to live with him. The two peaceful and simple souls were like children to all who saw them. Yet, the wisdom they carried in their love told of sages who wandered the barren escarpments of the world's tallest mountains.

• • •

The rest of Lucy's people left the valley, returning to their old encampment in the mountainous backcountry. She and Berto joined them. Their children and a few of their grandchildren paid regular visits. Their youngest son, Manuel, moved there with his new bride, and they had children.

Manuel, whom everyone called, "Manny," built a still for making his own whiskey. He handed down his know-how to his son, Aurelio, though some called it his "no-good." Manuel died, along with his wife, leaving their son to continue working the still and selling whiskey. Manuel was friends with Jiminy Walker and, later, Jiminy's son, Russ. Through his association with these men, Aurelio eventually met Robert Cadwallader, the Dreaming Man of Pine Valley. Aurelio befriended Robert. Robert helped with the still and Aurelio helped Robert to share his dreams, telling him they were a gift from God. Robert's other friend was Candelaria Hart's brother, Joaquin Mendoza. Robert and Joaquin were close friends throughout their lives and worked together at the county hospital as janitors.

While Aurelio Mendoza was arrested for distilling his own moonshine, Robert Cadwallader never stopped imbibing the drink for which he had an unquenchable thirst. His health gradually deteriorated. He checked himself into Spring Hill Residence & Infirmary in Edenville to sober up and restore his health. His co-workers and supervisors encouraged him to do so before he lost his job. Although his sobriety was short-lived, it kept him alive a while longer. Also, the time in the rest home sheltered him from The Big Bust in Laketon that shut down moonshining and the ramshackle tavern for good. Lucy was very old by then, but her dream for the valley continued to be held in her heart. She felt it gently nudging a younger generation of dreamers to awaken and carry the dream forward long after she was gone.

CHAPTER THREE

After her father sobered up, Sylvia visited the house on Fig Tree Lane where her earliest childhood memories were made. Her husband, Forty, was outside talking with her father, who had placed the house up for sale. It was nearly empty, but she wanted to explore it one last time. The rooms appeared much smaller than she remembered, though they sounded cavernous. Every step she took on the crackling old linoleum and warped wooden flooring echoed against the walls. Memories eluded her search, which left her feeling disappointed.

Returning outdoors, she held a few of her mother's dresses draped over one arm. An awful mildew odor arose the moment she thought she saw her mother standing in the kitchen. It gave her a headache. When she stepped across the threshold into the setting sun, the faint apparition called to her. Raising her hand to shade her eyes from the glare, she carefully went down the two concrete steps. Turning to look back, she saw only shadows. The sun was so bright upon her eyes, she could no longer make out anything inside the house. Even so, she knew her mother was there, tied to the house where they no longer lived. It was Sylvia's childhood home, yet it held no meaning for her. Her feelings about the place remained distant and as faint as the presence of a woman who had died years before that day.

Robert knew his daughter had seen what he had witnessed many times. He could no longer bear the sight, so he placed the house up for sale. Despite the eeriness of the subject, before Forty and Sylvia got in their car to leave, Robert told her what was on his mind, as well as in his heart.

He said, "I know it may have seemed like your mother didn't care about you, but she loved you in her own way."

Sylvia felt she might cry, so she mentally repeated a childhood reminder, "I'm not sad and I'm not sorry," which helped.

Her father embraced her, saying, "Your mother's needin ' your forgiveness, daughter. I think that's why she's still here."

Sylvia turned away as though forgetful of the moment and placed the dresses on the back seat of the car. Ignoring her father, she sat on the front seat, which signaled to Forty it was time to go, a familiar ploy of hers she used to escape uncomfortable situations.

"Goodbye! I love you!" Sylvia said to her father.

Dumbfounded, Robert shook his head, but returned the sentiment. "I love you, too," he said.

Though Sylvia's mind refused to acknowledge anything upsetting, the truth had left its imprint upon her heart. A scene delicately traced would re-surface one day, that of her father raising his arm to wave goodbye as she and Forty drove home.

•   •   •

Patty McGrew and her only child, Dottie, were among Sylvia's nearest relatives. They enjoyed a higher social standing in the community than that which Sylvia and her mother belonged. After the death of her mother, when she went to live with Aunt Justice, Sylvia's own social standing received a boost. She wore the best dresses, which Justice had made, and had her hair done in the latest styles by her Aunt Patty. The annual county fair provided an opportunity for Justice to parade her pretty niece before friends. Church provided the incentive to keep the attractive child on the straight and narrow. Sylvia's rambling Uncle Russ made occasional appearances, though had little to do with the family Sylvia knew—at least, the family she thought she knew.

Her grandfather, Jiminy Walker, was nicknamed, "Cricket," like Jiminy Cricket. But, unlike the dapper cartoon character, Jiminy was rough around the edges, like his hands from working in the orchards and driving tractor. He was often mistaken for a hobo, such was his lack of personal care, more like a vagabond who rode the rails, than a husband and father of four. His only serious flaw was his attraction to nighttime escapades, for which his son, Russ, developed a fondness. Running whiskey, then guns during Prohibition, tied in to all sorts of backroom and backwoods dealings. Both father and son were drawn to the lure of the chase, the thrill of secrecy, and the promise of it paying off big.

Jiminy's wife, Char Lee Rosebud, was from the same tribe that used to live in Pine Valley. It was through Char Lee that

Charity and Sylvia got their black hair and smoky-gray eyes. Char Lee was never the beauty her daughter and granddaughter had become in adulthood. Yet, her eyes were striking, lending her an air of mysterious intensity. She carried herself two feet planted firmly on the ground, one ear to the wind, and with eyes that saw far beyond the realm of man.

Jiminy wound up in prison during the war, so Char Lee packed up and went back to Laketon, where she was born. She left her grown children behind under her eldest daughter's care, which pleased Justice. Russ was on his own, or, as Char Lee said, "on his own recognizance." It was Justice, Patience, whom everyone called, "Patty," and Charity who were then left residing in Edenville. Like a dutiful mother, Justice took to checking in on her two younger sisters, both married with young girls to look after, Dottie and Sylvia. Russ had no one. He routinely visited their most recent family home in Edenville to mooch a free meal.

Sylvia was fond of her Uncle Russ. She would sit at the kitchen table to watch her aunt and uncle talk to one another until Justice shooed her out the door. The young girl usually hid around the corner of the house after that, waiting by the porch for him to come back outside. Curious about his friends who made infrequent appearances, she watched closely for any sign of them. They sometimes waited outside on the porch or in a car parked further down the road.

It was understood that Russ and his friends were about as welcome as larder ants or lice, but Justice allowed it, being in charge, more like a prison matron on the outside who bought none of his guff. Russ dared not say a word against her. He was a skinny one, wore thrift store clothes, like his father, which always needed washing or mending whenever he paid her a visit, Justice noticed. She washed his clothes and patched them. She fed him and let him bathe at her house before sending him on his way with a sack lunch packed full, like some bum who had come begging at her doorstep.

With sack in hand and placing his hat on his head, he thanked his sister for the trouble. "Thankee, Sister. You're a peach," he would say. Leaning forward, he would give her a smooth, freshly shaven and cologne-sprinkled peck on the cheek. Out the door he would go, mumbling, "gonna get a job," while looking far off, "waitin' to hear from someone about it." He would light a hand-rolled cigarette made from the leavings in cigarette butts he stealthily collected off the ground while remarking, "People ought not to be so wasteful. Plenty of tobacky left in these." No one in town paid any attention to him. Russ was more like a drift of smoke on the wind. You could always smell him coming, but then he would be gone, having drifted on his way.

He never changed. Though his short hair eventually grayed, he remained skinny, often seen wearing threadbare, brown work pants and work jacket, with a brown plaid shirt. He rarely shaved. His face was in a perpetual, stubbled, bewhiskered state. His skinny face grew drawn and sallow with age. His eyes that never looked at those he spoke to, were always into his thoughts and his schemes.

In the early 1950s, Russ landed in prison on two counts. He got into a big pile of trouble, making counterfeit money. While they had him, they learned he was also connected to the illegal whiskey distilling venture up at Laketon. By that time, prison became his permanent home. His father had died in prison, being upwards of eighty-plus years. Russ joined his father in The Big House Upstairs around 1960. The walls of his prison cell were covered in ink drawings he tirelessly, nearly obsessively penned, images of dragons and craggy mountaintops, castles and armored knights on horseback, running down the mythic roadways of his restless mind.

Russ physically harmed no one and rarely had an unkind word for a single soul. He simply had to do things he ought not to do, often remarking on it to the local deputy sheriff, who jokingly referred to him as, "Slippery Sam."

The deputy often said, "He's such a likable fella, always has such interesting things to say. Almost hate to lock him up." That was his undoing.

Russ would apologize and offer an explanation. "It's just who I am," he would say. "Sometimes the knight is the one who steals the crown from its rightful owner, the poor man, the pitiful stable boy with not a penny or a farthing to his name."

Slipping from sight, it would take a week, a month, or a year before the deputy caught him again.

Russ had taken after his dad, both in deed and in looks. Justice favored her mother but had fair skin and considerably more meat on her bones. She seemed to have been born with gray hair. Patty and Justice looked like twins, almost. While Justice was a bossy sort and often wore a stern expression, mulling over some wrong or another, Patty was kind and loving, affectionate, always chuckling and willing to listen. They tried to keep their youngest sibling on the straight and narrow. But, Charity, who also had a fair complexion, was born to the scheming ways of her father. She habitually stole things from the store and often paced the floor before sneaking out of the house, which Sylvia learned to do as well.

Her grandmother, Char Lee, attended Robert Cadwallader's funeral. Char Lee loved him like he was her own son. It was her place he stayed at when he visited Laketon. He brought her gifts of tobacco, maybe a discount ham or turkey. He and Joaquin Mendoza would fix what needed fixing and sit and talk with her over a smoke. Char Lee was sad about losing, first, her husband, then her two daughters, Justice and Charity, followed by her son, Russ. When Robert Cadwallader passed on, ending in such a tragic way, "she came down outta the mountains," which was how her daughter, Patty McGrew, described it to one of her salon customers.

At Robert's funeral, Char Lee stood outside the church, smoking a hand-rolled cigarette. She had long, gray hair in braids and wore a long, black dress, like she had stepped out of the Victorian era. She was aided into the church before the funeral by her other son-in-law, Clarence McGrew, who respected her. When asked how old she was, she replied, "Old enough, darlin', and smarter than them britches yer wearin', too!" The family knew she was at least in her nineties and probably very near one hundred years of age, maybe more. She was born in Laketon after the Massacre of 1855, which was all she knew. Her best friend was Lucy Shoseegan who, "beat her to the finish line," Char Lee said, meaning her friend died sooner.

Sylvia walked into the church, arm in arm with Tucker Stewart. Continuing down the aisle, she noticed an old woman sitting with her aunt and uncle. Her Aunt Patty, who was sitting next to Char Lee, gently hailed her.

"Sylvia, dear?" she asked.

Sylvia stopped and turned to answer, "Yes?"

Patty introduced Sylvia to Char Lee, saying, "This is your Granny Walker."

Sylvia about died, herself. She bent down to hug the old woman and receive a whiskered kiss on the cheek. The old woman's hands were like trembling claws, but her eyes, Sylvia noticed, had not lost their mysterious beauty. Sylvia smiled and they gazed upon one another like one would do with a friend from far away finally coming to shore.

"It's so good to see you, Granny," said Sylvia while holding her grandmother's hand.

Sylvia was one of only two grandchildren Char Lee Rosebud would ever have. Her other grandchild, Dottie, sat near them but was talking to her father. When Sylvia and Tucker resumed walking toward the front of the church and sat where they were directed, both Dottie and Char Lee watched them. However, neither were aware of the other's interest in the matter. They simply looked, then let their eyes wander elsewhere before looking back again.

CHAPTER FOUR

After her father's funeral, Sylvia asked Tucker to give her time to sit by her father's grave. She sat on the chair provided for her, recollecting the names and faces of relatives she had met that day, both Cadwallader's and Walker's. The workmen left with their equipment and shovels. People who had attended the funeral drifted away to their homes, since there was no food offered or gathering announced. They simply left. Patty McGrew peeked out the window of her beauty parlor and Char Lee waited in a car parked by the side of the road.

Sylvia looked at her parent's modest stone, the least expensive, which simply read: "Charity Cadwallader, 1910-1945; Robert Cadwallader, 1909-1967." A light breeze drifted through as though summoned. She lifted her head and looked far into the past. She heard the laughter of days gone by, when she was a girl and lived in that house her father had put up for sale. One time—it might have been her birthday—her mother baked a spice cake, frosted it with white icing, and invited Forty and Tucker over to share in it. They sat together on the back porch steps, including her mother, laughing and eating the cake with their fingers until it was gone. It was the best cake Sylvia had ever eaten.

She was aware she held on to the past, for those days, not the ones of neglect and abuse. How she yearned to walk up those steps once more, like when she was that girl, laughing and happy, sharing in the best cake ever with her best friends and seeing her mother smile and having fun. She held on to that house, too, and needed to let it go as well. The bungalow in which she was raised would not sell due to that strange, musty odor and an unsettling feeling to the place. Sylvia knew it was time. She would never be that child ever again. Her father had died and the past had died with him.

"Well, Mother," she began, "I think I'm about as old as you were when you died, but I still feel like your little girl." Tears ran down her face. "I miss you," she said. Her lips quivered as she said the words those in attendance were waiting for her to say. "I'm sorry you had it so hard during the war while Poppy was away. I miss him, but it's you he needs."

The truth, long dormant, slowly awakened in Sylvia's heart. The last time she saw her father, his hand raised to wave goodbye. The thought occurred to her that her mother was waiting for him.

"I understand now," she said. "I need to let you both go."

Sylvia sat for a minute longer, before saying the last she would say to them that day. "Goodbye, Mother," she said. "I'll always love you. I know you did your best. I know you both did."

She buried her face in her handkerchief and released her parents into their passing-on time. Experiencing the great rush of their departure, she sobbed from the sudden-felt loss. Tucker was at her side, gently touching her shoulder. Reassured and strengthened by his presence, she placed her hand on his.

"Thank you," she said.

Her grief passed and she calmed. Soon, she and Tucker were leaving the cemetery and walking homeward. The car by the side of the road carrying Char Lee pulled onto the pavement. The rear window slowly raised as hers and Tucker's eyes met. The curtains at the beauty parlor were still as Patty McGrew resolved to do what Father Jovial had requested of her. When closing time came, Dottie went home while Patty drove to Sylvia's house. It was the original Cadwallader family home, the house in which Robert Cadwallader and his siblings were raised.

"Hello, Sylvia," said Patty when Sylvia answered the door.

Pleased and surprised to see her aunt, Sylvia said, "Aunt Patty! Please, come in."

Her Aunt Patty promised to be brief. "I'm sure sorry about your father, dear," she said.

"Thank you," replied Sylvia. She looked down at her hands, trying to get used to seeing a bare finger where her wedding ring was worn. Turning to offer a seat on the sofa, her spirits fell, noticing the drab appearance to the room, unchanged since Forty's departure.

Patty tried not to look around, but she knew her help was sorely needed from the sorry state of that barren, empty room. She said, "Well, the reason I come by, Sylvia, was to ask if there was anything I could do to help you out. Since your divorce, you must have been thinking about how you're going to support yourself?" She made it a question, hoping Sylvia had given it some thought.

"I have," Sylvia answered. Dejected, she added, "I don't even drive a car." She recalled the dress shop whose owner offered her a job, and excitedly blurted out, "You know, I was offered a job just last week!"

Her Aunt Patty asked, "You were? Where?" Her joy could not be contained as she smiled exuberantly. "Oh, Sylvia, I can't tell you how happy I am!" she said.

"I'll have to pack and move there," said Sylvia. "It's in the Old Town section at the state capital."

Her mind working to solve the matter, Patty said, "You know, I just happen to be going that way myself, er, Daddy and I, that is. He's got to go see a doctor down there first of next week and needs me to drive him home." With her hand to the side of her mouth to share a confidence, she added, "Some sort of man-procedure, you know."

"Oh," said Sylvia. She did not know nor did she inquire further.

"So, tell me, dear," inquired Patty, "where's the job? What kind of place is it?"

"It's a dress shop!" said Sylvia. Her whole face radiated her excitement as she described the little shop, From the Heart. "It's perfect for me," she said. "I've never worked a day in my life, but I do know dresses!"

Patty promised Sylvia she would come by and pick her up in a few days. "Be sure and arrange to begin work there right away," she advised, "and for a place to stay, too."

The moment her aunt drove away, Sylvia remembered Tucker wanting to cook dinner for her at his house that evening. He said there was something he wanted to ask her. Wondering what that could be, Sylvia placed her palm on her growing belly. She knew she needed to tell him something, too, the thought of which brought her anxiety and unbearable shame.

The next day, she visited Father Jovial, to thank him for his help in counseling and supporting her during her divorce. She shared with him the news about moving and about her aunt being so helpful.

With a teary old twinkle in his eyes, Father Jovial asked, "She was? How wonderful!"

Early the following week, Sylvia was packed and ready to go. Her aunt had told her not to worry about the house, since she was already looking after the old Walker house next door and the McGrew place two doors down. She mentioned she was waiting for its new owner to take up residence in what was once her husband's family home.

When her aunt and uncle arrived, Sylvia stepped out the door and bent down to slip a note under the front door mat before getting into their car. She was wearing a dress that was her mother's, a white one with a floral print of green and blue flowers, set off with a lacy, bertha collar. She wore a white belt, blue heels, and earrings, plus a white, wide-brimmed hat. She had two suitcases packed, which her Uncle Clarence put in the trunk of his Chrysler New Yorker convertible, tail fins and all.

He left the top up for their trip, "for the ladies' sake," he mentioned. Although, he usually drove with it down when the weather was fine, like it was that day. He preferred to wear a hat to keep the wind from mussing his hair, but, "men don't wear hats anymore," so he was okay with the top up as well.

Sylvia handed the house keys to her aunt. More excitement and talking and laughing ensued as they turned up onto the highway and left Edenville. Sylvia felt her abdomen, mindful and protective of the secret she held within herself. She could not leave town fast enough.

Tucker left the newspaper office and was on his way to Sylvia's. He wanted to ask her if she would have lunch with him. She had canceled their dinner date the previous week, saying she felt unwell. Walking along Pine Way Junction, he looked forward to seeing her, but was also nervous. He planned a special lunch and was going to ask her to marry him. Arriving at her house, he saw no one at home. The hot sun was beating down on the old weathered structure. He peeked through the front window. Besides a pack of cigarettes left on the coffee table, the only sign of life was an envelope placed beneath the edge of the doormat. His heart sank into his gut at the sight of it. He snatched it up and called the dogs.

"Shep! Here, boy! Freckles!"

They ran toward him. Freckles tumbled and tripped over her front paws. Together, they left the house and walked home, a thoroughly disappointed man and two oblivious dogs.

Tucker asked himself, "Now, why can't I be more like them?"

He balled up the envelope, not wanting to read the words he feared would cause further pain to his second-time-around broken heart. Stepping onto the porch of his house, his shoes scuffed against the wood with plodding carelessness. Shep and Freckles lapped water from a bucket by the garden as Tucker wondered blankly what he was going to do, not really thinking in the moment about anything.

CHAPTER FIVE

Standing outside the newspaper office with Freckles and Shep, Tucker watched Walter Henry's truck approaching Pine Way. Sylvia was gone, having left town for good, he imagined. Jim Hart was dead. The troubled man's house was abandoned and sat in a weedy field like a haunted wraith. Neither wind nor rain could cleanse the horrors that took place within its crackled, sagging walls, he believed.

Searching the sky for an answer to his present quandary, Tucker sensed there was further change coming his way. With a touch of drama, he said, "I am but one man, you see. No need to fret the change that sweeps into the fiery dawn. For there are many who take up the sword for such causes as these, which call for courage, call for sanity, for a clear breath to carry us fearlessly into the waiting dusk."

He could not claim credit for words his father penned one evening after the bombing of Pearl Harbor. They were part of a lengthier poem written while Tucker, seven years of age, hid beneath the desk. After writing the poem, his father stood and stepped on Tucker's small fingers. He held his breath, trying not to yell.

The moment Walter Henry and Johnny parked in front of the newspaper office, Tucker further whispered, "What now?"

Seated in the truck cab, Walter Henry said to Johnny, "Go get the dog. We need to get back down here and clean out the barn. Some people want to take a look at it. Okay?"

Johnny replied, "No! Never wanted to come down here in the first place!"

Getting out of the truck, Walter Henry said to Tucker, "We'll take Shep off your hands. Tessie's pups all found homes, so she's safe for him to be around. I think she's missin' him now." He picked up Shep and helped him climb onto the front seat. Johnny remained sitting with arms folded tightly across his chest. The boy looked away from Walter Henry to gaze out the window. The old man sighed heavily and shook his head.

Trying to ignore the pang he felt when Shep was taken away, Tucker asked Walter Henry, "What are you going to do with the barn, now that Jim's passed on?" He thought, at first, that maybe he should have kept quiet, but rationalized it was merely a business-related question. He added, "I only ask, because..."

"Oh, I dunno," Walter Henry answered. He sauntered toward the barn, wishing he could simply tear the whole thing down, and said, "Johnny got Jim's half of the business, so I got to talk it over with my new partner." He grinned. Lowering his voice, he said, "I don't know when that'll happen, though. Me and the boy aren't getting along too good right now. You understand."

"Sure," Tucker said.

Tucker was uninformed regarding Jim Hart's paternal claim over the young man. Curious, he asked, "Why would Jim do that?" Walter Henry gave a disgusted, smirky look well-known to Tucker, that meant, "there you go bein' nosey again," so he let it go.

Tucker thought of his conversation with that man a futile exercise in tooth-pulling. The old blacksmith was the reluctant patient who would rather his teeth rot and fall out than face the pain of tooth extraction. No wonder he never got to know "the old geezer," Tucker thought, and went about his day, minus one canine companion.

Before leaving, Walter Henry said, "Probably rent it out for now. We've had offers. So, I thought I'd clean up the place."

Perplexed by the strange encounter, Tucker watched as the recalcitrant old blacksmith drove away on Pine Way Junction. Gradually, curiosity turned to surprising glee and Tucker laughed. He had come upon another story, that of linking Johnny to Jim Hart. With a smile on his face, he imagined the headlines reading, "Local Boy's True Identity Revealed Ending Rash of Gossip in Edenville."

Ready to start his day, he carried Freckles up the stairs to the second floor of the newspaper office. Before he sat down, he was told that another one of their staff members quit. "That skinny beanpole," Tucker said under his breath. He often pictured the man's bare cupboards and empty refrigerator. "Starving himself for some past deed of excess, no doubt, like bingeing on donuts or Twinkies," he further mused.

The editor was filling him in on the latest news. He stood near the front window with hands on hips and round belly straining the seams of his shirt. Tucker was still off in his imagination regarding his ex-fellow employee who sat at his desk like he was up to something, obsessing over some shameful secret or thought.

"Did you hear me?" The editor was familiar with Tucker's flights of imagination, but change had also hit the paper and needed to be addressed. "So, as I was saying, he defected to our competition," meaning The Big Guy, a real newspaper with a wide circulation, bigger press, more employees.

Tucker believed it was the promise of a bigger paycheck that lured away his co-worker. He wondered what he would do with more money. Freckles wiggled in his arms, so he set the puppy down, hoping she would stay out of mischief. He watched her sniff along the floor until she found something edible and ate it.

His boss said, "We'll stick it out long as we can, but you and I both know the days of the small town newspaper are over."

The editor turned away to look out the window, continuing to ramble. "Just the two of us now," he said. "When your dad ran the press, we had as many as five working here." Hands still on his hips, he examined the worn-out flooring, seeing its rough patches and warped boards. It earned a wag of his head, for it was one more thing piled on his overburdened shoulders. Looking at Tucker, he gave his prognosis of their future. "Yes, my friend, the days of anyone wanting to read in the paper what their neighbors are doing, well, those days are over," he concluded. He sat at his desk and fiddled with a pencil, looking around at nothing in particular as he rolled it between his thumbs and forefingers.

Tucker was drawn out of his mood by the expression on the editor's face. He had seen that look before on his father's face. He remembered, as a young boy, looking at his father and wondering if he had a pain somewhere. Since learning of his father's secret, Tucker knew his dad was entertaining a visit to Mrs. Cadwallader's next door. No matter. Tucker surmised the editor would share what was on his mind, so he sat at his desk and began work for the day.

"Uh...Tucker?"

Here it was. Tucker's low mood returned. The image of a coffin being carried across the cemetery lawn came to mind. Walter Henry and other men were leading the procession of mourners, delivering Jim Hart to the open grave ahead. Tucker was walking Sylvia home. She had turned to look back, so he did as well, catching a fleeting sense of something written in her gaze. The remembrance of seeing Jim Hart's coffin caught Tucker unawares. He wanted to yell. He wanted to yell openly and loudly, but was yet stifled by shock, wondering how one man as plagued with problems as Jim Hart could keep their little town of Pine Way alive, then snuff it out with his passing.

"So, when are we shutting down?" he asked.

His editor raised his eyebrows and took in a deep breath of air, then let it out. His hands went up in helpless defeat as he said, "I think today," before plopping them back into his lap. "I think it's already happened." He stared at the floor between his shoes as if a pool of water lay before him, showing him their future. Defeated, he said, "We can't afford to hire anyone now. It's just us. We can't run a paper on our own, let alone revive it."

Tucker swiftly reacted. "What are you saying?" he asked. "I'm out of a job? This was my grandfather's dream! You can't just decide to take it away and let it die! I won't let you!"

"What do you propose we do, Tucker?" his editor asked.

"Well," Tucker began, "we're a printing press, aren't we? The town needs one!"

The editor suddenly grew excited, his face changing from despair to joy, as though Tucker had touched upon his ideas. His change in demeanor so reminded Tucker of his father when he decided to pay Mrs. Cadwallader a visit and excitedly left the house.

"Well, you know what I was thinking?" the editor asked.

He told Tucker about his grand idea, to open a basic print shop, move the press into Edenville and run an ad paper, invest in a second press specifically for making business cards, brochures, and wedding announcements. Caught up in his excitement, the frazzle-haired editor was leaning forward in his creaking wooden office chair, reminding Tucker of Mickey Rooney. His large stomach slumped down between his legs. Tucker imagined his boss straddling an imaginary steed galloping full speed across the plains, hat waving through the air, shouting, "I've got an idea! I've got an idea!"

How could Tucker refuse such enthusiasm? He quickly blurted out, "When do we start?!"

"Well..."

A knock came at the door. The editor's ideas fell from the clouds and faced the empty reality before him. He excused himself and hurriedly got up to see who it was.

While he was gone from the room, Tucker telephoned his brother, Howard, to discuss the future of their grandfather's legacy. Howard was about to leave for work and said he would stop by the newspaper office. They agreed the press should not be moved until they could afford to start something new.

The editor's forgotten caller, none other than a bank employee, had informed him that his loan application to obtain funds to start up a new business venture was denied. The editor said nary a word when he returned inside. Instead, he addressed what was before them, getting out another edition of *The Edenville Weekly*.

Tucker wondered about the old woman Sylvia spoken to and hugged at her father's funeral. It seemed to him that her eyes could see right through them both, probably saw his insecurity over Sylvia's inherent restlessness.

He asked, "Would it be all right if I did a story on the Indians of Laketon for the paper?"

"Sure. Anything you say, Tucker," answered the editor. He looked around the room, avoiding Tucker's glance his way.

"What?" Tucker asked. He sensed there was more, something the editor avoided saying.

Answering Tucker, the editor said, "Oh, well now, we've got to plan everything out, pull together some capital." He stood up and put on his hat. "I'm off to the bank," though actually to the bar, "to discuss things. You know."

Since the newspaper was going bust, Tucker went all out on the next edition. After Howard's visit, he scooped up Freckles with one hand, went down the stairs, and was out the door, locking it with the other hand. Quickly heading down the road to his house, he planned on doing a big story, probably the biggest he had ever done. His grandfather had once put together a newspaper all on his own, and with only one man, Herman Mendoza, working for him. Tucker would keep the paper going, all on his own if need be, one issue at a time.

CHAPTER SIX

Jacket draped over one arm and suitcase in hand, Tucker boarded the bus that would take him to Laketon where he hoped to interview Char Lee Rosebud. Forested ridge after ridge held him in awe as the bus made its way up the highway, steadily climbing the mountain. The familiar scenery of yellow pine, oak, and maple gave way to majestic stands of sugar pine, fir, and cedar. The forest thinned and he viewed an open, granite-strewn landscape. The canyon gradually narrowed and the bus climbed even higher. Rocky knolls and stunted, twisted trees abounded as it reached the backcountry, an expansive wilderness of tumbling rivers descending into whitewater and deep pools. Turquoise-colored lakes dotted the open spaces, while broad meadows were yet blanketed with snow.

Despite the beauty of the mountains, Tucker felt anxious, as though something were amiss. A brief mental inventory revealed nothing. No one had questioned him why he decided to go on that trip. His brother, Howard, and Howard's wife, Mary, said nothing when he dropped off the dog for them to look after while he was away. In planning his trip, all he had thought about were the people he saw at the funeral, people he would soon meet again. He wondered if he would be welcome. Too late to turn back, he fretted, having lost the impromptu momentum of his initial decision. He was not yet ready to admit that his unease had nothing to do with a newspaper or being a journalist.

Guilty, as well as nervous, he fidgeted with a pen and notepad, continuing to pretend he was a journalist. He wrote meaningless notes as Grief summoned him to its side. Losing Sylvia again weighed upon him. He looked at his pen and the blue ink smudged alongside his fingers, then slowly raised his head to stare out the window.

The bus driver checked his interior rearview mirror and spotted the expression on Tucker's face. It reminded him of when he, as a young man, had left for the war, having to say goodbye to family and friends, and his girl, not knowing if he would ever see them again. Thinking to himself, "poor guy," he believed he knew exactly what Tucker was feeling: afraid and lonesome, the heartbreak kind of lonesome that could make a man cry. Grinding the gears as the road steepened around the curve, the driver returned his attention to his job as the bus chugged along further up the road.

After a two-hour drive from where the bus picked him up in Edenville, Tucker arrived in Laketon. The bus continued on its way, leaving him standing by the roadside with jacket and suitcase, questioning what he had done. His tan slacks, light-blue jacket, and light-green, twill shirt seemed like the wrong attire for what he saw ahead. It was a way of life too far-removed from his own, of that he was certain. Taking the first step to cross the road, he told himself that, if he wanted to return home, he would need a ride.

The mountain air was chilly, so he stopped to set his suitcase down and put on his jacket. Afterward, he continued walking toward the mountain village, seeing it as if he was looking through the wrong end of binoculars. He felt like he had put his shoes on the wrong feet. Looking down at them, they appeared normal.

"Why am I doing this?" he asked himself.

A corrugated tin shack was most prominent. Sylvia's father was not the only man from Edenville who spent many an hour in what was once known as Sammy's Tavern. It had become a storage shed or, perhaps, someone's house. An old toilet and pedestal sink sat outside next to a circle of lawn chairs placed around a fire ring. The market and cafe looked shut down. Both log buildings had rusted screens on their windows, be-draped in gossamer-like spider webbing.

In the stillness and quiet of that mountain setting, a lone raven called out as it flew through the tree tops above, breaking the silence. Tucker wondered derisively if it was a sign. Once he reached the buildings, the sweet-scented breeze passing through the forest uplifted his drooping spirits and calmed him. He was glad he had come, if only to have a peaceful and welcoming change of scenery. Standing before the two log buildings, a weathered wooden sign told him they were Arlen's Lake Town Market & Cafe. An ice machine sat outside on the porch. No one was around and not a single car was in sight. He thought he should first inquire about a ride home, when he heard a sound that startled him, like a bear growling. Slightly surprised, he discovered it was coming from a man napping on a broken-down piece of patio furniture.

"Hello?" Tucker asked. Not wanting to rouse the man from his nap, he knew he had to, if he wanted to get home. Raising his voice, he asked again, "Hello?!"

Another man came walking up, about to knock the sleeping man out of his nap and his chair.

"Oh! Don't do that!" Tucker yelled.

Regardless, the one man knocked the other into the dirt. With effort, the napping man stood, squinting and blinking. His long, black hair was messy with pine needles stuck to it and his dark-blue t-shirt, much too small for him, had come untucked from his blue jeans, revealing the top half of his buttocks.

Tucker quickly looked away and yelled at the other man, "Now, what did you have to go and do that for?!"

The two men walked away from him, entering the log store as though nothing had happened. Tucker followed them inside and was instantly greeted by a near-mummified black bear's head mounted on the opposite wall. Its gaping maw was set in a withered, vicious snarl. Next, he saw snowshoes hung on a nail. Black-and-white photos in dusty, crooked frames were hanging above the fishing tackle and poles. Beyond, a fireplace with a warm, crackling fire drew him over, where a coiled rug was placed on the floor. A wooden chair that had one leg missing was propped up by a stack of fishing magazines. The two men he met outside were sitting by the fire, a sight he found surprising given the heat wave the residents of Edenville had recently experienced.

Wanting to go home, Tucker asked, "Is Arlen around?"

"Arlen?" one man asked.

Tucker replied, "The man who owns this store. Is he around?"

"There's no one named Arlen here," said the man. "This is my store. I just named it that, cuz I like the name." He smiled, eyes twinkling.

Tucker began to say, "Oh, well, I'm—" but was interrupted.

"Hey, sorry to upset you earlier. Bear's my brother," the man explained. "He's used to me giving him a hard time."

"Oh," which was all Tucker could think of to say.

Still smiling, the man asked, "What can we do for you? Looks like you're going someplace, or coming. We don't have any lodging."

Tucker laughed nervously, lifting his suitcase up a bit. "Oh, this," he said. He no longer knew what he wanted to do, but he blurted out his original idea all the same. "I met a friend's grandmother," he explained, "Char Lee Walker, at Robert Cadwallader's funeral last week."

"Oh, Dreaming Man. Yeah, we were there, too. Hey, I remember seeing you." Lowering his voice, he turned toward his brother and said, "I told you we've seen him someplace before." He asked Tucker, "You live in Edenville?"

Ignoring the question, Tucker said, "Well, I was hoping to interview her for our town's newspaper, but I probably should have planned this better."

"Why? I know where she lives. Come on, I'll take you there," said Bear's big brother. He got up from the canvas beach chair he was sitting in, petting an enormous, one-eyed gray cat, to whom he said, "Gotta go, Snake Eye. You look after the store, now, hear me?" He grabbed a pouch of tobacco from a rack and handed it to Tucker. "Here. You're gonna need this." Tucker hastily drew some coins from his pocket to pay for it. The man motioned with one arm hooked through the air. "Come on, it's not far," he said. He pulled up his faded jeans as Tucker followed him outside.

The man had shorter hair than his brother, but was bigger, probably weighing around two-hundred pounds, Tucker casually deduced. They walked across the paved parking area, which was still absent of cars. They took a quick jog down a path into the woods. It was steep at first. Soon, they crossed a low-lying area dotted with branches and bits of trash, an old range stove, and a rusted car layered beneath the forest litter. Up the next hill, they climbed through a shaded area toward a small shed. Leastways, it appeared to be a small shed. It turned out to be a makeshift porch to a travel trailer which had rusted and was settling deeper into the earth. Tucker saw that it either had no wheels or they were buried. The man knocked on the door of the porch. Tucker spotted smoke rising from a stovepipe.

Char Lee shouted from inside the trailer, "Is that you, Bear?"

"No, it's me, Barclay."

"Oh! Clay! Come on in!" she said.

Barclay opened the door and, as he and Tucker filed in, announced, "Got a visitor for you, Char Lee." The first part of her name was short for "Charlotte."

"A visitor? You mean, 'sides you?" she asked.

They stepped across the porch, bending down through the doorway of the trailer. Tucker was suddenly reminded of when he was a boy. He and Forty and Sylvia were devising their plan

47

to build a fort, gathering old junk, later enclosing themselves within the tiny shelter. He never thought back then that it was junk or that it was dirty, unsafe, or unsightly. The same comforting sense of sheltering closeness he had felt as a boy, was what he experienced upon entering Char Lee Rosebud's burrow-like domicile. It was not a safety hazard or a junk heap, as it might appear to some, but something necessary, like the pretend Fort Sumner was to a small group of children long ago.

Seeing a brown couch, a tiny wood stove with a fire burning in it, an unmade bed off at one end, and a kitchen area at the other, gave Tucker the full tour of Char Lee's home.

"Hey!" Char Lee brightened. "I remember you! Met you just the other day at the funeral!" She looked concerned, her eyebrows drawn down, like she was recalling something, or making up something. Grinning slyly, she said, "My granddaughter left town, didn't she?" She laughed and laughed, giving her leg a slap.

Humiliated, Tucker answered, "She left a few days after the funeral."

Char Lee drew back in a pretend pout, ready to feel sorry for Tucker, and said, "Aw, well, don't feel bad."

She made that look again like she was scheming. It reminded Tucker of his Grandma Stewart when she was teasing him. Char Lee was teasing him, too, having a good laugh over his misery.

Char Lee went on to say, "My daughter, Patience, told me she was gonna help the poor thing, practically orphaned when my other daughter died. Didn't know she'd wind up stealing her away from you!" Char Lee laughed it up with a shriek and a cackle, saying to Tucker, "Come on! Sit down! Sit down!" She whacked Barclay with a swoop of her hand. "Move over and let the man sit," she playfully commanded. She continued to explain, "Well, you know, her mother and father never could sit still. I suppose she took after them," and winked at Tucker.

It was then that Tucker knew Char Lee liked him and was simply having fun, so he finally gave up and relaxed. Since Sylvia's departure was brought into the open, he thought about it momentarily, feeling like a chump for believing Sylvia would stay with him, even marry him. However, a slight thought occurred to him, which he quickly dismissed, exposing the doubt he harbored for even wanting to marry Sylvia. But he was not yet ready to investigate that possibility, so he let it go. That was a touchy one to contemplate, as quickly dismissed and forgotten as it had arose in his awareness.

Char Lee sat looking at Tucker with her hands clasped together, the old woman becoming more vulpine before his very eyes, then dramatically crow-like, or perhaps like a raven. Her hands were more like talons, intertwined, and her entire countenance shifted from humorous to someone seated in a cave one-hundred, maybe one-thousand years past, listening, waiting.

Tucker was both terrified and in awe. He recalled the raven he had heard upon approaching the hamlet earlier and a strange thought passed over him. "Well," he said in trusting resignation, "now I don't know what to do. I came up here to ask if I could interview you for the Edenville newspaper, but now I'm not so sure."

"Interview me? What d'ya wanna know?" she asked.

• • •

Tucker got his interview plus several pictures, and he got a ride home the same day. In listening to Char Lee, he heard a point of view not ever considered by non-Indians, that of the people who were driven out of Pine Valley. It explained to him why crying and screaming could be heard on the wind late at night certain times of the year, an eerie occurrence no one talked about anymore. The sense of peace many had dreamed of upon coming to Pine Valley had come at a great price. Peace had many sides and many faces, he learned.

At the end of their interview, before he took his leave, he told Char Lee, "I'm-I'm sorry," sincerely apologetic for the way the natives were treated. He knew she was done teasing him when she solemnly replied, "It's not your fault." Tucker took his leave, thinking of all the women in his life having gone away, like Sylvia. The words Char Lee spoke, he realized were in consolation of his own loss.

CHAPTER SEVEN

Char Lee Rosebud was a reclusive woman the residents of Edenville barely knew existed. Therefore, they failed to notice when she moved to Laketon and, years later, passed away. Tucker wanted to honor her. He took it upon himself to make the last edition of *The Edenville Weekly* unforgettable and reflective of his values, principles, and long-ignored creative talent. The entire newspaper was put together to the best of his abilities, using his skills to craft something of which he knew his grandfather and his father would have been proud. On the downhill side of health, Tucker's father could no longer read a newspaper, so it meant even more when the paper was finally in the hands of its readers.

They sat on benches in the Edenville town square, at the library, and on their front porches. They later gathered to discuss what they had read. Tucker knew he had done good as "fine job" and "great story," plus a pat on the back from his editor while praising him, reached his ears and then his heart.

"I'm proud of you, Tucker. I knew you always had it in you," said his editor.

Tucker felt he could finally move on. Besides the praise he had received, the paper caught the attention of The Big Guy, who subsequently offered him a job. Wanting to pay homage to his last day working at the newspaper office, Tucker got a chair and, with Freckles napping at his feet, sat out front of the building like his grandfather used to do. He planned to read the entire paper. He began with Char Lee Rosebud's obituary, the old woman's passing only then striking a blow.

The obituary read: "The village of Laketon lost a prominent and well-loved citizen, Charlotte Lee Walker, better known as Char Lee Rosebud, when she died Saturday of pneumonia. Born in Laketon, she lived part of her life in Edenville, before returning to the mountain village where she lived the rest of her life. She is survived by her daughter, Patience McGrew, and her granddaughters, Dorothy Ann McGrew and Sylvia Sumner. Graveside services will be held at 10:00 a.m. Thursday at the Edenville Community Cemetery, where she will be laid to rest beside her late husband, Jiminy Russell Walker, her son, Prosperous Samuel Walker, and her daughters, Justice Marie Walker and Charity Charlotte Lee Cadwallader. All who knew her loved her. Donations may be made to the QSN Fund (Quit Smoking Now)."

The interview she had granted Tucker, combined with the tribe's history, created a memorable piece he would always treasure. He had entitled the article, "The Pine Valley Massacre of 1855."

Before he began reading the article, he noted the many familiar sights of the season, like the tall green grass in the shade, where the air was yet cool. He noticed the late spring foliage of the elm trees. Birds were busy everywhere, singing, building their nests, or feeding their young. The house sparrows that nested anywhere and everywhere, seemed to always be first before they put out a second batch, he had observed. They had one brood begging to be fed. The tumbling, feathery, fat balls of fluff hopped on the ground nearby and stuck their wings out, all a-quiver. They were peeping and cheeping from their gaping yellow grins until something gruesome was shoved into their mouths by their exhausted, beleaguered parent.

Watching the birds, Tucker's mind wandered to that unforgettable day spent with Char Lee Rosebud. He would never forget her telling a story told to her and handed down to all the children, imagining them gathered around their cook fires or huddled in their shelters. In that rickety, ramshackle travel trailer, surrounded by what he knew some people would call, "abject poverty," the old woman brought the past to bear. He listened to her near-monotone voice while the ghosts of the past, that had yet to find peace, began rising up and sharing their suffering. The experience transformed into a dance of memory that yet lived as Barclay lit a sage bundle and Tucker became mesmerized with its smoke.

•   •   •

"This is the true story of a man by the name of Caruthers whom my people have called a hero," Char Lee began. "He came from back East to strike it rich in the Gold Rush. The mountains drew him and, like the trickster that it was, the gold failed him. He joined the army and soon became Sergeant Caruthers. He was sent with a detachment to Pine Valley, his first, real, field assignment. The year was 1855. The mission was the same as it was everywhere by then: 'Let's finish this once and for all.' That was the exact order from his commanding officer, Lieutenant Harold J. Caufield, and it shook the young sergeant out of his daydreams of fame that he had planned to write home about.

"Once the shooting began, he saw what was happening, yet couldn't do the same. Abandoning his men, his uniform, and his country, Sergeant Caruthers helped the fleeing, screaming women and children scattering into the cover of trees, old ones barely able to run and the men who never had the chance to protect them. He had fallen behind the rest of his company who had come charging on horseback through the village, shooting as they went, so they never saw what he was doing behind them. He rushed to pick up those who had fallen, placed as many on his horse as it could carry, wrapped his coat around an old man, his bedroll swaddling a screaming child. Because of what he had done, he became part of our story and no longer a part of the one his country would tell for generations. Every shred of the soldier was cast aside when he chose to hurry off with my people who were fleeing ever deeper into the woods.

"The trail they followed was the summer trail, the one normally taken to the backcountry here, to follow the deer and to gather the wild onions and the sweet shoots of herbs and other plants that were used for seasoning a stew or a haunch of deer or maybe an elk. But there was no time for gathering, only running. Every last person left alive was on the run, including the man who could no longer call himself, 'Sergeant.' He was a deserter who had aided the enemy and who chose to become one of the people whom he had helped. Such was his heart, uncontaminated by the world in which he had been raised. He only knew that he cared about those who were being exterminated, routed out, destroyed before the tide of 'the angry swarm of ants,' as one of our elders once described it.

"That first night on the run came too soon and it grew cold. They asked one another, 'How many survived? Who was lost?' One man, who later gave himself the name, 'Hector Shoseegan,' lost his wife. He had gathered up his children, thinking his wife was right behind him, but she was shot down and left to lie there with all the rest in the valley, unburied until his return several years later. In their camp, they asked Caruthers his name, pointing to him, but all he said was, 'Michael. Just Michael.' They didn't know each other's language, but Hector knew enough of the soldiers' ways to know that Michael Caruthers had placed himself in danger by helping them. Because of that, Hector and all our people, have always been especially grateful.

"Under the best of conditions, the trip from Pine Valley to the summer encampment here took three or four days, some on horseback, some walking. This time, with many of them injured, with old ones and young children, most of their horses stolen from them, it took weeks. By the time they made it here, some had died along the way and many became ill from the fever. Setting up a permanent camp was pretty sad business and talk began amongst a few about wanting to return to Pine Valley. Only fifteen or twenty adults, plus their children, would make the trip, Hector and his children being among them.

"My mother lost her husband in the massacre. She had been pregnant and gave birth to a baby boy in 1856. Michael Caruthers married her when a priest came through on the

Emigrant Trail. The priest baptized the baby, 'Michael Caruthers Holy Savior,' named after the man who had helped them to escape slaughter. She was only eighteen years of age. Later, she had another child. That was me. Everyone called me, 'Char Lee,' for our hero's mother, Charlotte Lee Caruthers, of Lancaster, Pennsylvania. It was from her I got my gray eyes, though I never told anyone about that until now.

"My father never returned to his former life, having died from the fever soon after I was born. One man, before he left with the others back to Pine Valley, promised my mother he would return and take care of her and her children. That he did and, afterward, they were married as well.

"Life was not the same for those who returned to Pine Valley. They eventually retreated back here to Laketon. The last ones to leave the valley were Hector Shoseegan, his children, Lucy and Dexter, and Lucy's husband, Berto Mendoza, and their son, Manuel. Lucy's and Berto's other sons, Jesse and Herman, stayed in Edenville. They would occasionally visit. Herman worked for the newspaper and Jesse was the Edenville Elementary School janitor until he died in 1950.

"It was back in 1892, when I met and later married a Pine Way resident by the name of Jiminy Russell Walker, who was close friends with my brother, Savior. Jiminy came here to visit him. I lived with my husband, for a time, first in Pine Way, then in Edenville, but my heart was always in these mountains. I finally returned in 1943, and have been here ever since. It was Jiminy who named me, 'Rosebud.' Said it was because I was not yet in full bloom. I've always liked that."

CHAPTER EIGHT

Tucker waited for his brother at the newspaper office. The printing press loomed from behind where he stood beside the sliding shop door. Turning his head, he imagined his grandfather standing in the room and became downhearted. He reassured himself he did everything he could to keep his grandfather's dream alive. "Times have changed," he said to the imaginary presence in the room. "Time to let it go," he said.

Howard's sedan rounded the corner. Like the lead car in Kennedy's motorcade, the approaching vehicle conveyed a premonition of impending death, which Tucker felt ill-prepared to receive. His brother had said earlier that he was bringing their father to the newspaper office "one last time."

A fleeting sense of awareness came to him as his brother parked the car. He wanted more time, though none was being granted. He imagined a teacher informing her students to "turn your papers over and set your pencils on your desks." Time had run out and there was nothing he could do about it, except pray that he would not fail.

Car doors opened and closed. He drew in his breath and released it. Stepping aside so Howard could push their father's wheelchair into the room, Tucker was thankful. At least the surviving Stewart men had come together to acknowledge the end of their family business.

Howard looked upon the printing press as if he was considering retiring the old, but faithful family car. He said, "Well," lightly pounding the edge of the press with his fist, "we can always come back. Who knows? You and I will be around for a while yet, little brother. The town council assured me we can keep it stored here as long as we want, just check in on things now and then." He waited to see what his brother had to say.

Tucker believed there would be no going back, only forward. In his mind, ideas stirred, one of which was to preserve the entire town of Pine Way as a historical district. Sliding his fingertips to skim along the press's metal edge, he said, "This is a museum piece." Looking around the room in which they stood, he added, "This building, the whole town, Howard. It's part of history."

Howard's eyebrows creased in wonder. He was about to say something, but was distracted by their father and forced to let it go.

Their father's illness had advanced to where he could no longer speak. He tried to say something, but grew frustrated with the effort. His hand was shaking as he grunted incoherently.

Tucker was stunned by the effort, not knowing what to do.

Howard carefully placed his hands on their father's shoulders to calm him and said, "I better get Dad back over to

Spring Hill. I didn't exactly get their permission to bring him out here. You know how that one nurse gets if you break any rules."

Tucker was relieved his brother took care of their father's agitated behavior. He threw a canvas tarp over the press, then followed them out. The shop door was slid back into place and locked. The moment Howard drove away, the printing press was forgotten.

Before heading home, Tucker stopped to look back at the small town. It appeared deserted. Plywood sheets covered the windows of the brick buildings, like eyes closed in death. The post office on the corner was recently shut down when funds were approved to build a new one in Edenville proper, on Edenville Loop. However, until the new building was up and running, the mail would come through a temporary facility. The old store went out-of-business years ago, but the reclusive sculptor, Tommy McGrew, still used it for his studio.

Tucker recalled one evening years ago, when he chanced upon the older man sitting on an upended crate behind the store. Jim Hart was sitting nearby on a tall round of wood. Tommy's quiet, deep voice contrasted with Jim's loud and hysterical fits of laughter. The two men were drinking together before a small warming fire. Tucker realized that was a frequent occurrence with them. The sculptor looked more like a mechanic, or a convict, wearing coveralls and work boots, and holding a fat cigar, Tucker had thought at first. By the smell of the smoke drifting on the wind, he knew it was something other than tobacco. Tucker never forgot that day, a combination of having witnessed the two breaking the law and wishing he could have joined them, that they had even asked.

Reflecting on that experience exposed the truth about himself and Jim Hart. Theirs was a complex relationship. Tucker was drawn to Jim, to his darkness. Whatever light Jim held was revealed to no one, he believed. Like two halves of a whole, Tucker held the light that Jim was likewise drawn toward. Yet, it was that small piece of darkness, which Tucker harbored within himself and would reveal to no one, that kept Jim at bay. For that, Tucker was especially ashamed. It touched upon his secret obsession over Sylvia. So similar, he and Jim were, yet fated to be rivals from birth, both chasing after a girl who had learned at too-young an age how to ply her feminine wiles. Sadly, Tucker thought, it was only after Jim's death that he finally saw the man's light.

The barn, further down, was relegated for use as a storage shed. Once a huge building, it seemed to have shrunk in size, dwarfed by modernity and the advent of much larger and more imposing structures. To witness the industrious and grand blacksmith shop and livery stable reduced to a dilapidated old dust bucket of weathered, gray boards, brought such sadness to Tucker. He believed that Edenville's historical heritage was held, not only by the one office, but by the whole town, that place on the map. Not a single mention of saving it from complete decay had Tucker heard. Pine Way was like the forgotten village of Laketon. It had its day, its purpose, at one time, but lost it somewhere, some time ago.

Tucker remained living in that isolated place, loyal to what it had meant to the Hart's, the Henry's, the McGrew's, the Cadwallader's, and the Stewart's. It was a place to set their dreams to canvas, to paint upon the landscape a vision of their idea of peace, an orderly town, bricks and paint, doors and windows, a community. To the earliest settlers and the native people once living there, peace meant simply the beauty of the place. For them, all things occurred in cycles, like the seasons, birth and death, growing up and growing old, when to plant and when to harvest.

Tucker searched the sky for purpose. He believed he was losing his with the need to start a new job and buy a car. Reading the sky, seeing the mare's tail clouds swept across the blue above, his eyes opened to possibilities.

"All things in their time," he said.

The words lent him hope and made him aware that he knew what the future held but needed to be patient for its arrival.

He continued looking down the road toward the end of the forsaken row of structures where he lived. Like a boom town gone bust, the houses had emptied, one by one. He wondered where their occupants had gone. One woman, Eunice Chapman, held on to the house across from the post office, but Tucker rarely saw her. Though Walter Henry and Johnny, and even the sculptor, occasionally showed their faces, he was as good as alone on that street, unable to deny the loss he felt. His father's recent decline had gone unnoticed by him until that day. It was yet another life drifting away along with the town.

Freckles sauntered about, sniffing various plants and stalking the curious rustling of leafy debris beneath the bushes. While observing her, Tucker admitted to himself that he missed his father. He could recall the activity in old Pine Way, doors banging shut, storekeepers briskly sweeping their doorsteps, shouting out their "good mornings" to one another, and children running and playing. Tucker helped his father at the newspaper office, learning how to run the press, how to set the type, everything to making a newspaper. It was a craft, his father said, a skill that took time to learn.

He recalled one incident from when he was a teenager. His father stood by watching him apply the ink after they had set the type, tasks Tucker was learning how to do. But, apparently, Tucker botched the whole thing.

His dad became impatient with him, shouting, "No! No! Not like that! Look what you've done!" Gruffly pushing Tucker aside, he began correcting the mistake.

Tucker felt like a dumb kid when that happened, hurrying outside to get away from his angry father. His feelings were hurt, not by his father's words, but by his actions. He was not yet fourteen years of age, still wishing his mother was alive, but she was not. His father had also forbade his going out for sports, saying he needed to help at the office and with his grandmother. The only consoling thought for that crushing assault on his youthful pride and dignity—and for all the conflict he experienced while working at his father's side—was the fact that plenty of arguments drifted into hearing range from the barn as well. The same father and son confrontations rose and fell, from heated words shouted within its walls to silence pervading the empty spaces of their lives. Because of that, Tucker had heard Jim Hart's father wanting Jim to help at work and not go out for sports, either.

Tucker's wounded pride was soothed that day while basking in the hazy sunshine, watching flies lazily circling through the dusty air. He lingered outside, watching Jim lead a horse around in front of the barn and carefully inspect its glossy brown coat. Jim lightly ran his palm along each of the horse's legs. His sensitivity and obvious love of horses made an impression on Tucker. Jim's dad came out of the barn and patted the young man on the back, which brought a smile to Jim's face, receiving praise for a job well done. Tucker watched as Jim led the horse down the dirt road a ways, before turning around to return to the barn. Jim looked his way, noticing Tucker observing him. Only then, did Tucker look away and return inside the newspaper office.

Saddened by the memory, Tucker wanted to stop dwelling on the past. He called to Freckles and walked home. On his way, he continued pondering the incident from that long ago day. Resigned to the past's insistence on being heard, he asked himself, "Why did my dad get so angry?" It was in 1948. The memory of war still beset Pine Way and Edenville. Wounded veterans congregated each day in the Edenville town square. Wartime posters, albeit weathered and torn, yet held fast to buildings.

At his house, Freckles settled onto her blanket in the kitchen, so Tucker got his notepad and pencil from the table and sat on the sofa to write. The significance of the era in which he had come of age carried an important lesson he yet struggled to grasp. He wanted to know what that was and what it had meant.

"It was not the war that held us all enthralled by fear and loathsome terror," he wrote. "I believe it was peace, occurring in all the quiet places yet prevailing in our lives amidst conflict and terrible loss. How vulnerable and precious our lives had become because of war! Parents feared losing another son or daughter, their livelihoods, and everything they had worked toward in times of peace. It was an era that called upon us all to serve, whether in another country or at home."

Tucker was thankful for what he believed was the lesson from that period in his life and came to appreciate his father's efforts. His dad was not simply trying to pass on what he knew about running a printing press, no more than Jim's father was only teaching his son how to groom or shoe a horse properly. They were teaching their sons about life, how to be men, how to be responsible. They were teaching their sons how to be a father, how to hold that hard-won peace sacred and, most especially, how to carry on in spite of war.

Nearly twenty years had passed since then. Pine Way's businesses were no longer bustling with activity but were shut down and silent. Beyond their sleepy town, the country was in chaos over the Vietnam War. Protesting, rioting, anti-war demonstrations, all of which he chose not to write about for the paper, he had left for others to address. But the importance of his father's lessons, and the lessons taught by all wartime eras, opened his eyes to serving in a cause greater than himself.

Tucker finished writing what he needed to say. He added, "Peace on the home front is as important as freedom being fought and died for on the battlefield. To serve our fellow citizens in the preservation of peace, as well as freedom, is the sacred duty of all Americans."

Setting aside his notepad, Tucker asked himself, "How can I serve?"

Considering how badly he treated Jim when they were growing up, Tucker resolved to make amends. In the same manner in which he knew soldiers would do for one another in times of war, Tucker vowed to be the kind of friend he knew Jim needed. Feeling hopeful and inspired, he left his house and walked to Edenville.

CHAPTER NINE

Tucker left Pine Way but, before it fell from view, he turned to look back. The dirt road to the old town looked abandoned, since so few people drove it anymore. Like the village gate slowly drawing to a close, to shut, then fade into an earlier dream, the woods and fields on opposite sides of the road were inching closer together, reclaiming what was once theirs. Tucker was not only the last one left occupying a house in Pine Way, or nearly that, he was its guardian. He watched over the vestiges of the past, the wooden and brick vessels that once carried the lives of an era no longer in existence. His childhood during the Great Depression was gone, the war years had passed, then his coming of age. Sylvia, Forty, and Jim were so much a part of that, all gone away.

"Why was it so?" he asked. "Why all the troubles, the striving, when it would amount to mere dust?" He pondered these questions and more. What had it meant? Why did he hold on to it so? An old town once thriving lay dying. "Each person took something with them when they died or moved away," he said, "but they left something important, too, something of value that we need to honor."

He turned down Peach Tree Lane to visit the cemetery. Passing through the entrance gate, he saw his family's burial plot. Each of their headstones came into view, except that of his eldest sister, June, because she was buried in the town where she had lived. The most recent one marked where his brother, Dewey, was laid to rest. Recalling the ceremony, Tucker was disappointed that only one of his sisters had attended. That was Marjorie. She said that Lois could not get away. Tucker sensed otherwise. He remembered overhearing Howard whisper in his wife's ear, "I told you," meaning he suspected all along that Lois would not attend.

They had a big family, eight children, but too few remained. His parents only had four grandchildren, which were June's and Marjorie's kids, living elsewhere. Tucker wished he could talk about that with his father. He wanted to thank him for teaching him so much about life and how to be a dad. He wanted to tell his father that he understood the responsibility to value freedom and to uphold peace, to safeguard it.

Believing his father could no longer be reached, languishing away in a rest home, Tucker instead stood over his mother's grave and said, "I know you wanted your sons to have children, too. But there's just me and Howard left to carry on the Stewart name. I'm afraid it's too late for Howard, but there's still time for me...I hope."

Hands in his pants pockets, he glanced around that sunny day. He noticed the green of the trees blown by the wind, shades of light-green and dark turning autumn-gold.

Announcing to the air, the sky, and the wind, he said, "I'd like to try my hand at fatherhood...I think I'm ready."

The sight of green lawn, with its rich, earthy smell, brought to him one day playing baseball at the elementary school. It was hot that day. The spectators were fanning themselves with whatever lay at hand. He was up to bat and Jim Hart was pitcher. He feared the other boy was going to hit him with the ball and give him a fat lip.

Tucker smiled and laughed a little. He knew why he thought of that. Hart had pitched the ball that gave Tucker his first home run. Because of that, home plate, where he stood that day with all eyes on him, came to represent something more than a game.

"Home is the beginning of all great things, there within our grasp," he said. If he wanted to be a father, then he would be one. If he wanted to preserve Pine Way, he would do it. At the back of his mind dwelled his promise to befriend Jim Hart. Looking across the fields and orchards toward the old brick buildings of Pine Way, then allowing his gaze to sweep across the valley, he said, "I'm gonna try."

Adding one last comment to his mother before turning to leave, he said, "I think Dad might be joining you pretty soon, Mom. When you see him, thank him for me, for having faith in me. He'll know what I mean."

•   •   •

With Freckles trotting faithfully alongside, Tucker left the cemetery and made his way toward the back of the elementary school grounds. Soon, he spotted the lone house on Walnut

Lane he was seeking, which stood across the street from the Pine Valley Marketplace. A weathered sign on the lawn read, "Vet's Office," which the veterinarian who ran his business there apparently found convenient. It was a white house, more like a cottage, built after the First World War as a veteran's administration office. To Tucker, it was merely a white house with green shutters. An immense rose vine clambered up one side of the building while a Bermuda grass lawn and white picket fence constituted the front yard.

Approaching the front door, he saw the nameplate and read, "Joseph Cadwallader, DVM." Tucker disbelieved his own eyes. The vet was another one of Sylvia's relatives. "Oh, boy," he said. Rubbing the back of his neck, he momentarily glanced away and shook his head. When he looked back, he noticed another sign hanging inside the door's window. It had a cartoonish picture of a sheep, saying, "Be right baack."

Unmoved by the veterinarian's humor, Tucker sat on the doorstep, thinking instead about fatherhood and marriage.

"Well," he grumbled, "Sylvia's one woman who's not going to make me a father."

Freckles shot her head around to look straight at him.

"What?" he asked her. Pretending to reprimand her, he said, "Not a word from you, young lady. And, in your condition."

Freckles licked his face and peered intently into his eyes.

He stroked her fur and asked, "You remember Sylvia, don't you?"

Freckles whined, then snorted with a jerk of her head as though she had nearly sneezed, before looking at him again.

"Well, she left me," said Tucker. "She left us both." He was suddenly glad he kept the dog. He would manage somehow. "We'll be all right, girl," he said. "Just you and me, huh?" He scratched along her neck, which always made Freckles close her eyes and sway a bit.

They perked up at the sound of an old and faded blue BMW sputtering its lopsided way down the street toward them. Its driver parked in the driveway. After the engine was shut off, the car shook and rumbled before letting out what sounded like its final gasping breath.

Noticing the wire holding the engine compartment closed, Tucker said, "Well, girl, let's hope he takes better care of animals than he does his car."

When the driver got out of the car, he said, "Hello! Who might you be?"

"Hi, I'm Tucker Stewart."

"Oh? Well, you must be little Tucker James all grown up," said the man. Smiling, he extended his hand and said, "Good to see you!"

The veterinarian was a smiling man. He had snow-white hair and wore a rumpled white linen suit. Laughter came easy to him.

After they shook hands, Tucker inquired, "Well, I know you're related to Sylvia Cadwallader somehow. Are you a distant relative?"

"I'm her uncle!" the vet answered.

Following the man into his office, Tucker immediately noticed a sickening odor he imagined must be from a mixture of dogs and medicine or disinfectant. Freckles turned to make a quick dash out the door, but Tucker grabbed ahold of her and closed it. She started whining and shivering.

Sylvia's uncle asked, "What can I do for you?"

Momentarily distracted by the dog, Tucker ignored the question. But he also wanted to inquire further about the veterinarian's connection to Sylvia. "So, I know Sylvia's dad had a few brothers. But I don't remember a Joseph Cadwallader being one of them," he said.

"Oh, I've rarely been addressed by my given name," the vet explained. "Everyone usually calls me by my middle name, Reginald, because our father was also named Joseph. While he was Joe to most everyone, I was Reggie. Like yourself, you and your father had to be differentiated, did you not? So, you were Tucker James and your father was Tucker Howard. Am I right?"

Tucker was forced to sit down and hold on to Freckles in his lap as she continued to tremble in fear. Even though he wanted to listen to the vet, he needed to get Freckles' issue addressed and be on his way.

"Well, apparently, my dog has gone into heat, but I don't want her to have any puppies," he said.

The vet said, "Okay, well, we can schedule her to come in and get spayed." Looking at his calendar, he inquired, "How about the end of the month? My assistant only works mornings, so it would have to be then. Oh, but you'll need to drop her off the day before." Pointing out which days on the calendar, he added, "So we can get her ready...say, around noon?"

"That would work fine," answered Tucker.

"And," the vet continued, "I'd like to keep her overnight, just to see how she does."

Tucker worried about the cost. "Uh," was all he said before the vet interrupted him.

"Until then, these might be of use to you, for when she's indoors," he said.

He handed Tucker a small package after rummaging through whatever was behind the counter. Tucker had no idea what he was given, merely stuffing it into his back pocket.

The vet added, "Oh, and you should purchase a leash and a collar, so you can keep her under control." He again began rummaging around behind the counter, informing Tucker, "I've seen her, you know, all over town. She has friends everywhere. It wouldn't be long before she had puppies. It's a good thing you're having her spayed." He then asked, "Is she up to date on her shots?"

"Shots?" Tucker halfway expected the vet to pull out a loaded syringe from behind the counter.

Seeing Tucker's look of surprise, the vet said, "Okay. Why don't we include that in her visit." He scribbled some illegible notes on a scrap of paper and handed it to Tucker. "Here are some instructions. Be sure to follow them," he said.

In a daze, Tucker put the collar on Freckles, clipping the leash to it, not at all happy with having a dog at the moment. Freckles tried wriggling out of the collar, tugging on it with her paw to pull it off. Tucker paid for everything. However, a blank look formed on his face when he was told the additional charges for Freckles' surgery. Turning to stagger out of the vet's office, he muttered under his breath, "How am I supposed to pay for that?"

Despite Tucker's difficulties, the vet cheerfully chatted on. "You know," he said as he stepped from around the counter and rested his elbow on it, his hands clasped, "my brothers and I used to come here when this was a real vet's office." He chuckled, momentarily looking downward into his memories, before he continued, "Bobby would bring his daughter, Sylvia, with him. He adored her. And, she adored him. Tragic end, my brother...getting murdered." Looking at Tucker, he said, "I think I'm still in shock!" He followed Tucker out the door, squinting in the sunlight as he continued talking. "I remember Sylvia saying once that she wished her house had a white picket fence and rose vines, just like this one. We all doted on her! Moved away, I hear."

"Hmph. Don't remind me," Tucker mumbled under his breath as he, the reluctant new owner of her cast-off puppy, hastily waved goodbye.

CHAPTER TEN

Tucker turned his head to see Katie Winters hailing him from the Hillview apartment complex. An impulsive urge came over him at the sight of her. He felt like he might trip over his feet or tear off down the road. Considering the string of dates they had enjoyed over the years, it occurred to him that she might have assumed they would eventually marry.

At the sound of Katie's voice, Freckles struggled to pull her head out of her collar, straining on the leash and whimpering. Katie ran toward them, first stopping to greet Freckles.

"Hello, girl," she said. She began petting the dog and cooing at her.

Freckles was wagging her tail. She folded her ears back and licked Katie's face.

Katie said to Tucker, "I'm glad to see she found you again. She paid me a visit. Didn't you, Freckles?"

According to Katie, Freckles had a regular route through town to visit and mooch and socialize with other dogs. She visited Katie at the library and was a regular at the playground during recess, according to Johnny, she said.

Tucker was astounded. "What?! I don't believe it," he said.

He crouched beside the dog to ask, "What's this I hear about you, young lady, cruising around?" He scratched and petted her. "What am I going to do with you?"

Playing it safe, he said goodbye to Katie and continued on his way home.

But Katie followed along beside him, asking, "Mind if I join you? I get so little exercise."

"Uh, I don't mind," answered Tucker. Trying to conceal his anxiety, he smiled and said, "We'd love to have you along. Wouldn't we, Freckles?"

Soon they were walking down Walnut Road together. Katie was wearing the comfortable clothes she liked to wear at home, denim capris, a boat-necked, light-green pullover sweater, and black, cotton slip-on shoes. Her reddish-blond hair was down, loose, and curled at the ends into a "flip."

Tucker noticed and was admiring her. He felt very comfortable around her, which brought a smile to his face. Setting aside his worries over marriage, he took her hand in his as they leisurely strolled side by side. Noticing Freckles had finally stopped fighting with her new leash, having settled down, Tucker relaxed and enjoyed their walk together.

Walnut Road curved around the houses and walnut orchards, where it followed alongside Pine Valley Creek, eventually meeting up with a dirt road. Continuing along, the noise from the highway grew faint as the sound of the wind and the swishing and clattering of the cottonwood leaves, grew louder. The water in the creek was low, but Tucker imagined hearing it trickling and bubbling when they walked closest to it.

It was Katie's turn to admire Tucker. They had known one another ever since she moved to Edenville. They began dating a couple of years later, after she started working at the library. Dating was not on her mind at first. She had moved to Edenville primarily to be close to her son, Johnny. Secretly, she had wanted to reconnect with Johnny's father, Jim Hart, but that never happened.

She pointed to a path that went up the hillside and said, "There's that trail."

Tucker saw the trail and recalled that Katie had been at Jim Hart's funeral. He wondered how she knew Jim. Yet, another thought came to him, something about Jim from when they were children. He shared it with her.

"One time," he began, "a bunch of us kids were playing here by the creek. We must have been, oh, eight or nine...about the time the war started and my brothers signed up." His pace slowed and he looked at Katie. She was rapt with attention. Continuing his story, he said, "Jim Hart's uncle had also enlisted. I guess we were all talking about that, about how all the men were going to war and what it meant." He stopped walking and fixed upon that distant image he was recalling as he questioned, "What did we know? We were just kids. But I'll never forget something Jim said."

Katie waited for Tucker to tell her. She was slightly frightened, worried, her breath quickening.

Tucker's voice had a slight quaver to it as he said, "I guess it was because we were afraid, worried our brothers and uncles,

Sylvia's dad, would all get killed. But Jim said, 'Dying's not so bad. It's living that's the hard part,' and we all got really quiet."

Tucker asked Katie, "How can a little boy be so wise?"

Katie hugged Tucker, realizing only then that they were both grieving Jim. However, she grieved him so much that it hurt. She felt the pain in her heart again, remembering the day she returned to Edenville with Johnny and learned that Jim had married. That was 1954. Thirteen years had passed. She wondered how that could still hurt her so much and, yet, how she needed the man who held her. She felt his strength, his arms around her and how safe his embrace made her feel. In her thoughts, she said, "I love you, Tucker," and knew she could withstand any loss so long as he held her close.

Tucker appreciated Katie's friendship. However, feeling a mix of emotions, specifically regarding Jim Hart, he stepped away from her and asked, "Why did I have to be so mean to Jim? Why couldn't I have been his friend?" Looking at Katie, he told her, "He needed a friend, not another person making fun of him."

Katie told him, "Don't be so hard on yourself. Jim had his own problems that had nothing to do with you."

Momentarily wondering again how Katie knew Jim, Tucker let the matter go and continued walking. Katie's head lowered as she joined him. They were on the dirt road, gradually wandering beyond Pine Way Junction, having missed the turn to go to Tucker's house. They were following an abandoned road into the woods, neither of them paying attention to where it might lead.

At some point, Tucker stopped and looked around, saying, "Hey! This is where we used to come for picnics! I think."

They were standing in a cleared area in the forest that was filling in with shrubs and tall grass. A pathway led through it, which they followed for a while, eventually stumbling upon an old cemetery. Katie remembered Jim sharing it with her. In her memory, she saw him kneeling beside two graves in particular. His dark, wavy hair had grown long, nearly to his shoulders that summer. He took a small pouch out of his shirt pocket. Digging through it with his fingertips, he drew out something which he then held toward the sky, as though in offering. Katie remembered wanting to kneel beside him and place her arm around him, telling him, "I love you, Jim," but she had held herself back. Her head lowered again, knowing it was fear that kept her in silence regarding her true feelings toward Jim, as well as toward Tucker.

The sun was setting. In the pine and fir forest at the edge of the mountain, it was more like dusk. On impulse, Katie looked for the tiny white headstones that Jim had shown her.

"What are you looking for?" asked Tucker.

He watched as she walked between the bushes, looking up and saying, "They should be here. Oh, look! I found them!" She bent down and began to clear pine needles, branches, and leaves away from two white quartz headstones showing above ground. Using a stick, she carefully dug around them.

"What are those?" Tucker asked.

"This is the Indian cemetery," Katie explained as she continued digging, "from the Pine Valley massacre. The Hart family buried two of their children here. Jim showed me."

She stopped digging and looked up at Tucker. Her entire countenance had changed. She looked younger somehow, but also scared.

In that moment, Tucker knew why Katie had attended Jim Hart's funeral. Walter Henry had said that Jim left his half of the business to Johnny. Tucker was among those who noticed how much Johnny resembled Jim. It dawned on Tucker that Katie had arrived in Edenville not long after Johnny had arrived. She was working odd jobs before she started working at the library.

Knowing full well what had happened, and trying to not let his anger and disappointment show, he reassured her. "Don't worry," he said. "It's okay. I-I know about you and Jim."

Slightly aghast, Katie asked, "What do you mean, you know? How? Who told you?"

"I-I figured it out," answered Tucker.

"Oh," she said.

She stood up, tossing aside the stick she had been using. She pushed her hair from her face with the back of her hand and wiped her nose. Looking down at the ground, she suddenly felt defeated by the years, by loss and what could not be for her, not then and not ever, she believed. She lowered her head and cried, her shoulders shaking as she sobbed.

Tucker placed his arms around her, not knowing what to say, except, "I'm-I'm sorry."

Katie let him hold her in his arms as she grieved the loss of one man and her youth and what never got to be for her and Johnny.

Tucker knew in that moment that Katie had loved Jim and that she still loved him. Furthermore, she was entrusting him with that knowledge, that secret.

Wanting to be a good friend to her, as well as to Jim, he said, "Let me try."

He bent down to clear more weeds and grass from the area. Even Freckles started digging and pulling on the weeds with her teeth. Once the names were unearthed, it all came back to Tucker. He remembered seeing Jim's mother pregnant and even holding a baby at different times during the war, but the babies disappeared. What had happened? He stood and straightened his back, sniffing from a runny nose and sweat, looking up and around. Acres of land needed to be cleared, he realized. Years of neglect had gone by since the war. What happened?

A dull ache grew in the pit of his stomach and he said, "I don't know if I can do this."

"Do what?" asked Katie.

Tucker confessed to her, "I promised just today to make it up to Jim for how I treated him. I had no idea what would come of that. This day..."

He promised Katie he would come back later and clear a wider area around the headstones. Looking at their dirty hands and disheveled clothes, he said, "We can wash up at my house. Come on, it's getting dark anyway."

CHAPTER ELEVEN

In all the years Tucker had known Katie Winters, he had assumed their relationship would remain the same. They dated and shared in a meal now and then. They enjoyed spending time together and, though it had gone unnoticed by even the most observant of townspeople, their friendship had blossomed into more than "just friends." However, Jim's death had affected even that most intimate aspect of their lives.

Walking to his house with her, Tucker placed his arm about her waist and asked, "Are you okay?" She nodded. Once at his house, he took off his shoes, placing them outside on the porch. While he unlocked the door, Katie removed her own shoes and set them neatly beside his, which made him smile.

They took turns washing their hands in the bathroom. Katie could hear Tucker in the kitchen struggling over something involving Freckles, who was apparently being uncooperative. When Katie came out of the bathroom, she saw them looking very embarrassed and humiliated.

"What's that thing on her?" she asked.

Looking embarrassed, Tucker said, "Oh. The vet gave me these-these-*things* to put on her while she's in the house. Evidently, she went into heat."

Katie pitied Freckles, who was standing there whining, as though mortified, her rear end hitched up in the air, not liking how "that thing" felt on her. The dog sighed quickly with a snort, the whites of her eyes showing as she looked away in worry and embarrassment.

"Freckles doesn't look very happy with that on," said Katie.

"No, she doesn't," Tucker said. "And, believe me, I'm not liking any of this either. But this is the last time. Isn't it, Freckles?" He explained to Katie about the dog's upcoming surgery.

"Poor girl," said Katie.

Soon, they were both petting and cooing at Freckles, who was then ready to eat her dinner.

Tucker and Katie prepared a meal together, laughing over little things, enjoying one another's company. While potatoes baked in the oven, they played Parcheesi. Tucker had, at first, set up another game, Sorry, but Katie looked at his choice and then at him, before they broke into laughter. When everything was cooked, they sat and ate their baked potatoes with Salisbury steaks, a salad and buttered bread. All seemed back to normal between them.

Eventually, their easy conversation made its way to the subject of Katie's involvement with Jim Hart.

Tucker gently asked her, "How did you and Jim meet?"

Ready to let the secret go, Katie said, "Oh, it was the summer before Jim's senior year. I was staying at Sister Ruth's, at the retreat center up the hill. You know, where Walter Henry lives. I was very young, and she was helping me. Jim and I just ran in to one another. You know how it is, unplanned. It just happens. I was walking up that trail I pointed out." She pointed her fork at her food and said, "This is really good, by the way."

Tucker could only imagine she and Jim had many such meetings and Katie had gotten pregnant with Johnny. It was shortly before he and Sylvia had their own fateful meeting out in the woods. That happened similarly, unplanned. It dawned on him that Sylvia could have gotten pregnant, too.

"Young and in love," he said. "Must have been going around."

"Don't tell me, you and—who?" Katie asked.

Tucker laughed out loud and said, "Sylvia."

Together, they laughed. Their predicaments in life, unmarried, with Jim and Sylvia's presence seemingly summoned into the room...it demanded they see the humor in it, and let it go. After all, it was nothing new. Young people were doing the same since Adam and Eve, Tucker mused. Although, he needed to clear the air of what clouded it long ago.

He asked Katie, "Did he ever tell you about Beth?"

"No," she answered. "I found out after they were already married."

"Sylvia?" he inquired further.

"Definitely not," said Katie. "He never said a word. I think he was juggling at least the three of us, all the while planning to make his big escape!" She grew irritated with that last admission, hastily finishing the last of her food, before collecting their plates to rinse them off. Afterward, she sat down again.

Confiding in Tucker, she said, "I had a child, you know, a boy. I tried to raise him on my own." She rolled her eyes. "That didn't work out," she said.

Tucker knew she was referring to Johnny, and was about to say so, when Freckles began nudging Katie's leg and whining.

Katie reassured her, "I'm okay, girl," and pet the dog.

Freckles returned to her bed. The pad Tucker had put on her was dangling down and ripped. The dog had been quietly pulling on it with her teeth while they were busy talking to one another.

"Aaah!" Tucker took the useless thing off. "This isn't working," he said as he tossed it into the trash can.

Momentarily distracted, they finished cleaning up after dinner. Tucker took a carton of ice cream out of the freezer and scooped up two bowlfuls. Though he had feared the subject, he said what was lingering on his mind.

"You know," he reluctantly began, "after Jim died, I couldn't figure out why his German Shepherd, Shep, kept following me around."

Tucker ate his Rocky Road ice cream, his favorite, while Katie looked at him, as though waiting for him to say more. He took a chance and asked her, "Do you think Jim's still around? I mean, do you think that, when people die, they don't really go away anywhere? Maybe they're all still here, only we can't see them."

Katie smoothed her ice cream with the back of her spoon and said, "I don't know. I've never noticed." She ventured,

"Sister Ruth used to tell me, we come into this life for a purpose, but it doesn't end when we die."

Tucker listened carefully. "Oh?" he asked. He wanted to hear more.

Katie went on, "We just...keep to our purpose, like a-a path. You know? We walk this path before we're born, during our lives, and after we die. It's continuous." She paused before saying, "It's like all of it is our life, not just this part, here, as-as people. We're already living before we're born and we continue living even after this life, as this person, ends."

Tucker caught on to what she was explaining and said, "So, you think—it seems to me what you're saying is that 'we' are spirit." In awe over their discussion, he shared, "I think our being here together, having met and dated, meeting up today, is part of our path."

"Yes, I think so, too!" said Katie. She smiled.

The conversation lagged. Katie went outside and put on her shoes. Having followed her outside, Tucker stood near, appreciating the night. He reached for her hand, wanting to tell her something important. Thanking him for dinner, Katie stepped off the porch and was gone.

Tucker was alone, but he was not lonely. He and Katie had drawn closer, yet they also became more distant. What would come of that was an unknown. Tucker needed only to trust in the spirit, in himself, for he knew that was why they were there, everyone, perhaps even plants and animals. That realization gave him a newfound appreciation for Freckles, whom he knew was not simply a dog, no more than he was simply a person, only human. She had a purpose, too. It was like Shep, following him around, because of Jim Hart having died, and needing to help Sylvia with her purpose. It was connected, like a thread connecting them all.

The night was cool. Slipping on his shoes, Tucker went down the steps to look up at the stars. Seeing the bright flickering of a multitude of luminous beings, the stars that were so far away, he touched upon that sense of awe he had felt earlier while talking to Katie. It was an expansive feeling, his awareness drawn up into the air by a force. Gazing upon Orion, the Big Dipper, the North Star, Cassiopeia, and the moon, left him in awe. Why Earth? He questioned. Why this planet? The reason for it was larger than him, greater. It was an unceasingly amazing mystery.

He heard footsteps coming down the road and turned to see who was there. Someone was walking past his house. Pine Way was devoid of streetlights, except one in the alleyway by the old post office. At Tucker's end of the street, it was dark. He saw a man, minding his own business, walking on past. It seemed strange to Tucker. He went into the house, which felt odd. So, he went back outside and sat on the porch steps when an enormous ball of orange flame in a myriad of colors and light shot across the sky. Stunned, he looked around in the dark as though others were near and he was asking them, "Did you see that?"

Pleased, he said, "thank you," for what he had witnessed, for the evening, and for Katie as he hurried back into the house to call her and ask if she had seen it, too.

CHAPTER TWELVE

Tucker spent the morning clearing grass and weeds from the Indian cemetery. Freckles stayed nearby as he worked. Once he finished, he stood back and surveyed what he had accomplished. A well-worn path, he noticed, came from the direction of where Ev Mendoza's house once stood. It ended at the two headstones.

A cool breeze swept through the clearing, like a sighing breath. It carried upon it a story relived, a massacre yet crowding the airwaves of Time. Screaming, and gunshots blasting away at a race, a people and their home, Tucker did not hear, yet he knelt in silent homage to its victims, their presence known only for two white quartz headstones.

He imagined Jim Hart's mother yet visited the graves and wondered why her babies were buried in such a forgotten place. The thought came to him that her two baby boys were taken from her, and feared it was true. The entire valley was once awash in blood and death, according to Char Lee Rosebud. The burials of two tiny babies were an offering, he supposed, to those who had come before them, the ancestors. It horrified him and, yet, broke his heart.

While he had not the words, his prayer, with eyes closed and head bowed, was felt. "Let there be peace," it said.

Gathering his tools and wheelbarrow, he called to Freckles, "Let's go home. Okay, girl?"

She had her appointment that day so, after bathing her, Tucker returned to the little cemetery, leaving the dog in the house. He could hear her whining and barking, even scratching and banging at the door as he walked away. Once he arrived at the burial ground, the same man he had seen the night of the meteor was standing there as though in prayer. Tucker knew the man was Indian and probably had relatives buried in that cemetery. He quietly set the flowers he had picked from his garden between the two tiny headstones. The man turned and approached him.

"Hi." Friendly and smiling, he asked, "Are you Tucker Stewart?"

He was younger than Tucker, of average build and height, and had dark-brown hair, which was at collar length. He wore a dark-brown cowboy hat with a ragged turkey feather poked in its brim, blue jeans, and a pearl-button shirt. A very congenial young man, his temperament was similar to Tucker's when much younger and more happy-go-lucky than of late.

Tucker answered, "Yes, that's me."

"Name's Harvey Six-Bits," said the man.

They shook hands and Tucker said, "Hello, Harvey."

A bear sauntered into the burial ground as they turned to walk away. Harvey saw the bear, knowing why it came. He also knew why Tucker had come.

Patting Tucker on the back, Harvey said, "Hey, thanks, man. For what you did here."

When they reached the old McGrew house, he informed Tucker that he had bought it with his own money.

Tucker raised his eyebrows in amazement. He was proud of the young man, and asked Harvey, "You-you did? You own this now?"

Harvey nodded and smiled.

They stood in front of the house, looking around the property.

Harvey grew serious and asked Tucker, "You know what my people call you?"

Tucker hesitated, expecting the usual teasing. He thought about how these people of the old, old way of life in Pine Valley had come into his life. He appreciated it, even if they enjoyed teasing him. Taking a chance, he answered, "What do they call me?"

Harvey said something in his native language. Tucker asked him, "Uh, what does that mean?" He heard Freckles yapping in the distance from the direction of his house.

"It's a sacred name my people gave to you when our healer, Lucy Shoseegan, was still living," said Harvey.

Harvey sat on the porch steps, but Tucker remained standing, wanting to be serious, but not sure what to do or to say as he listened to Harvey explain.

"She said you would be the last man left in our original village site and that it would be your job to watch over it, protect it for our return. It basically means, 'The Keeper of the Dream,' or something like that." Harvey looked up at Tucker and reassured him. "It's true, man," he said. "You ought to feel honored that Lucy knew your purpose. After the massacre, when everyone was living up in Laketon, she started envisioning us returning home one day. Until then, she said that you would be asked to watch over the valley, to protect her dream."

Tucker remembered his high school graduation. Afterward, he glanced at the Hart family gathered around Jim, congratulating him. There was a short and weathered old woman looking his way, who then turned to place her palm on Jim's head as he bent toward her to receive a blessing. Was that Lucy? Everyone was making plans during their senior year, where they would go to college, where they would go to work. They were eager to marry, eager to move away. Tucker eventually dismissed it, knowing that he would stay, he would remain.

He was the last man standing in Pine Way. The businesses were closed. Many of the homes had burned or became neglected or abandoned. Eunice Chapman lived at the other end of his street, but only he took care of his home. He devoted his time and attention to it. It was his responsibility, taken upon himself, to watch over that forgotten end of the valley. The power of that knowledge brought greater clarity to the upset of the past several months since Jim Hart's death. Like a Great Turning or Shifting, the dream was coming home as Lucy's vision had foretold. He could never leave the valley. He loved it, and wanted to bring Pine Way back, like in its heyday. That was in his heart. It was his secret. It was sacred.

Tucker never shared his secret, though, for he barely knew it existed. Not something he could yet put into words, but he imagined a great circle of people of all races and ways of being, living together in peace. Ideas and creative ways of doing things differently would be welcomed. At the center of his secret was Jim Hart's mother, Candelaria, the central figure in his imaginings of what would be created in a new Pine Valley. It was his sacred dream. Standing before the house, with Harvey looking on, Tucker cast his thoughts adrift into his inner visioning. He let his dream come forward, seeing Harvey's people living in Pine Way. He could see gardens, flowering plants, and joyful activity. Some were creating art and music, others were dancing. Change? Yes, but toward peace, not chaos, not violence.

"Thank you, for telling me that," he said to Harvey. Knowing it was Freckles whining and yapping from his house, he hurriedly added, "Sorry, but I need to go let my dog out."

"Okay," said Harvey. "But, come on back, all right? Got some friends coming over to help me with the house." Nodding his head back toward it, he added, "Gonna fix it up."

"All right," said Tucker.

He hurried home to find Freckles made a wreck of the house. She was agitated, almost unmanageable as though she knew her appointment was drawing near. Tucker was appalled. "What did I get myself into?!" he cried. An image of Jim Hart's dilapidated shack came to mind and Tucker feared his perfect little house would be ruined should he allow Freckles to continue her bad behavior. Groaning, he took her outside and, as he was about to tie her to a metal stake he had pounded by the yard, a familiar car slowly drove past his house.

The driver waved and said, "Hey, Tucker! How's it goin', man?"

It was Barclay, whom Tucker had met in Laketon. Tucker waved at Barclay and his brother, Bear. Tucker assumed they were on their way to Harvey's house. A young woman was sitting in the back seat whom Tucker recognized, Aurelia Mendoza. Wondering what she was doing with them, he quickly took care of what he needed to, put Freckles on her leash, and walked back to his neighbor's.

Tucker's dream was coming to life. Reassured, he knew that Harvey and his people would help to rejuvenate the little town that was slipping away. Lucy's vision of a new Pine Valley edged closer and Tucker caught a glimpse of its true light.

CHAPTER THIRTEEN

When Aurelia saw Tucker approaching Harvey's house in the mid-morning sun, he enraptured her heart and soul. She was attracted to the tall, light-haired man, unselfconscious of how she appeared as Tucker returned her warm smile.

"Hi," she said. "So, we finally get to meet. I'm Aurelia."

"Hello. I'm Tucker. I remember you used to live over here with Ev Mendoza," he said.

Oblivious of anyone or anything else, they continued their conversation, occasionally joking and laughing, though mostly gazing into each other's eyes and smiling.

Harvey was busy talking with the other men about the work to be done on his house. He failed to register the encounter between Aurelia and Tucker until Barclay nudged his arm and directed him to look their way. Harvey saw his girl talking quietly with Tucker and how they were getting along so well.

He said to Tucker, "Why don't you help us unload these tools?"

Tucker remained standing near Aurelia. She was petting Freckles as they took turns pointing out the various instances in which they had come across one another in the past. Harvey and his crew made trips to and from the porch, unloading saws, sanders, toolboxes, and other items, like the cooler.

Candelaria Hart approached the house from the direction of the Indian cemetery. She immediately noticed Tucker and Aurelia behaving so friendly with one another. Assuming that Harvey cleaned up the burial ground, she was stopping by to thank him. Seeing Tucker, however, caught her off guard. She asked herself, "What's *he* doing here?" Upset with Aurelia, she wanted to tell the young woman to stop flirting with the man. Yet, she stood by, behaving as though she had a sliver of wood in the bottom of her foot she was too stubborn or proud to take time to remove.

Why Tucker felt the loss of his own mother more keenly around the woman, was unconscious. He believed Candelaria was angry with him for taking it upon himself to clean the Indian burial ground. Uncomfortable with the awkward situation, he joined the other men at their task, pretending to have something to do inside the house. Two white headstones appeared in his thoughts. He deemed it wise to avoid a confrontation.

Tucker never forgot his family's earliest associations with the Hart family, especially Candelaria's kindness toward him when he was a child. Her daughter, Rosa, used to come over to his family's house to visit his sisters, Marjorie and Lois. Sometimes, Dottie McGrew joined them. They would do homework and study together, bake cookies or make sandwiches, maybe listen to music and practice dancing. Tucker recalled vividly that, whatever they did, it usually involved him playing their date, their model, or their child. Guinea pig, is what it felt like to him. Rosa would fawn over him, saying, "Aw, look how adorable he looks." It was humiliating for him, riding in the wagon, dressed up like a baby with a pretend diaper and bib on, so they could take turns pulling him around. Before he had started school, Rosa would bring her little brother, Jim, in tow. The boys served as their pretend children when the girls played house. Their two families once owned businesses in Pine Way, working side-by-side, yet they drifted apart and he knew not how it happened.

Aware that he was standing around doing nothing, Tucker wondered where the other men had gone. He heard their laughter coming from the backyard. Soon, Harvey, Barclay, and Bear returned inside the house, bringing with them a telltale odor. Tucker knew what they had been smoking. He smiled slightly at the thought, then shook his head, checked the time on his watch, and attempted to help them set up their work station in the living room. He tried not to notice that Candelaria was still outside, petting Freckles and talking with Aurelia.

Grinning slyly, Harvey began teasing Tucker about the encounter with Candelaria. "Boy, Tucker," he said, "I think maybe you and Aurelia's cousin love each other, or something." Bear and Barclay giggled.

"What?! No, no." Tucker lifted his hand to tell them to stop. "That's enough," he said. After all, he was older. He wanted their respect.

Barclay, who nudged his brother, Bear, could not resist joining in. "Yeah, Tucker, when's the wedding?" he asked.

The three jokesters laughed, with their helpless target standing beside them looking forlorn and embarrassed.

"All right, all right. I said that's enough!" demanded Tucker.

It was not enough. Barclay chimed in again with, "Maybe you and Harvey, here, could have a double wedding!" He literally doubled over and fell to the floor, holding his stomach as he rolled with hysterics.

Tucker gave up. He knew it was no use trying to stay serious, though had to defend himself, somehow. Trying not to yell, he raised his voice. "She's Jim Hart's mother, for goodness' sake. He just died not that long ago. Haven't you any respect?" he asked.

"Uh, sorry, man. I feel really bad now," said Barclay.

By some mysterious signal, the joking trio left for various areas in the house to begin their work, leaving Tucker to wonder for which task he was needed, other than being the source of their fun. Checking his watch again, he decided to go home. He had to take Freckles to the vet by noon. Informing Harvey of his decision to leave, the young man objected.

"You can't go now," said Harvey. "We need you to help." With hammer in hand, he was busy pounding nails into the wood flooring where boards were warped or creaking.

"I only have a short amount of time before I have to go," Tucker said.

Smiling, Harvey flipped the hammer around and handed it to Tucker, along with the nails. He patted the older man on the back and left the room.

When it was nearly noon, Tucker told them he had to leave right away to take Freckles to get spayed. He went outside the house and discovered that Aurelia and Candelaria were gone and that Freckles was gone, too. He looked up and down the road, went back inside the house, and asked, "Where's my dog?!"

Bear, usually the quiet one, answered Tucker's frantic questioning with, "How should we know? We're just here to work."

Bear's job was to sand the floors once they were ready. He went about plugging in the sander and untangling the cord. Barclay's job was to varnish and seal the floors, but he and Harvey were having a discussion in the kitchen about their work schedule.

Barclay laid the back of one hand onto the palm of another, saying, "We should've checked the foundation first." He was concerned they were getting ahead of themselves.

"Foundation? There's no foundation in these old houses!" said Harvey, grinning.

Barclay's concerns did not end there. His hand went out in each direction as he pointed out, "Well, what about the roof? Or-or-termites?"

Harvey became surprised at Barclay's worry. He said, "Why are you all of a sudden worried, man? We went over all of that. The house is sound. We agreed the floor was where we'd begin, then we'd do the finish work."

"Okay, okay." Barclay took a moment, then said, "I think maybe it's lunchtime. I need to eat something."

"We just got here!" Harvey was exasperated and simultaneously doubted his renovating plans. "All right," he said. "We'll stop for lunch. I'll go over the house again to make sure I know what we're doing. Okay?"

So it went, the three of them, Harvey and his crew, the volunteer builders of modern-day Laketon, going through their usual round of issues that typically revolved around Barclay's eating habits. Barclay dug into his ice chest for a soda and a half-eaten deli sandwich, sat down and took a bite and, with mouth full, announced, "I'm gonna go get some pizza." He left the kitchen to roust Bear into going with him. "Come on! Let's go get pizza," he said.

In disbelief, Tucker asked Harvey, "How do you ever get any work done?"

Harvey good-naturedly defended his loyal crew. "Hey, we built nearly all of Laketon together," he said. "If we can do that, we can do this." He nodded his head in proud affirmation.

Tucker rolled his eyes and muttered, "No wonder." Their work ethic, in his opinion, left little to be desired.

Harvey was digging in his pockets for money to give Barclay with his own instructions. "No pepperoni, man. That stuff's bad for you. Gives me gas, too," he said.

He turned to Tucker who, completely lost as to what to do now that he had wasted nearly his entire morning, stepped out of the kitchen in a daze.

"Tucker, why don't you go with them? They can give you a ride over to the vet's office," said Harvey.

Tucker threw his hands up in the air. "I have to find my dog first!" he said.

Harvey reassured him, "Oh, don't worry. Ellie probably took her to her cousin's house. Clay'll stop by there on the way."

"Yeah, sure, man. You can say 'hello' to your girlfriend," teased Barclay.

They roared in laughter all over again, as Tucker closed his eyes, wondering what he was doing with these people.

"We'll get your dog, Tucker," Bear asserted. "We know you don't wanna be a father, or nothing."

They were all standing together when it dawned on Tucker why he was there. In all his struggle since he first went to Laketon, pretending to know what he was doing, and worrying, because he had not a clue as to what he was doing and, in all their joking, he had acquired friends. His heart warmed at the thought. He had friends.

He said, "I'll be right back, then, and help some more, too."

"You better!" said Harvey. He smiled and put out his hand to shake Tucker's with a smack and a clasping grip. "You're all right, Tucker," and added, "Keeper of the Dream," in his native tongue.

Aurelia sat out front of Candelaria's shack with Freckles. She had argued with her older cousin, because she refused to help make sandwiches for the men. Candelaria had mentioned to her that Harvey was probably expecting to get married, so she had better learn how to take care of him. Aurelia hated the idea of being the kind of wife Candelaria had in mind, aproned, standing at the stove, cooking for a man, and having his babies. She secretly wished a big hole would open in the earth and swallow her up. She plotted how to get out of her predicament, when she spotted the cloud of dust coming up the road, which signaled her escape.

She vowed angrily, "No one's gonna turn me into Susie Homemaker!"

Soon, she was riding along with the men on their way to the pizza parlor. She had seated herself in the back seat next to Tucker and behaved opposite to what Candelaria had advised.

Riding in the old Pontiac, with tires so worn, they bubbled, blue paint so faded, rust showed like scabby wounds, Barclay's trusted steed, that had not yet failed them, went galloping off down the road once more.

CHAPTER FOURTEEN

That night, Aurelia wanted to see Tucker again. She put on her sneakers and said, "Uh, Laria? I'm gonna go for a walk. You know, just sort of enjoy the evening."

Candelaria was quick. "Aurelia," she said. She was very clear with her younger cousin. "Don't do something you'll later regret. Do you hear me?" she asked.

Aurelia rolled her eyes and said, "Look. I'm only going for a walk and then I'll be right back. Is that all right with you?" She tied her shoelaces.

Noting Aurelia's tone and her restlessness, Candelaria guessed what the young woman was doing. When her younger cousin stepped outside, departing on foot into the night, Candelaria watched her from the porch. Aurelia was walking toward Pine Way, hands in the pockets of her jacket, going somewhere in mind, to see someone in mind.

"Remember what I said!" yelled Candelaria.

On the porch of her little shanty, Candelaria continued watching what could very well have been herself long ago.

Growing sad and wistful, she looked on, even after the young woman disappeared into the dark. She asked herself, how many times had her husband, Jimmy, waited for her in the night before they were married? Growing chill, she rubbed her arms, though she was not yet ready to return indoors. Thinking of her husband and her youth, she felt the nights were never so feared as they had in later years become. The night was their safe place where their love was held close and treasured. When had the night become something to fear? She knew. It was the night their son, Jim, purposely cut himself and they thought he would die.

Tears fell across Candelaria's face from eyes that saw a long ago day held painfully in her heart. Tempted to step further into the memory, something told her, "no." A light breeze swept through, tumbling piles of dry leaves further down the road. It drew her out of her sadness. Time to go indoors, she thought, and let rest the weary memory of her son.

She quickly bathed and donned her nightgown and robe, since the nights were getting cold. Even though she sat in her token living room before the television, she sat quietly, not watching anything, merely content to soak in the quietness of being alone in her home. Thinking further about the young man, Tucker Stewart, she was reminded about the time when he and her son were boys.

Candelaria pondered the cost of raising an angry child. She longed to love her son once he had outgrown his cuddly baby stage and became the tough kid with flying fists. She had lost both her baby boys as well. Tucker was that sweet little boy down at the newspaper office she wished was her son. Hearing about Addie Stewart's sudden death, when Tucker was only nine or ten years old, her heart went out to the boy whose grieving father yelled at him. She thought he blamed the boy for his wife's death. He was also too busy philandering to pay any attention to his children. It was all Candelaria could do to keep herself from asking Tucker Howard if he needed any help with little Tucker James, so she could bring him home with her.

An unexpected rise of grief, from down in the depths, nearly overcame Candelaria, but, before she could allow for its release, Aurelia opened the door, teary-eyed and sensitive. With her came the night air and its alluring mystery.

Not wanting to pry and not feeling up to anything emotional, Candelaria merely greeted Aurelia. "Hi. How was your walk?" she asked.

Unfortunately, for Candelaria, the young woman was in need of unloading what was on her mind.

"Can we talk?" asked Aurelia. She hoped Candelaria would be okay to talk to about something difficult for her to share.

"Sure," answered Candelaria. She got up from the sofa to sit at the kitchen table.

Aurelia poured herself some milk and served up a piece of cake that Rosa had made for them, some kind of banana-spice-nut-raisin-and-chocolate chip thing that Aurelia loved. She tentatively shared her feelings. She further confided in her elder cousin, saying that she was attracted to Tucker Stewart and had decided she would definitely not marry Harvey.

"I don't know why everyone thinks we are. It's not like he asked me or anything," she said.

Candelaria surprised herself when she supported her younger cousin's decision. "You're not ready, Aurelia. Maybe you're still looking for the right one. But I don't think it's

Tucker Stewart, do you?" She tried to contain her laughter, imagining him and Aurelia walking down the aisle together with little children in tow. One would be Little Tucker and one would be Little Ellie. Candelaria had to force herself to stop those silly thoughts before she burst out laughing.

"Did you hear what I said?" Aurelia asked. She rinsed her dishes at the sink and remained standing.

Candelaria snapped out of it. "What?" she asked.

Aurelia repeated herself, "I said, I think it could be important, you know, not a crush or like I want to marry him, or anything like that. Just, like it means something." Seeing Candelaria's blank look as though she had no clue as to what Aurelia was talking about, Aurelia merely added, "Ugh! I don't know what I'm trying to say."

Candelaria shook her head, saying nothing as she got up from the table to go watch tv.

Aurelia followed her to the sofa, asking, "What?"

Candelaria turned on the tv and flipped the channel to the show she wanted to see. Letting out a big sigh, because she was too tired to play games, she plainly asked the young woman, "Why don't you just admit that you like him? What's the harm in that? He's a likable person. I like him, too."

Aurelia agreed. She liked Tucker, period. However, once the lights were out and each of them retreated into their private thoughts before falling asleep, Aurelia knew she more than liked Tucker. She was attracted to him and wanted to continue seeing him. Lamenting her situation, she wondered how to tell Harvey. Recalling the day and how she felt when she first saw Tucker approaching Harvey's house, she realized that one of Harvey's friends was watching her. Harvey probably already knew, Aurelia thought.

Barclay told Harvey that night in Laketon around their campfire, "Hey, I think your girl's in love with Tucker, man. Sorry, but she was all goo-goo eyes with him and everything." Barclay made it clear.

"All right, all right. I'll talk to her," said Harvey. Recalling Aurelia's behavior earlier that day, acting disinterested in him, he admitted to himself that Barclay was right. "Oh, well," he said, "it's not like I wanted to marry her, or anything." He drained his beer.

Trying to get back to his discussion with Barclay and Bear about restoring the old house, Harvey gave his final say on the day's revelations. "Sh—!" he muttered to himself.

•　　•　　•

Meanwhile, Tucker was over at Katie Winters' apartment. They were enjoying a filling meal of pot roast with potatoes, onions, and carrots, plus a nice gravy, dinner rolls, and a salad. For dessert, Katie purchased a berry pie, which never got eaten.

Katie asked Tucker, " Do you want to watch television together? There's a special on I'd like to see."

Tucker was thinking about Aurelia, when they met at Harvey's and, after that, when she visited him at his house before he left for Katie's. Instead of answering Katie's question, he told her, "I was over at a friend's house today and met Candelaria's cousin, Aurelia Mendoza." He described her behavior, wanting Katie's opinion on what it meant, adding, "Candelaria showed up and was acting peculiar. I think she was mad at me for cleaning up the burial ground."

Annoyed, Katie informed Tucker, "Well, from what you describe, it sounds like Aurelia might have a crush on you." She tried to hide her anger regarding the young woman who was taking an interest in the man she had hoped to marry. Irritated, she gathered up the dishes and set them by the sink. Caught up by emotion, she unthinkingly added, "And Candelaria was probably concerned. Like a mother." That assessment on Katie's part only made her more angry, knowing what had taken place between Aurelia and Tucker. More to herself, she said, "If there's one thing I learned from Sister Ruth, these are the times when we simply need to trust."

Tucker overheard her. "Trust?!" he argued. Tossing his napkin aside, he got up from the table. He said, "You didn't see them today! They were—" Wiping the palm of his hand slowly across his unshaven jaw to rest over his mouth, he imagined his own mother standing in Harvey's front yard, looking from Aurelia to Tucker and back again.

Trying to understand what had happened, he said, "It all started when we began digging around those two graves." Believing that something had been unearthed in the process, he remained standing in place. He smiled through tears he would not let run, not knowing what to do.

Katie asked him, "Tucker? Are you okay?" She was worried, but let it go as she nervously wiped the kitchen table down, saying, "She loves you, Tucker." He flashed a look at her. Yet she continued, "For whatever reason, or however it happened, she just loves you," and was shocked that had come out of her mouth. She was referring to Candelaria, but it sounded like she meant Aurelia.

Katie became quiet after that and directed her attention to filling the sink with water, squirting in some dish soap, and beginning to hurriedly and vigorously scrub.

Tucker slowly stepped out of the kitchen area and plopped onto her couch, wanting to change the subject. He knew Katie was angry, and rightly so, but wondered whether to leave or to pretend he was ignorant of what got unearthed right there in that room. He decided to pretend.

"All right. So, what's this tv special about?" he asked.

Standing before the sink, her hands braced there, and without looking his way, Katie answered, "I don't feel much like watching tv now. Why don't we call it a night?"

Tucker learned that pretending was not working anymore.

CHAPTER FIFTEEN

Aurelia was softly crying, watching the lights from a car make their trek along the walls of her nighttime cell. A burning deep in her groin and a soulful yearning for something unseen, somewhere unknown, clearly rose within her. Calling her soul to task, it came unbidden and lightly crept into her bed, lying beside her, then entering her consciousness. She floated up and away into the night sky, soaring among the stars and the moon, high above the trees and the rooftops. Like into another realm, she drifted, seeing a dreamscape so real, it would change her. Like a river on the wind, her hair lightly blown, she was carried along until she came to rest upon a soft patch of earth. Nothing could be seen except the lighted, blue morning sky. All else was in shadow. It was as if she stood on the edge of Time, the end of primordial Earth where it met the backdrop of dawn and where her truth met her knowing.

Aurelia sank deeper into sleep, then awoke in the early morning, aware of what she needed to do. She told Harvey, "I can't see you anymore, Harvey." With her head down, she added, "Sorry."

Bravely setting his hurt aside, he said, "Tucker's the Keeper of the Dream, Ellie."

Humbled, though interested, Aurelia sat with Harvey on a sofa he had rescued from the dump and placed on his front porch. He continued, saying, "Lucy's dream is coming home. It's sacred. You need to honor your purpose, why you came to live here in Pine Valley." Aurelia nodded her head in agreement.

Over the next few days, what helped was to ask herself what role was she to play in bringing Lucy's dream home? She knew, first of all, that expressing herself was definitely needed. How she could express herself, she yet did not know. Candelaria had her writing, but Aurelia was not interested in keeping a journal. Rosa, she noticed, liked to cook. Aurelia enjoyed her walk that evening some nights before, so she took long walks in the forest.

Candelaria was not the only one who had shared in her mother's strolls in the forest around her house. Aurelia had oftentimes joined Ev, listening to her stories and enjoying Ev's thoughtful consideration of each thing that caught her eye, whether a bird or a flower, something she picked up off the ground or saw in the trees. Aurelia never shared that side of herself with her boyfriend, the fireman who turned out to be an arson and burned Ev's house down. She told her elder cousin as they reminisced about Ev Mendoza.

Following in Ev's footsteps while on her own walks, Aurelia took her time investigating whatever interested her. She would bring her findings home, adorning the top of the porch railing with them. Various sun-bleached animal skulls and interesting pieces of wood accumulated until, running out of room, she had to set them around the porch and the front steps.

Candelaria commented, "Don't you think the skulls are a bit morbid?" Seeing Aurelia's expression of sadness and worry revealed to Candelaria it was something her cousin needed to do. She hugged Aurelia and reassured her while rubbing her on the back. "It's all right," she said.

Feeling disheartened, Aurelia said, "I wish I knew how to carve the wood. I can almost see these animals in each piece I bring home."

"What do you mean?" Candelaria asked.

Aurelia's mood brightened as she excitedly told her, "Like this one. See how it bends here and the way the wood's grain flows over this way."

Candelaria smiled and knew Aurelia was finding her way, her true way, like she, herself had found her true way through writing.

Aurelia went on, her eyes wide with excitement as she shared, "It's as if I can see the finished piece, but I don't know how to do that, how to get there. It's so crazy! I feel like the animal is in the wood, calling to me to free it!"

Candelaria was pleased. She knew Aurelia had a gift and told her to look for someone who could help her learn woodworking, which brought even greater joy to the young woman. Aurelia appeared as though she could hardly keep from running down the road in search of whomever that might be. Candelaria finished what she needed to tell Aurelia. "I think you'll find the truth this way, what you've been needing to understand," she said. "I'm so proud of you!" She hugged her young cousin again, who was crying with joy.

Having arrived home from work, Candelaria entered her little house to gather up their laundry that needed washing. She felt the heaviness of grief building within her heart. Jim's death had taken place earlier that year. She thought it best to lay down for a while. With the memories in her vision of her two baby boys and her son, Jim, she sank into a state of depression so debilitating that she remained in bed.

The following morning, when Aurelia arrived at home, having stayed the night somewhere, she nearly stumbled over the bag of laundry by the door. Concerned, she peeked in Candelaria's bedroom before getting ready for work. She got a part-time job at KaZoo, the pet store in the Pine Valley Marketplace, and was trying not to be late her first day of work. However, she wanted to be sure her cousin was okay.

"Larie, are you all right?" she asked.

The light, sheer curtains in the shaded room were blowing gently and the room was cold. Candelaria was still and quiet, as though barely even breathing. Aurelia stepped into the room and closed the window. Returning to the bedside, she asked again, "Are you okay, Larie?" She was shocked to see Candelaria's eyes slightly open, but showing no recognition. Worried, Aurelia gently covered Candelaria with a blanket, then telephoned Rosa. Thankfully, Rosa was soon at their house.

Having seen that behavior in her mother before, Rosa saw to her mother's comfort, then closed the door again. She asked Aurelia in a hushed voice, so as not to disturb her mother, "What happened?"

Feeling guilty, Aurelia said, "I don't know. We've been talking a lot lately…about…things. She was helping me with some ideas I have. I don't know!" She threw her hands up in her honest innocence of what Candelaria was going through, then hurriedly blurted out, "I'm gonna be late for work if I don't go now!"

Rosa drove Aurelia to work, asking her to be sure and get the laundry washed. Afterward, she returned to her mother's house. Not having any classes until evening, she looked downward, patting her very pregnant belly. "It's not like I can do anything else," she said. She cleaned the kitchen, noticing that neither her mother nor Aurelia seemed to be at all interested in housekeeping. Once she was finished in the kitchen, she sat on the sofa to watch a game show, hoping her mother would snap out of it soon. Rosa dared not think about it, but knew that, even though he had died, her brother lived on in her mother's mind. Being pregnant, she wondered what kind of mother she would be, what kind of children would she bring into a changing world. Becoming a teacher, she realized, was a very important goal to have.

CHAPTER SIXTEEN

Winter in Pine Valley was in its deepest chill, bringing over two feet of snow during one storm in January. When the storm ended, fog shrouding the hills lifted away and the sun shone a glaring white. Comments were exchanged between men shoveling sidewalks and excavating their cars hidden beneath drifts of snow. Snow plows were in short supply, so those who worked in Edenville, either on the Loop or at the Marketplace, gave up on their cars. They trudged through the fresh snow to work. Stories were told of the coldest years, wettest years, even the hottest and driest years, but none could recall a snowfall like they had received.

Children appreciated its novelty. They slid on icy sheets created by long-frozen puddles and threw snowballs at each other on their way to school. Coats and mittens, knit caps and rubber boots were dug out of the hinterlands of their closets.

Grown-ups yelled after them, "Don't leave without your coat! Put on your mittens!" They complained of the mess and inconvenience, dreading the gas bill's arrival after a second month of unusually cold weather.

Higher in the mountains, roads were closed, and the people of Laketon found themselves cut off from everyone else. Bear and Barclay had to dig out Char Lee Rosebud's old trailer. Another one of their elders, whom everyone called, "Pappy Jack," had moved in and found himself trapped during the storm. The trailer's makeshift add-on collapsed under the weight of snow. The old man had no dry wood to put in the stove. He was nearly frozen by the time they dug him out and carried him over to the store where a nice fire was blazing. They wrapped him in blankets and gave him a cup of hot cocoa laced with brandy to warm him. Soon, Snake-Eye, the one-eyed cat, was settled in the man's lap as he contentedly dozed. Barclay and Bear spent the day rebuilding the collapsed porch and keeping the fire going in the store's wood stove, walking back and forth on the pathway they had shoveled.

No one knew if that would be the last snowfall of the year, but Walter Henry rolled his eyes at the comments. He could well remember real record snowfall years, back when he was in his twenties and could put in a full day's hard work. He recalled one quiet and still morning, startling the deer that came to nibble on the tips of young fir trees poking out from under the snow. They would kick it with a hoof in one move, then fall through the drifts in the next, struggling to keep aloft. A rabbit darted away from his very doorstep where crumbs, hay, and seeds were tossed for the birds and other creatures by his sister, Lulabelle. The snow blew up in the air as the rabbit's big hind feet back-kicked to leap away, the spray of powdery snow glistening.

Lulabelle, like a frightened rabbit, herself, scolded him from inside the miner's shack. "You scared it! I was gonna make a pet out of it!" she said.

Walter Henry both loved and grieved at the memory. Nearly sixty years had passed since then. Lulabelle was well over ninety years of age. Her retreat center was winding down, the winter all but shut it down, but she still talked of plans to improve despite it being the very last year of her life.

It was nearing spring and still the snow and ice hung on. Lulabelle refused to bathe. Crusts of crud crept out of the ground, it seemed. It grew on her ankles and wrists and was visible on her neck. An odor fumed from her scalp, where matted clumps of her snow-white, mere token wisp of hair was hidden beneath her woolen scarf wrapped around to cover her head.

Walter Henry had a funny feeling about her and told Millie, "Reminds me of when we had to go catch her out in the woods back when ole Josiah killed my papa."

One day, when Millie addressed the diminutive woman as Sister Ruth, Lulabelle stared at her and asked, "Who?"

Lullabelle, Walter Henry knew, had become his big sister again, wild and going to seed like all the wild things she loved.

"Bless her heart," Millie said to Walter Henry when they found Lulabelle after she stumbled in the snow over an unseen boulder. Fortunately, they saw her when it happened and hurried over best they could, or lest they might fall as well.

Lulabelle explained, "I thought I caught a bit of spring coming. Thought it was a flower, but it was this here itty bitty thing."

They had her lay on her bed after carrying her back into her cabin. From out of her soft, knitted mitten, there rolled a tiny, limp warbler. The small bird was but a streak of yellow, like a spring wildflower, which Lulabelle's keen eye had spotted. They let go of trying to bathe her or cut her hair. It was the right decision, because Lulabelle Henry, who lost all memory of ever being Sister Ruth, the spiritual director of the retreat center, passed away a few nights later. She was still decorated with tiny feathers from her frozen friend, a migrant warbler caught in the cold night air.

Walter Henry was more than a decade younger than his sister, yet grew concerned and thoughtful of his own mortal end. He was about to turn eighty years of age, but Millie assured him that she would be by his side, not knowing her time was coming due as well. She had a cancer scare the year before, not long after Jim Hart had passed, and it would resurface to claim her and carry her away from Walter Henry and Johnny, the diner, and Pine Valley. Not knowing what was to come, Walter Henry quietly made preparations for his demise, making two coffins, one for Lulabelle and one to store in the woodworking shop, not knowing how soon he would need it. He signed everything he owned over to Millie and Johnny and spent all the time that he could closing up the retreat center for good.

Walter Henry still found time to keep up his faithful duty going to the blacksmith shop and livery stable, even though it was rented out and used for storage space. Aurelia's timid ventures there to speak with him, only to be sidetracked at the sculptor's studio, were not missed by the old man. He saw her behind the old Pine Way store, nearly flashing back to another young woman whose memory was not yet neatly forgotten.

"Sylvia Sumner has a replacement, I see," he said to himself.

One day, the sculptor, Tommy McGrew, walked over to the blacksmith shop to warm himself at the forge. He told Walter Henry something he had observed about Aurelia. "She's an artist, Walt," he said. "She wants to work with wood. You should show her how. My place here, you know, having a lot of dry wood laying around wouldn't be such a good idea." The sculptor was afraid of fire starting in his studio as he stroked the charred and scorched memory of a beard he had long ago shaven away.

"Hmm," said Walter Henry. He knew he owned the only woodworking shop for miles around, but he thought it best to avoid Aurelia Mendoza. He drew the bellows downward, saying, "Mighty cold today," thus giving the sculptor his view on the matter.

Tommy McGrew's attention picked up out of disappointment, knowing the old man was refusing to share his shop with, "that girl," as Walter Henry often referred to Aurelia. Something else he sensed about the young woman, though, told him to steer clear of her, himself, so he let the matter go.

The sculptor was a pondering sort, envisioning how colors of burnt orange and green, aquamarine and red, like blood could be achieved. It all depended on the heat he applied, the metal he worked, and the luck and patience of his skill. On an upturned wooden crate, he would sit, thoughtfully smoking a cigarette. He sat looking out to the road, to the fields and orchards beyond, to the mountains draped in trees, and to the sky. He saw none of it, for his artist's gaze was directed inwardly, imagining, dreaming.

Slightly heavy-set and broad-shouldered, he was well into his fifties with graying hair. He kept it closely shaved on his rounded head, while his square jaw was set and always shaved smooth. A small scar was visible on his chin. Few knew the story of how his beard had caught fire from a shower of sparks as he worked in his studio. Jim Hart would tease him about it, but it was no joke to Tommy McGrew, who felt it best to keep a close-cropped head of hair and a bare-skinned face. He wore a leather jacket he had found, though its owner, stepping outside Klucky's one night, would swear otherwise when he discovered it missing from his bike. The man had stolen it, himself, and that was that. Tommy also had a motorcycle and appreciated the find on cold days he rode into the hills or out across the great valley beyond into the thick blanket of fog.

Jim Hart liked the older man. Starting back when he was in his teens, he would often wander over from the barn to peek in the back of the store to see if the sculptor was around. Younger than his parents, the man was more like a friend to Jim, sharing whatever he was smoking and, after Jim graduated, whatever he was drinking.

Aurelia had encountered the reclusive sculptor upon occasion back when she lived with Ev Mendoza. It was only a few months before Ev's house burned down and she died, but long enough for Aurelia to have scoped out all the men at that end of town, including Tucker Stewart. She tried to avoid the sculptor, following Ev's warnings about him, "smoking the devil weed" and drinking far into the night with her grandson, Jim.

Aurelia remembered seeing Jim with Tommy once. Her car was broken down, so she had walked to the drugstore that evening and was on her way back before sundown. She had a small sack of goods clasped in her arm, which contained some tooth powder and cotton balls, a box of crackers on sale for fifteen cents, and a can of tuna. She heard their laughter. Tommy McGrew's deep voice came with a quieter chuckle followed by a hoarse cough and a hawking spit. Jim Hart was loud and gleeful, as though he was being tickled. They were sitting behind the store-turned-studio, the green grass growing tall in the latter part of spring where all it had done was rain. The patches of bright-green moss on the aging, red brick structures had come alive, spongy with dampness, growing and creeping and spreading. Those buildings, she thought, could almost be seen crumbling down in the graying evening and the weariness of what to her was a ghost town, a town of ghosts.

Jim Hart was her elder cousin by almost ten years, but she thought him good-looking, very good-looking. She wondered how he could have ended up with Bethany Clark, who got to be so fat, Aurelia imagined she could fit her whole body into one pant leg of Beth's stretch-nylon work pants. She remembered what Ev had told her about him and Sylvia Sumner shamelessly committing sin after sin up in the loft of that barn at the end of the row. Aurelia could almost picture herself with him up in that loft, but stopped herself. Good thing, she thought. Something about him made her skin crawl and, yet, strangely drew her curiosity. So, on that one evening she walked into Pine Way and spotted him sitting there, she looked his way for much longer than she ought, catching his eye. At that moment, she realized she already knew him, from Laketon. She swiftly turned her head away in her own shame, and in fear.

When she got home to Ev's, she asked, "Why's he so—" She failed to find the word that described a dark fox in the shadows, when talking about a man. She was unaware of her own inner pain, becoming hungry for relief and retribution, that had espied his own. The she-beast that prowled within her depths, like a panther black velvety smooth, was better suited to slinking amongst the Southern bayous, for all its restlessness, cunning, and heat.

Ev saw it, especially when Aurelia's boyfriend, the fire bug, came by to pick up Aurelia and take her out to dinner. Ev knew better. God did not make her young once for nothing. She told Aurelia that day, "Ay! Mujer! I know what you're up to!"

Ev caught a man looking at her like that when she was a teenager. It was around 1890. She was a teenager working at the Pine Valley way station with her mother. Feeling the eyes on her as she was dusting the parlor, she turned to catch the stalking beast in a man, a guest smoking by a window, as its presence disappeared from view. The man stood, buttoned his suit jacket, and went out to the front porch. He stood looking into the distance as he continued smoking. That was the first time Ev feared one of their guests. It was the same reasoning why a lady did not walk unaccompanied in those days, if she were a lady, and why men dared not look at a woman like that, if he presumed himself a gentleman. By the look on her grandniece's face, Ev knew that Aurelia not only saw the stalking beast in her grandson, but had become one as well. However, Jim was older and married. Ev feared he had sunk lower.

"Oh, he's a troubled one," she told Aurelia. "You stay away from him, you hear me?" She added with a half-hearted laugh, "Even your plotting, fire bug boyfriend cannot compare to Jim when it comes to stupidity!"

Aurelia flashed her a look, mouth agape at Ev's nerve, but Ev quickly blessed herself with the sign of the cross and put her head down to cover her face and cry. She was aggrieved and said, "Oh! I should not speak so, Aurelia! He's my grandson and I love him." She was ninety-years-old and very weepy and forlorn at times. She knew she could do nothing more for Jim. But she also knew that Aurelia had troubles of her own, even though they were yet hidden and easily denied.

Ev went back to her sewing, but had lost interest. Gathering her sewing basket and mending, she muttered, "Vaya con Dios, mi nieto." She sensed Jim's fate was not a good one and did not want Aurelia to get mixed up in it or, worse, come to share a similar fate. She pushed herself up out of the chair with her wobbly, old, wrinkly arms and went to put her things in her room. Running a shaky hand over Jim's football medal on a shelf in her bedroom, draped over Grandma's Brag Book, she reminded Aurelia, "Best to stay away from that one. He's got problems you're no match for."

Aurelia did as she was told, but only after she was tempted and spoke to him once in passing. She immediately regretted having done so and avoided him after that, even avoided attending his funeral. He knew who she was and gave her clear warning to stay away from him. He told her a native phrase he learned from his great-grandmother, Lucy, that, in English, meant something like, "stop playing the fool and wake up."

Aurelia visited Jim Hart's grave once, to place flowers and to talk to him. She told him "thank you" for what she yet kept secret. She also dreamed about him, dark, shadowy dreams. In one, she saw water pooling up in a cave, dripping from above, unseen, except for its glint as each drop released and fell below. Rings slowly rippled across the dark liquid. After the dreams began, Aurelia stop believing what Ev had told her about Jim. It bolstered her decision to continue paying the sculptor a visit, figuring that if Jim was friends with the older man, then maybe she could be as well.

CHAPTER SEVENTEEN

After work one day, before Candelaria could say anything, Aurelia left the shack and walked to Pine Way. The back door was open to Tommy McGrew's studio. Aurelia peered into the old building, her breath in fog before her, and stepped inside. Examining the sculptor's set-up, she wished she had a shop. He had gutted nearly the entire bottom floor and built himself a sturdy workbench with a large vise. His tools were neatly hung along the wall. A flight of steps led to the upper floor. One foot on the bottom step and her hand resting on the banister, she glimpsed toward the room above, tempted to explore.

Tommy McGrew had stepped out for a smoke earlier, but was at the blacksmith shop talking to Walter Henry about the weather. The old man was getting in his truck to go home. He had it running awhile to warm the engine.

"Yeah, it's darn cold! I'm gonna head on up the mountain," said Walter Henry. He waved goodbye and drove off, looking forward to a hot meal. The sculptor finished his smoke, dropped the stub end onto the ground and stamped it out.

Aurelia walked over to her new friend's house. Several times, in icy patches, she slipped and almost fell. The light jacket she wore provided little warmth and she grew chill and shivered. She pulled her knit cap down to cover her ears better as she walked, her arms wrapped about herself to stay warm. It was after sunset by then, the snow quickly refreezing and crunching beneath each step.

She looked forward to seeing her new friend. He worked with her at the pet store and had invited her over for dinner. He told her they were going to order pizzas and buy some beer. Although he was younger than her, Aurelia found him attractive and had hopes for how the evening might turn out. She had purposely neglected to tell Candelaria, knowing her elder cousin would disapprove. The house she was looking for was on the corner of Magnolia Lane and Walnut Road. Her co-worker shared it with other young people who pitched in to make the rent and pay the bills. It was Candelaria's uncle's old house. Herman Mendoza owned it from the time it was built until his death when it became a rental. It had slowly gone downhill. The front lawn was more like a field. Loud parties of late drew complaints from the neighbors.

Earlier, Candelaria had seen Aurelia go through the back entrance to the sculptor's studio and grew concerned. Tommy McGrew was younger than Candelaria by several years, but she knew better than to go poking her nose in that man's business. She made a mental note to tell Aurelia why. She never forgave the man for being a bad influence on her son.

After she returned inside her house, she assumed Aurelia was still in Pine Way. A chill had set in, though. She knew she was coming down with a cold. Usually, when she felt ill, she would call Rosa to come over and help, but since the baby was born, she avoided bothering her. Betsy Marie. Candelaria loved the name. She drew a hot bath to soak in and warm herself.

She needed to keep earning money, but with the snow, there was no farm work, except what the men usually did. The packing sheds were cleaned out, any waste and debris burned in big bonfires. The pruning in the orchards was underway. They kept her on after she pleaded with the foreman. She wished she had saved her husband's big coat, but she had kept his gloves and was thankful. With the freezing cold all day and the draft in her Villa Borracho shanty, no matter how much newspaper was stuffed into the spaces around the crooked window frames, she had trouble staying warm.

She was receiving regular checks in the mail for her writing, but it was not enough to get a better place to live, definitely not enough to quit her job, not nearly so. All it paid was enough for paper, pencils, pens, erasers, and ribbons of ink for the librarian's typewriter. She was invited to her very first speaking engagement, about which she had mixed feelings. It was being held in a high school auditorium by an organization that wanted her to address women's rights. Things were looking promising for Candelaria. For the time being, though, she needed to take better care of herself.

She undressed in the icy cold room before slipping into the hot water, feeling her tired, aching bones thank her as she gave a groaning sigh.

"Oh, Aurelia," she lamented with eyes closed, "what are you doing with that man?"

Candelaria had hoped Aurelia would be more helpful when she moved in, but worried her instead. She wondered about the young woman, not interested in getting married, all but tearing down Tucker Stewart's front door to be with him. Candelaria's mother had not failed to mention to her the look on Aurelia's face when she had spoken of Jim. What was it about her she was so attracted to men too old for her? Candelaria quickly forgot, but would soon remember once Aurelia came home the following morning.

Rosa called her mother to say she saw Aurelia at her Uncle Herman's old house where a party was going all night, which left Candelaria in a mood. She was shocked and furious with the young woman.

"Don't you even care what other people think of you, Aurelia?" she asked.

Surprised, Aurelia asked, "What are you talking about?"

Candelaria told her, "Rosa said she saw you at that house where all those boys live. You were there all night, weren't you?"

"Rosa?" Now, Aurelia was irritated. She said, "Oh, who cares what people think! Besides, I'm old enough to do what I please!"

"Not if you want to live here with me!" countered Candelaria. "I thought you were more grown up than that. I hoped you'd at least help out around here!" Her tone quieted as she tried to regain a sense of calm. "I-I wanted to be there for you, but your behavior has me worried. You're acting like a—like—" She tried not to say it. Aurelia's look of surprise and even tears welling up in her eyes let Candelaria know she had gotten through to her.

Candelaria withdrew and went back to making coffee. She had cooked a large breakfast of chorizo scrambled with eggs, heated tortillas, and even made a big pot of hot oatmeal. She wrapped the leftover chorizo scramble into the tortillas and then tinfoil for her lunch. Soon, she was pouring the coffee into a thermos she had bought at the thrift store for a nickel. She was sick, but needed to work. Being the only woman hired that winter, she was prepared to conceal her illness from everyone, especially the foreman who told her not to expect any special treatment. Arguing with Aurelia wore her out and her voice became hoarse. Fortunately, her younger cousin was too preoccupied with herself to notice Candelaria's difficulties. She was getting a bath and was going to work as well.

Candelaria announced through the bathroom door, "I'm going over to the orchards, Aurelia! See you this afternoon!"

The porch was icy, so Candelaria was careful going down each step. The cold air was a shock. She had the oven on to heat the kitchen, so she felt she could bear the cold until she got to work. But she worried how she would make it through the day and the rest of the winter. Rosa gave her long underwear for Christmas, which she wore, along with double layers of socks and an extra shirt. But she had no coat. She prayed for the end of the cold weather, because she could not afford to buy one. Arriving at the worksite, she noticed someone walking up to her carrying a coat. It was Esther's husband, Jorge Gutierrez, her neighbor.

"Here, Laria," he said. "Esther asked me to give this to you."

"But—why did you—where did you get this?" she stammered.

"The thrift store," said Jorge. Seeing Candelaria's worried face, he told her, "Relax. It only cost thirty-five cents. Esther's idea."

"Thank you, Jorge. Tell Esther, I said, 'thank you,' okay?"

Esther had washed and repaired the coat. Candelaria put it on and felt better already. The workers set out to get started, each grabbing a tool or a ladder. The rungs on the ladders were icy, so the foreman told them all to be extra careful.

He said, "No accidents, hear me? I need every one of you. Let's get to work."

The men disbursed to various trees to get started. They were bundled up with woolen caps or hats with ear flaps, heavy gloves, extra layers of clothing, and heavy boots. Some of them would be out all day to oversee the work that was done. Their lunches and thermoses were in a couple of large ice chests, without the ice, to protect everything from freezing. They sat on the foreman's truck bed for break time and for lunch. A warming fire nearby was kept stoked with wood, melting the surrounding snow.

Candelaria grabbed a pitchfork to collect the pruned twigs and branches and heap them into piles to be burned. She said a prayer to God and to her mother, Ev.

"Dear God, make me well. I can't afford to lose work. Oh, Mamá. How did you do it all alone in your house after Papá died? I'm sorry, I was so selfish I didn't help you out more.

Thank you, God, for Aurelia. She helped you, didn't she, Mamá? Thank you, God, for the coat. Thank you, for good friends. Take care of them and take care of Aurelia." She made the sign of the cross and kissed her closed hand afterward, feeling stronger and more able to face the day.

CHAPTER EIGHTEEN

In the earliest part of the 1950s, when Jim Hart was a living, breathing, young man who yet commanded the attention of the girls at school, and who was considered a hero by their small town, his father fell from grace and became just a man.

They were at one of the racehorse breeding facilities where Jim and his father worked as farriers. When he had finished his work, he went to look for his dad, wondering when they could go home. Walking alongside the stables, then further down where the office was, he heard his father talking low with the secretary, Joan. Jim was about to step into the office, but his father closed the door. Jim heard their voices, playful flirtations and laughter, followed by silence. He was shocked and, though he felt sorry for his mother, anger for both his parents dominated his thoughts.

Later that evening, while having dinner at a roadhouse near the stables, Jim noticed Joan had entered. She was standing inside the doorway. Her jacket was draped over her shoulders and a fresh coat of lipstick was "slathered on," he thought angrily. She was looking for his dad, no doubt. His dad turned to see her, then looked back at him. It was then that Jim, himself, began to fall. His dad could hardly stay in his seat, wanting to go to her and, yet, kept looking back at his own son the way someone does with an ugly little dog who keeps chewing on their ankle, wishing they would "git."

Out riding, Jim asked his horse, "Why do my parents act like they can't stand me? Don't they love me?" He mused, "If I could stay upon a horse and ride a thousand miles, would I find myself in the end? If I turned aside from this town, this family, would the girls I love, who have become women like my mother, demanding, needing, set me free? If I could ride a thousand miles across a land I've never seen, would I lose myself and, then, no longer care what my parents think of me?"

"Why can't you be more like that little fella, Tucker James?" his father said one scolding moment back when Jim was nine years old. Crestfallen, the walls closed in on him as the thought arose, "If I were dead, then they'd love me."

Getting ready for the end of high school, the end of all that was certain, he asked his horse, "If I could ride a thousand miles upon a horse, across the prairie sea, would I lose the pain I carry? Would I finally then be free?" No answers came, only a deep desire to belong where he was at. Why would any place else be different? Why leave into further uncertainty, when the unknown of his life faced him every day where he was at?

Jim knew about his rival's father fooling around with another woman, and often teased Tucker about it in their locker room bantering after football practice. However, he was ignorant of the details of which Tucker, himself, would one day learn, the lurid particulars of a man Tucker called, "Dad," but who, like Jim's own father, was just a man.

•   •   •

Tucker sat on the couch by his front window, gazing at his frozen yard and the road beyond. He felt trapped in the house with nothing to do and nowhere to go. He had no money with which to buy a book to read and avoided the public library since his last, disastrous date with Katie Winters. Amusing himself, he dug through some worn-out boxes he had retrieved from the closets. They contained various items that were left in the house by his grandparents, he had assumed. It was their house once, which his grandfather had built. Some of the furniture used to belong to them. One piece was an end table placed beside Tucker's bed, upon which a small lamp was set. It had one drawer, which he had never opened.

He went into his bedroom. Slowly opening the drawer as he sat on the bed, he retrieved each item and examined them beneath the lamplight, which shone dimly on that dreary, clouded day. Meaningless items, a couple of fountain pens, a knife-sharpened pencil, a small screwdriver, some paper clips, and an old wrist watch, were all the drawer contained, he thought. However, at the bottom of the shallow compartment, beneath some loose papers, he spotted a slender tobacco canister. His father told him that, before he and Tucker's mother were married, they had exchanged love notes by using a tobacco canister as their secret mailbox.

Tucker was curious. He wondered if any love notes remained under Prince Albert's royal charge. Lifting the lid to peek inside, he froze. Inside, was a slip of paper very much like other scraps his father had kept in a little black box. Tucker withdrew the familiar, yellowed note and read the words carefully penned.

"My darling, I have such wonderful news! Bobby has agreed to move to Edenville! Your parent's old house will no longer do! Love, C. C."

Tucker closed his eyes in horror, then yelled, "Dammit! This house!" Tucker lived in it. "They met in this house!" he yelled again.

He stuffed the note back into the canister and slid it into his shirt pocket. Hurriedly, as though he had caught his father and Charity in the act, Tucker grabbed his coat, his gloves, his hat, the dog, and went outside to get into the car and drive. He was not used to driving on icy roads, but he cared less. He drove as one fleeing the scene of a crime, not paying any attention to where he was driving, only that it was away. But, before he knew it, he had driven to the back entrance of Spring Hill Residence & Infirmary. His father was no longer there, because he had died. His father was dead. Tucker sat for a while until he was cold and Freckles started whining. He started up the car again and drove to his brother's house. Howard would know what to do, he believed.

At his brother's house, he showed Howard the tobacco can and the note. Howard welcomed him inside, along with the dog. Calling to his wife, he informed her that he and Tucker were going to be "discussing something" in the office. Leaving Freckles to her own devices, which Mary usually managed, they went into Howard's home office and shut the door.

"Sit down," said Howard.

Before a crackling fire in the fireplace, he began telling his younger brother everything he knew that took place before Tucker was born, about which only he, his brother, Dewey, and their sister, June, had known. Howard, of course, never knew the whole story. But, what he did say, was enough.

Afterward, when Tucker entered what used to be his happy home, he turned on the lights, his eyes surveying the scene. Determined to stake his claim, he began going over every inch of what had become defiled by the things Howard said about their father, things Tucker never wanted to know. What items he did not want, he piled by the front door. Discoveries relating to his father's ill-gotten gains, the affections of a bitter young woman, he threw into a box to take out back and burn in the incinerator—never mind what the fire department said about not using them anymore.

One item particularly disturbed Tucker. Like the spy deftly riffling through what does not belong to them, he took in his hand a strip of pink ribbon. It was in a thin volume of poems by T. S. Eliot, marking the page of one verse that, Tucker believed, said it all. Reading aloud the words, Tucker's low voice discovered in them the man who once had lived.

"April is the cruelest month...mixing memory and desire..."

In his grief, or because of it, Tucker developed a different attitude, not so disgusted and angry anymore. He missed his father, not the invalid he had become in later years, but the man he was, when he and Charity were...in love? Tucker tried not to think about that. All he could do was lay on his bed and let flow the pain that was stifled by the years he long-obsessed, himself, over Charity's daughter, Sylvia, wondering why, what for? He closed his eyes and rested while Howard's cryptic comment he would not repeat, floated amidst Tucker's other thoughts.

"Silence is a cruel master, little brother. In the end, it'll kill you."

CHAPTER NINETEEN

Jiminy Walker held little Charity Charlotte Lee Walker, bouncing her in his arms and shushing her. He stared down the road, contemplating his next move. "Let me see here," he said. With one free hand, he scratched his crusty beard stubble and pondered his prospects. It was 1910 and there was no work driving tractor, which was his usual fallback occupation. Competition in the moonshining business was tough and his luck at the draw in cards was down so low he could not see his way back "through stygian darkness," he related to friends. Thankfully, the midwife accepted eggs for payment.

Seeing further down the road, Jiminy spotted the dust raising and he heard a sputtering rumble. While the baby worked herself into a loud scream, the source of the dust and rumble appeared.

"Praise God Almighty!" Jiminy cried.

He ran inside the house, thrust the baby into his eldest daughter's arms, grabbed his hat and coat off the rack by the door, leapt from the porch, bounded across the yard, and jumped into the puttering vehicle as it came to a rest before his house. One arm was laid across the top of the seat, his eyes directed on the road ahead. "Let's go!" he instructed the driver. Jiminy Walker's prospects had taken an advantageous turn.

Meanwhile, Justice Walker, sixteen years of age, changed the whimpering child's diaper. She carried the baby upstairs to her parent's room where her mother was sleeping soundly. Tugging on her mother's bedclothes, she retrieved a breast with which to attach little Char Lee Junior. Justice ran a gentle finger across the baby's face to catch the tears, dabbing them with a corner of the infant's blanket, one Justice had made. Switching the baby to the opposite breast, she propped up the child until sleep came. Justice covered her mother again, tucking in the baby, so she would not fall from the bed.

Seeing that all was well, she returned downstairs and checked on the soup bubbling along and the two loaves of bread set to rise. The soup was poor man's fare, at best, disguised and prettied-up with herbs she had gathered, maybe a weed or two, and vegetables she had dug from the family garden. Floating in the thin gruel was corn from the chicken's feed she picked through, having discarded the weevils. Her father had chopped the head off of one of their skimpier laying hens, plucked it, and instructed Justice to use every bit, except what filled its craw, the head with eyes still blinking in surprise, and the feet it tried to use to run away.

The Walker family was used to such primitive means of making a meal, though Justice swore as she reached for her bible on the table by the door, "I'll not be so poor I resort to stealing, like Father does!" She stepped out the front door, sat on the porch steps, opened her bible to a marked page, and began to read aloud from one of her favorite verses.

"Seek ye first the kingdom of God and his righteousness." She looked out toward the road as one would in thought, pondering the words. Having grown up poor, the only riches she had ever known were those her father stole from others. In pitiful sadness, she wondered why she was born to such a man. She read aloud from another saved passage, "Let him that stole steal no more...working with his hands...give to him that needeth..."

The young woman's heart was one of goodness, but it was ruled by a disapproving temperament. Strict determination to lead a righteous life guided her, never mind her father's ways. She closed her book at the sight of her brother, Russ, coming down the road with his schoolbooks, hardly even in hearing distance before Justice knew what he was saying.

"I ain't *never* goin' back! I *hate* that teacher!" he announced.

His hair was a blondish-brownish frazzle. His mouth was held in a gaping scowl. The bib overalls he wore were much too short, yet they fit his skinny, bony body like a sack, faded and threadbare. Barefooted, his shoes were tied together by the laces and slung over his shoulder. His shirt sleeves were rolled up and his shirt hung unbuttoned and fanning out the sides of his overalls. Holey socks peeked out of one pocket. He walked like a hungry dog. Justice knew that her father had his apprentice in the making.

Their little sister, Patty, walked beside him. She had run down the road to meet her brother, so she could carry his books and pretend they were her own schoolbooks. However, she was trying not to listen to Russ mouthing off about the ills of a world she had only begun to experience.

Regardless of anyone listening to him, Russ ranted on, fist raised in defiant protest. "I *swear!*" his latest proclamation began. "Nuthin' is the way it ought to be in this world! Can't a man even rise up out of the dustbin where his fate has tossed him?! I'm a man, I tell you! I've got dreams! I'm gonna be like Robin Hood and stealeth from the rich, so I can giveth to the poor. Says so in the bible."

Justice rolled her eyes, stood, and went into the house to see to the baby, her mother, and the family's dinner. She never gave her brother's words another thought, especially because Russ had gotten further along in school than she had, not having reached the sixth grade, herself.

Muttering and grumbling, Russ instructed Patty to leave his books by the door. His nose and his complaining, empty belly directed him to the kitchen.

"Mmm. Smells good. Can I eat?" he asked Justice.

Justice cuffed his hand before he stuck a grimy finger into the soup pot and answered him, "No! Wait 'til Father gets home."

Russ circled the kitchen, prowling around and poking into wherever else he might find something to eat. He settled on a carrot left on the chopping board and began to gnaw away.

"Where'd he go?" he asked Justice.

"Off," she answered.

"Oh," he said.

"Wash up. I'll get this bread in the oven," Justice told Russ. "Mother's sleeping," she warned.

Russ tiptoed upstairs and peeked into his parent's room where Patty was nestled among the peaceful quietude of her mother's presence. Further down the hallway he entered his own room, one of three small bedrooms upstairs. The walls of his room were pasted with sketches, drawn on paper collected through any means, paper sacks, newspaper, flyers, whatever scraps he had found. Books stacked by the bed, a crate on end with a candle melted to a flattened can, and hooks on the wall for his clothes, were all that furnished it. He opened one book and flopped onto his bed to read for a while. He read voraciously every tale of adventure he could find that told of places he would never see in his lifetime, like Robin Hood, Sinbad, Aladdin, Huckleberry Finn, and Tom Sawyer. Like a well-used set of encyclopedias, his books were in various states of disrepair due to the repeated need to refer to them.

After washing, once his father was home, he grabbed a clean change of clothes, which Justice and his mother had washed with the tub and scrub board and hung to dry. It was the only show of respect for all that Justice and her mother had done, to wash before eating and to say, "thank you," before heading out the door again.

The years passed and the future Justice foresaw had arrived. They were sitting in the parlor talking one evening when Russ and his father returned from somewhere no one dared ask, except Justice.

"Where've you been?!" she shouted.

"Never mind, Daughter. Never mind," said her father.

"You can fool your neighbors, but you can't fool me!" shouted Justice. She stormed off, yet determined to lead a righteous life.

Patty and Charity followed her up the stairs to their bedroom where they then lay upon the floor to hear the truth via the floor vent directly over the parlor.

Deadly serious, their mother spoke first. "Tell me, Cricket," she said, "I can see it on your face, so might as well tell me." Her raven-like demeanor held court before the men of the family.

"Buddy o' mine came by last week," began Jiminy. "You remember Gus. Gus Harper? He co-owned the feed store with Charlie Goodman," and so the story began.

Justice listened to the evil doings of her father. Her mind raged like a burning fire until she saw him as the Devil, himself. Her mother's countenance was grave, her back to them, seated in her high-backed chair, like a queen or a raven-princess, each word spoken directly.

"It was a set-up, Cricket. I told you not to trust that man," said Char Lee. She wagged her head at her husband's mistake, adding in her anger, "It's obvious, there was something in it for him!" Her voice raised to a shout with the last words.

Justice drew away from the vent to go to bed and let rest the horror of the night. Patty folded her arms beneath her face, sobbing quietly upon the cool wood flooring. The dust blew away from her stifled, panting breath. Charity climbed into bed with Justice.

"Is Daddy goin' to jail, Justice?" Charity asked.

"I don't know. Get some sleep. I'm sure we'll find out tomorrow," answered Justice.

"What about Russ? Will the sheriff take him away, too?" Charity asked in a worried tone.

"Go to sleep now. We'll have to wait and see," Justice said. She drew her younger sister in close to comfort her, adding, "Maybe they won't, since he's underage."

Hearing his sisters from the hallway, Russ disappeared to his own bedroom, not daring to ask for something to eat. Their parents talked late into the night by the light of the lantern, their shadows looming like dark giants leaping, bobbing, and circling 'round. Before he blew out the candle in his room, Russ looked down over the parlor. He saw his father's bent body where he sat on the sofa, sobbing into a conscience so dirty it would never wash clean.

"I'm sorry, Rosebud," Jiminy sobbed. "I'm sorry. I can't ever seem to do the right thing. I'm just a bum. That's all I'll ever be." Jiminy was truly sorry for doing things against the law, doing what he later knew was wrong, but what seemed right at the time.

Patty went to bed, nudging Charity to move over. Russ retreated to his room for the night. Their mother softened her tone and rose from her chair to sit beside her husband on the sofa, tenderly placing her arm around him.

"Never mind," she said. "We'll figure somethin' out. We always do. We'll manage."

Jiminy, smaller than she, leaned into her embrace as she comforted him. She dreamed of going back to Laketon where she was born, back to her people. She was thinking a lot about her mother and missed the life they had in the high mountains. Every night, she lay awake remembering the deer and the bears she used to see in the meadows. She remembered the quiet and grieved the beautiful, forested scenery. Something in her soul, a kind of yearning for home, held its memory close to her heart. At that thought, Char Lee cried and, together, she and Jiminy held one another and dreamed about a place called Home.

CHAPTER TWENTY

By the time Charity Walker was nine-years-old, she had a head full of dark brown curls that sprang up and down as she walked. With hands drawn into fists, she tromped along the center of the road as one aiming to fight for what she wanted. She made it her sole mission in life to demand, to finagle, and to greedily flaunt the riches of life she would thus acquire, however crooked or wide the course she had to tread. On her mission one day in June, when the high buzzing of cicadas and the songs of birds were at their height, she planned to inquire whether one article she had specially requested came in at the store. It had not. For that, she drew back her leg and gave the storekeeper, Sam McGrew, a swift kick in the shin.

"Ow! Oh! Oh!" cried the storekeeper.

He hobbled around on one leg, rubbing his shin and wishing death and destruction upon the little rascal that inflicted such terrible pain. With finger wagging, he told her, "Now, listen here, little girl," as she squinted her eyes up in his direction, hands on her hips, "just because you want something and then order it, doesn't mean it's automatically going to appear."

Like she had planned all along, he reached into a jar on the counter and pulled out a licorice stick, mainly to be rid of her, and said, "Here. Why don't you take this and run along, all right?"

"Two of 'em."

She laid out her palm, the other hand on her hip and, with a heavy sigh, Sam McGrew relented, getting a second stick of licorice.

"Now, *scram!*" he shouted.

He walked away from her too soon. Behind his back, her tongue was thrust in his direction. She grabbed a small mirror from the shelf and slipped it into the pocket of her dress. Pleased with herself, she sauntered about the store, while Sam McGrew went about his business, mumbling, "One of these days..."

Smiling in her impish hopes, Charity skipped out of the store and over to the newspaper office. She often plied her youthful flirtations on Tucker Howard Stewart, who treated her to some trinket or other such indulgence. Hoping for a similar gift, she strolled along and nonchalantly slipped into his office. Harry Stewart was busy setting the type for the next edition of *The Pine Way Weekly Journal.*

He noticed Charity standing by the doorway. Knowing full well why she was there, he glared straight through her intentions and said, "Boo!" Reminding himself she was only a child in need of some attention, it hardly being her fault she was a conniving—he ignored her.

Charity slowly slunk back out the doorway, innocently humming. She was pleasantly surprised to see Tucker Howard appear, having come from the outhouse in back of the store. He was on his way home and in the process of re-harnessing his suspenders, when his father yelled, "Tuck! Get back here!"

Knowing his father was waiting to either shout an order or reprimand a wrongdoing, Tucker Howard instead hurried down the alleyway, for he dared not be late. Rounding the corner, he spotted Charity. He thought she was cute and great fun to have around. The sight of her brightened his day.

"Hello, Charity! What brings you into town?" he asked.

He had outgrown his knickers and the wool made him itch. His wife was at home with their first child, who had the colic. With his father's expectations bearing down upon him, the world at the moment was intolerable. Charity brought a smile to his face. He reached into his pant's pocket to retrieve a little something he had saved for her. It was a shiny, realistic-looking ring he had dug out of a box of Cracker Jack's.

"Got something for you," he said.

Handing her the prize, he was pleased to see her timid look grow joyful. He knew her family's plight and doted on Charity, wanting to be nice to her. Although, he was unaware of their shared fate being written in that simple act.

Several years later, Charity had grown into a beautiful young woman. Her hair had darkened considerably, black as charcoal, and it had lost its springy curl. But, it was her eyes that, in their smoky midst, caught many a man off guard.

Tucker Howard had five children by then, plus a mortgage weighing on his shoulders. He lacked the necessary immunity in a very married man. Easily swayed by her emerging womanly attractiveness, he saw Charity in a new way. He had stayed youthful and physically fit, walked everywhere he needed to go. His wife had grown heavy-set and often beleaguered him with complaints. Not what you would call hen-pecking, but merely tiresome. He was in need of a change, and saw in the young Charity Walker the diversion he was seeking, unbeknownst to himself, which was unfortunate.

He had left the newspaper office and was on his way home, walking toward the new town of Edenville where he and his wife lived on Fig Tree Lane. Charity was running to catch up to him. She enjoyed their easy friendship. Once she reached him, she playfully tugged on his shirt sleeve.

"Hi, T. S.!" she said.

Charity called him that, because he always talked about being a poet, like T. S. Eliot, and they shared the same initials, somewhat. She liked Tucker Howard Stewart, her T. S., since he was the only man who paid her any mind. She practically worshiped him. It was not because of the gifts he gave, but for the treatment she received from him, like she was someone who mattered to the world. She dreamed of marrying him and secretly wanted to run off with the man. At the very least, she settled for a moment here and there when they could have such encounters and laugh.

One look at her smile, a hint of the scamp as she looked up at him, and Tucker Howard felt a flash fire strike him down. Her smoky-gray eyes stood out in the mid-day quiet, asking him, no, needing him, and he was drawn toward her. He stopped to take stock of what he was feeling and knew in an instant what had been in the making somewhere back down the road.

He confessed to her, "Well, Charity, girl, if you haven't found your way into my heart." He reached out to touch the loose strands of hair that had strayed and wrapped them gently around her ear. Seeing her as nothing less than breathtaking, his need for some enjoyment in life, the ache within him to express the poet in his soul, to give it voice, rose in his awareness. So softly, the wind carried his words aloft, he said, "Now, if I weren't married..." Before he could add, "and if you weren't so young," he was caught in the net of their entwined fate and simply let it take him. He bent forward and kissed her on the lips. Having thus met with the poet of his soul, he turned away to continue homeward, lost in a daze from which he would not recover for many years.

Charity remained standing in the road, tears welling in her eyes. A sudden yearning arose in her heart to call out to him, to run after him. Feeling cast adrift, she looked around and wandered back toward her parent's house. On the way, she saw Robert Cadwallader passing by her family's home. She tried to avoid being seen by him. Not wanting to go into the house yet, she lingered in the cool shade at the back of the house where their vegetable garden grew in careful orderliness in a scant patch of sun. She stopped to look at it. Not really seeing what was before her, she suddenly hated it and craved instead the wild brambles of berry vines and the weedy disarray beneath the alder trees where she was taught not to go, warning her it was dangerous. She felt an impulse to run through it, her arms getting torn and scratched from thorns, and thrilling in it. The wind swept through in a breezy gust, lifting her hair and loosening those few stray strands from behind her ear.

Touching them with her fingertips, she knew with all certainty what she had to do next.

She went inside the house and searched for a scrap of paper on which to write her feelings. She wanted Tucker Howard to know that she loved him. Her mother was sitting in the parlor in her high-backed chair, carefully rolling a cigarette.

Charity asked her mother, "Mama, do we have any paper?"

"Paper?" asked Char Lee. "Only this here piece I've wrapped some tobacky in." Char Lee shook her head at her daughter's question and laughed, saying, "You know Russ cleans us out of every strip and scrap of paper from here to the county jail whenever he's around." She saw Charity's disappointment and asked, "Why? What do you need paper for?"

Char Lee stuck the crumpled result of her efforts into the corner of her mouth and lit it with the last match she owned. It was matches she had sent Charity to fetch at Goodman's Hardware Store, along with some candles and kerosene. She looked intently at her daughter, wondering first at the knowledge her daughter had forgotten to take the kerosene can with her to have it filled and, secondly, with the vision in mind of a certain remembrance.

They were at the brand new store, Forbush's Market, when Robert Cadwallader walked in, noticeably happy to see Charity. Char Lee liked the young man, but she knew her daughter thought of him as a hopeless clod. She witnessed Charity snappily turn her back on him with her nose in the air, pointedly ignoring him. But, when Tucker Howard walked into the store with two of his sons, little Howard and Dewey, the look on her daughter's face was all Char Lee needed to see. Charity was trying her best to suppress a grin, while giving sly, sidelong glances toward the man. Pretending to look at the items before her, Charity slipped a bit of pink ribbon into the pocket of her skirt.

Char Lee saw that look again on her daughter's face, not two days having gone by. She looked on as Charity danced off to her room.

Charity had found an old greeting card, tore the sentiment half off, which was a "Happy Birthday, Sweet 16" from her Aunt and Uncle Walker. They lived in a big city on the coast where she dreamed of living one day. The money they had sent her was going to be the first of her savings to help her leave town. With that goal forgotten, soon as it was made, she expressed her love, uninhibited by guilt or social convention.

"Dear T. S.," she wrote. "Today, you kissed me! I knew then I was in love. If we cannot marry, is there yet hope for us? Tell me, there is! I love you so. I can't bear the time we are apart. I know you feel the same as I. I know it's true! What are we to do? I dare not ask you to leave your wife and children, only that you love me." The young-and-in-love woman ran out of space before she had finished her letter. With her tongue poking out the side of her mouth and her head tilting in her concerted effort to cram every passionate avowal of her affection onto that greeting card, she continued writing up the side of the paper. She signed it, "Yours truly, C. W."

Charity's love note may have been the first, but it was not the last. She and Tucker Howard would exchange many love notes over time, during which they went one step further. He betrayed his wife's loving trust in him, all so he could love another, and so Miss Charity Walker could have her spoiled, petulant way yet again. She may not have had a head full of curls any longer or determined fists and shin-kicking feet to get her way, but she had something far more dangerous to a married man. She held, in the shadowy places of her soul, pure, unadulterated savagery over which her conscience would never hold sway to her dying day.

Tucker Howard sought only to enjoy life as the poet he was imagining himself to be, while she, yet a young woman, was in search of nothing less than the whole world. That one step further, when they met in secret, awoke the young woman to the freedom she sought, opening her eyes to the real possibility she could leave that town and move to the city. For Tucker Howard, their romantic liaisons merely provided the missing piece in a life he had no desire to change.

His parents were having difficulty living on their own in their cottage in Pine Way, so they moved in with his and his wife's still-growing family in Edenville, leaving the Pine Way house unoccupied. The furniture was yet to be moved, but Tucker Howard procrastinated, making excuses, planning to keep it there for him and Charity to use. No one was the wiser, he had assumed. Meeting one another in the house that would one day belong to his son, Charity eventually became pregnant.

That dreaded inevitability was what Char Lee vaguely discerned in her daughter's future when Charity asked if they had any paper. Like she had done with her husband, she did with her daughter, telling her once what she thought of her behavior, and never again.

"Why couldn't you have fallen for an unmarried man you could actually live with and, who knows, maybe even be happy with?! Tell me that much, Charity!" she said.

In a saucy manner, Char Lee's daughter looked away, grabbed her sweater and was out the door. However, Char Lee knew a thing or two about Fate. It was not always so sure what It had done.

Suspecting her mother would follow her, Charity hid on the side of the house. Her mother strode down the road as though she had some serious business on her mind. Charity followed behind and was aghast when her mother encountered Tucker Howard on his way to his parent's old cottage.

Like syrupy molasses oozing from its spigot, Char Lee addressed him, "Well, good afternoon, Mr. Stewart. I thought I should inform you that my daughter's pregnant. Now, you can't marry her, I know that much, but what do you propose to do?"

Charity saw the shocked look on his face. She saw him nervously glance her way before speedily turning around and walking away as fast as he could without breaking into a run. When her mother walked past her on the way back to their house, Charity screamed at her, "Why, you stinkin 'old *witch!* How *could* you!"

Char Lee figured that if she could not move back to Laketon, she was at least going to move to a better house. Justice had told her there was one available, "rent-to-own," she called it. Patty had married Clarence McGrew. They were living with his parents. Russ and Jiminy, well, Char Lee never took them into consideration anymore. Charity swiftly tricked

Robert Cadwallader to believe she loved him enough to marry him and they left town. All Char Lee and Justice had to do was pack up and move, having rented out their old house, "that drafty old haunt," Char Lee commented. After she moved back to Laketon, Justice presided over the family who remained in Edenville, hoping and praying that all would be well.

CHAPTER TWENTY-ONE

Tucker Howard Stewart and Adelaide Jones were married in 1913. She was the wealthy daughter of one of Pine Valley's first settlers, Bartholomew Jones. Bart had lost his first wife on the Emigrant Trail, but married again after settling in the valley. It was many years before they finally had a child, sweet Addie Jones. His homestead of one-hundred-and-sixty acres later became the town of Edenville. He died before there was an Edenville, leaving the land to his wife and daughter. His wife sold it parcel by parcel, gradually accumulating the greatest wealth of anyone living in the valley. Her enormous bank account eventually became Addie's dowry.

Addie was a little on the plump side, had a pretty smile framed by handsome, silvery-brown curls, and eyes the color of the summer sky. It was not solely the money that attracted young men, but it certainly sweetened her allure and, truth be told, intensified the competition. The shy young woman with dimpled cheeks and fair skin, would blush when any young man said "hello" to her. She played coy when her future husband first greeted her and when he later held her hand in his, asking her permission to give her a kiss. Always the gentleman, Tucker Howard wooed her all the way down the aisle. The love notes they had exchanged during their courtship, Addie saved, and summarily burned thirty years later, the day her daughters told her what they knew.

Addie's eldest daughter, June, was close to giving birth to her second child, so Addie treated her other two daughters, Marjorie and Lois, and their friend, Rosa Hart, to a family visit. Tucker James, but eight or nine years of age, begged to go with them, so their all-girls vacation turned into a plus-one-tag-along-boy vacation. The older boys had gone off to war, so Tucker Howard was a free man until his wife's return.

Charity had convinced her husband, Robert, to move from the old Cadwallader house in Pine Way to a new house conveniently located next door to the Stewart's. Sylvia was born by then, which gave Charity reason to buy the house.

She told Robert, "You don't expect me to take care of a baby in this old barn, do you?"

Robert agreed, so they moved into the bungalow on Fig Tree Lane. Her father, Jiminy Walker, was in prison, where he could "rot, for all I care," were her indelicate words. Her sister, Justice, lived in the family home on Magnolia Lane, one street over, yet worlds apart.

Justice knew about Tucker Howard's and Charity's arrangement, rarely saying a word, except in prayer, which she did daily. Taking care of her rose garden in the front yard, she saw plain as could be when Tucker Howard made a fast dash over to Charity's, not five minutes after Addie and the kids drove away in their big black Chrysler. She foretold the future under her breath, right there on the spot.

"Oh, sweet Jesus! I see another pregnancy comin' on!" she said.

She later warned her sister, whose husband had also gone to war, leaving the coquettish tart alone and "vulnerable," as Justice saw it. She believed that, if "that man had kept his you-know-what where it belonged all these years—" She held her tongue, hateful of the sneaking scoundrel, yet feeling sorry for her youngest sister, not knowing what to do.

Meanwhile, it was at June's house, after the baby was born, and about the time they were getting ready to pack up and leave, when the Stewart girls held a meeting. Surrounding their big sister, June, as she nursed Little Baby Patricia Catherine, Marjorie and Lois discussed" whether-or-no" their mother should be confronted regarding their wayward father. They neglected to take care once the subject of an affair was broached. Rosa quickly got up and excused herself from the room. The minute she opened the bedroom door, Tucker James fell flat on his face into the room, having been eavesdropping. Embarrassed, he hurriedly ran out of the house, followed by Rosa. They helped Addie to load their things into the car, while the three Stewart girls conferred. After weighing all the potential outcomes, one way or the other, they finally decided that, "yes, Mother must be told."

Leaving June in her room with the baby, Marjorie and Lois went out to the front yard where June's husband was busy handing out cigars, as well as flyers about a sale down at the car lot where he worked. They hailed their mother to come back into the house, saying, "We need to tell you something." Again, they gathered around June's bed and told their mother what they knew. Knowing what they were discussing, Rosa distracted Tucker James in the front yard, playing a game and singing songs. However, it was not long before they heard the commotion in the house. Addie had fled the bedroom in tears, hurrying out the back door, with the screen door banging shut behind her.

Marjorie said, "We're sorry, Mother! We shouldn't have told you!"

Lois asked, "It'll be okay, won't it?"

"No, it won't be okay, Lois!" Addie yelled between sobs through her sodden handkerchief that was about as effective as a postage stamp. "You girls run along and finish packing the car, hmm? I need some time alone." They held fast by her side, though, worried and afraid. "Run along!" their mother shouted.

They were soon back on the road for home, having said their extra-teary-eyed goodbyes, each giving the baby one last kiss before parting. Everyone was noticeably quiet on the return trip. Tucker James knew something was terribly wrong. He asked, "What are you all so sad about? You'd think we just got the tax bill, or something," quoting one of his grandfather's favorite expressions.

It was then that Addie pulled over and began to cry some more. Marjorie leaned toward her mother, placing a hand on her shoulder to console her. Lois sulked in the back seat by the window, hating her father, and vowing to leave home when she was old enough and never return.

Rosa placed her arm around Tucker James and held him close to her, saying quietly, "Now, Tucker James, we're all just sad, because we miss the baby. And your mother is feeling extra sad, because she loves it so."

Tucker James's lower lip quivered as he started to cry. He whispered to Rosa, "I miss the baby, too."

His mother and everyone heard. Soon, they were all crying, yet smiling through their tears. Marjorie and Lois also missed Little Baby Patricia Catherine, whom their mother had nicknamed, "Kitten." Regarding their father, well, they would see when they got home.

Once they arrived at home, Tucker Howard, a little over-enthusiastically, came out of the house to hug and greet everyone. During, and long after everything was unloaded, nothing changed. The only thing that came of it was that Addie dug from her handkerchief drawer every love note from her husband and, without hiding what she was doing, took them out to the backyard where she promptly set them on fire. Their words had become about as meaningful to her as dried grass on the withered Kansas plains during a deep and burdensome drought. She told her husband nothing, gave him nothing, and felt nothing, until the following year when they got word their son, Henry, was killed in action. She grieved doubly hard, once for her son and once for her lost love. Soon afterward, Adelaide Stewart literally dropped dead in the backyard in front of her youngest son, Tucker James, after she had resolved to confront her husband. She did not confront him. Her heart had broken and her strength had failed.

When Marjorie and Lois left home, planning never to return, they could not foresee the inevitable, for which Marjorie, alone, made the trip homeward, first for Dewey's funeral and then for her father's. Lois stuck to her vow and eventually became estranged from the family. When their father's funeral was over and everyone drifted away, Marjorie lingered at her father's grave. She waited until no one was around, then spat on the fresh mound of dirt.

"You good-for-nothing *snake!*" she yelled. Afterward, she walked away, got into her car, and left town.

Tucker Howard may not have seen his wife burning their love notes, but he felt it coming from her eyes that would not dare look at him the last year of her life. When, by chance, they had, he saw there his guilt, written upon the blue dawn azure of the summer sky for all to see. Too late, it was, for him and his wife to repair the damage done. The chariots would not bring their bright message to him anymore. That awareness was held in his thoughts for nearly twenty-five years, until he lay in his bed at the Spring Hill Residence & Infirmary, hands and head uncontrollably shaking and wobbling. He managed to swallow the pills he had saved. So ended his life, leaving his two sons, Howard and Tucker James, to pull the family name out of the tragic place where it had fallen, and carry on.

The day they had met at the newspaper office, with Howard and his youngest, surviving brother discussing the future of the printing press, their father had become agitated. He was trying to speak, desperately wanting to have a say in the matter, but could not, not then and not ever.

What he was trying to say, was, "I'm sorry. I'm sorry, for everything."

CHAPTER TWENTY-TWO

The day drifted on a somber tone, its shades and hues drawn in gray and shabby brown. It was November of 1967, the same year Jim Hart had died, before the winter of the big snow. In sadness and regret, Tucker James Stewart walked the dirt road through Pine Way. Before turning the corner to continue toward Edenville, he noticed Walter Henry sitting in front of the barn. The gray-haired man was whittling and talking to himself, even gesturing as though in conversation. Tucker also saw his father standing in front of the shuttered newspaper office, dressed in his brown suit, donning his brown fedora, and holding his briefcase. The vision seemed real.

Tucker could remember the exact day his father stood at that location. It was in his senior year. The locker room bantering between himself and Jim had ended, since football season was over and their class schedules no longer matched. Their entire life in school was nearing a close. Tucker thought about attending the community college to study journalism, maybe leave town and work for a large newspaper. He had mentioned that to a friend, someone he had known on the team. Arriving home from school that day, he unloaded his books and changed into other clothes before walking to the newspaper office to help out his dad. When he reached the corner of the row of brick buildings, he overheard his father talking with someone and hesitated. Slowly continuing on, he saw it was Jim.

He heard Jim say, "I'm planning to go to college, too. I already sent out my application."

Jim sounded hopeful, yet Tucker sensed an inauthenticity to Jim's words. It seemed as though Jim was merely making up a story about going away to college, as if to conceal an unspoken truth. Listening to Jim, Tucker realized their rivalry was as strong as ever.

Struck with the memory and with the sight of his father fading into that sunny day back in '52, Tucker knew that Jim was fully aware he was not going anywhere, but needed to pretend he was in front of others. The pressure was on, building toward graduation. Everyone talked and made plans. Why was it such a big deal?

Tucker remembered his father's reply. "Well, Jim, that's a real nice goal. Let me know if there's anything I can do to help," he said.

Balancing on one foot, Jim looked at his other foot as he tapped the edge of the wooden door step with it. He had his hands in the pockets of his jeans and a smile on his face. He looked like someone who was being praised and felt shy, but proud. It all changed when his own father, Jimmy Hart, stepped out of the barn and hailed him.

"Son? I need to talk to you," he said. He turned and went back into the barn.

Tucker approached his father after Jim walked away. He felt badly, like he had witnessed something not meant for him. Yet, only that day, he had shared his ideas about going to college with his supposed friend. Those ideas had made their way to Jim's ears.

Tucker tried to let the memory go and kept walking toward his brother's house. He felt like the whole world was looking at him, like everyone knew why he was walking through town that day. His father had died. He wondered about the vision he had seen, whether his father was trying to show him something. With that in mind, he tried recalling more of that one day.

Jim and his own father had argued. Jim said he wanted to leave town, to go away to college, but his father said, "You don't want to go to college anymore than I do!" Tucker heard every word of their argument, feeling sorry for Jim. Afterward, Jim stormed out of the barn and hurried down the path to go home, looking angry and hurt. What Jim's father had said made Tucker think twice about going away. He no longer wanted to go. It was only a thought, never a plan, only something expected of seniors before graduation, to talk and to plan. He regretted telling anyone.

Looking back on that day, Tucker saw it as a turning point in his life, one turn down the road of life he did not take. Regardless if he ever wanted to go away, or if it was even possible, he remained remain in Edenville, and so did Jim. Why? Tucker believed the vision of his father was trying to tell him something important he needed to understand.

At his brother's house, Howard asked his wife if she could watch the dog while he and Tucker drove to the rest home. The director of the Spring Hill Residence & Infirmary had requested they come in and sign papers regarding their father's death. However, Tucker objected.

"Drive?" he said. "We don't need to drive."

"Now, Tucker," said Howard, "I'm not walking over there to talk about our dead father with that man."

"Howard! I'd feel foolish driving across the highway and parking barely a hundred yards away," said Tucker.

"Oh, it's further than that!" argued Howard. "You're exaggerating!"

Howard got into his car. Mary took the leash in hand and led Freckles into the house. Tucker threw his hands up, giving up, and got into the car as well.

Howard knew how their father had died, but had kept that part out of the telling when he called his younger brother to give him the news. He was plainly in shock and did not want to walk anywhere. At the rest home, they met with the director and both heard their father had committed suicide. Tucker reacted instantly to the news.

"What?!" he asked. "That's ridiculous!"

Howard looked out the window, the palms of his hands gripping the arms of the wooden chair in which he sat.

The director looked at him and asked, "Uh, Mr. Stewart...Howard? Didn't you tell your brother?"

Howard remained silent.

Tipping his head downward to look over the top of his reading glasses, the director looked from one to the other before he said, "I had assumed you both knew by now." He noticed Tucker was equally unreceptive of the devastating news, but needed to proceed. "It's really not that uncommon in people with—" He changed his approach. "Maybe we could discuss this some other day, give you time to make arrangements. There's no real hurry. Just need some papers signed." He picked up the forms he was going over and set them before Howard, adding, "It's standard."

Howard took the papers and they left the director's office. Howard went out the back entrance to the parking lot and got into his car while Tucker went out the front entrance and walked away. From where Howard sat in his car, he could see Tucker cross the highway, go down the embankment, then cut through the orchards. Howard knew his brother was simply going to get the dog from the backyard and go home. He hurried off in his car, reaching his house the moment Tucker entered their backyard. Howard followed him and saw Mary handing over Freckles' leash, commenting that she barely had any time to spend with the dog before they returned.

Tucker saw Howard and said not a word, imagining that he would rather push his brother aside and walk on past through the open gate. He found he could not actually do so, for he was again struck with a vision of his father's memory. His brother looked exactly like him. Howard had become his father and Tucker felt like a teenaged boy again, seeing his dad walking into the backyard.

"Now, Tucker," Howard began. He wanted his brother to hear him out, to be more understanding, to be reasonable, not to be mad. But Tucker was dumbfounded, because Howard was very much like their father, the mustache, his expression, even the "now, Tucker," his father so often used to say. How could he be mad?

Tucker stood before his father-brother, holding the leash and looking down at the ground but out came the words that spoke for how he felt. "I was surprised, Howard," he said. "Shocked! I'm-I'm-I'm still shocked!" One hand held on to the leash, the other hand was on his hip or flying out around in the air as he yelled, "How do they know?! Were they there?! Why didn't they stop him?! Why Howard?! Tell me! *Tell* me!! *Why?!*"

"Tucker! Stop!" Howard shouted in return. "I'm just as shocked with the news as you are! All this time I believed Dad was doing better. I thought he was." He brushed past Tucker to sit in one of the lawn chairs near the barbecue grill.

Tucker realized they needed to work together. It was up to Howard and himself. He absentmindedly dropped Freckles' leash and joined his brother. He sat in the other lawn chair, in which one of the cloth strips was torn through, causing him to sink through the hole it had made. He could not have cared less. He thought of the native people he had met who lived in Laketon. A broken chair never bothered them.

He asked his brother, "What about Marjorie? Have you called her?"

"No. It was hard enough just to call you," Howard answered.

Howard's usual levity toward serious matters was absent from their discussion. The issue before him left him shook up and ill at ease. The last death in the family was Dewey's, another suicide. Howard was overwhelmed and looked up into the high tree tops of elm and maple to avoid looking at his brother, to stave off what was coming. He feared he would begin ranting on and on as he felt like doing, shouting inappropriate obscenities, smashing and breaking things. He pressed his thumb and index finger against his closed eyelids as though he could hold back the rising tide moving within him. Leaning forward and hunched over, he could only relent, as a wave of shock and grief erupted into hacking sobs. Mary ran to him from the back porch where she was watching the two. She knelt beside her husband and placed her arms around him.

"Oh, Howard. It's dreadful. Just dreadful!" she cried.

Giving the house one last look behind, Freckles wandered away down Fig Tree Lane, dragging her leash behind.

It was but minutes later when handkerchiefs were drawn from pockets and noses were blown. They each stood and hugged one another. Howard and Tucker patted each other on the back.

Mary looked for the dog, spotting the open gate, and exclaimed, "Oh, no!" She chided herself for not shutting the gate, but knew it was not negligence but circumstance that prevented their attentiveness to a dog that ran off every chance it could get. She dismissed it. The two men in her life promised to get through the current crisis together. With no parents or siblings of her own any longer, Mary vowed to devote herself to them, her only family.

Reassuring his brother, Howard said, "We'll work it out, Tucker. We'll sign those papers and get things rolling on this. Could you call Marjorie, at least once a date's been set for the, uh, you know..." He besmirched the thought their two sisters rarely, if ever, kept in touch. "Not that she cares," he said.

Tucker shot him a look of concern and asked, "Why do you say that?"

Howard explained, "Well, that's been my impression. Leastways, she can figure out how to get the news to Lois."

Gathering in Howard's office afterward, the necessary arrangements were set in motion. Exhausted, Tucker said his goodbyes and went outside to search for his dog. After he closed their front screen door, he turned to go down the porch steps, when he was met by another vision of his father. The man appeared as he used to look when he came home from work, surveying what Tucker had done around the house. He was dressed the same, his brown suit and hat.

Back then, it was only himself, his father, and Dewey at home, the three of them, since his Grandma Stewart had passed away. Dewey was having emotional problems and had trouble keeping a job. Howard was living out of town and Tucker was set to graduate from high school. His father had asked him and Dewey to mow the lawn, pull weeds in their neglected garden, clean the bathroom, sweep the kitchen, and wash the dishes. Tucker was fed up with Dewey for not helping. They fought and, right when Tucker decided he was going to move into Grandma and Grandpa Stewart's old house in Pine Way, his father came home. Tucker had his head down as he strode with purpose down the front sidewalk to the street, down the steps, only then seeing his father.

"What's this I hear about you planning to go to college, Son?" his father asked.

Finding himself once again immersed in the past, Tucker became disoriented and tried to stay present. He needed to look for his dog, but was struggling to cope. He sat on the porch steps and heard Howard and Mary talking about him. He had neglected to close the front door. In the very air, it seemed, came the voices of children at the school. He heard them shouting and laughing on the playground, the chain from the tether ball clinking, a teacher's whistle blown. It was off in the distance as though coming to his ears through a flange, wrapping around and around in sound, spinning into him and out again, and circling back.

His brother's voice was heard among the other sounds. He said, "Why don't I give you a ride home, Tucker? You don't look so good." Howard opened the screen door and let it close behind, his keys jingling as Tucker stood and walked only by instinct, getting into the car as though in a dream.

Driving down the street, Howard asked, "Are you gonna be all right? I'll ask Mary if she can bring some dinner over for you."

Tucker said, "I just need to take some time to—I-I need to find my dog!"

"Forget about it!" said Howard. "She'll come home. You'll see. She's probably visiting with someone right now," which proved to be true. Turning the corner, Tucker caught a glimpse of Freckles running from the school toward the diner, right as Walter Henry's truck was parking out front.

Once at home, Tucker lay on his bed. He wished he knew no one, so he would not have to care and feel so hurt when they were lost. He wished he was like some people he had seen, rushing forward to grab something someone else had chosen, not caring about anyone, unaffected. His father, whom he had known and loved all his life of thirty-three years, was gone for good, yet was still very much alive. It haunted Tucker, the strangeness of it. He wished he could understand what his father wanted him to know. He thought of his ideas about going away to college after high school and his regrets over the rivalry between himself and Jim Hart. Had he failed Jim somehow? Had he failed himself? Those questions held him enraptured in a past long gone. Yet, in the stillness and quiet of his simple cottage, which sat like an island of life amidst a dying town, Tucker knew intuitively, without words, that his father was merely seeking his forgiveness, showing his son that he, likewise, needed to forgive himself.

CHAPTER TWENTY-THREE

On the day of his father's funeral, Tucker sat on the steps of his childhood home on Fig Tree Lane. His sister, Marjorie, was leaving the cemetery in her gray Chevy sedan. He caught its movement beyond the parsonage and the Community Church gardens across the street. She had barely said hello at the funeral. Apparently, as he watched her continue toward the highway, she had not planned on saying goodbye.

"Well," he said, "at least she came." His comment referred to the fact that his other sister, Lois, did not show up at all.

Hands clasped before him, Tucker looked at his shoes, studying them. He noted the scuff marks his brother had pointed out to him. Sighing deeply, he debated whether he should go inside the house, but thought his hands and his fingernails deserved a look. He listened to the conversation drifting among those who came to pay their respects and give their condolences.

"What's Marjorie up to these days? Wasn't she at the funeral?" asked one guest.

"Oh, she's living out-of-town. I think she works at a market," said Howard.

"What about Lois? I didn't see her at all today," inquired another guest.

"Oh, she's busy. Lives too far away," answered Howard.

"That's too bad. She was in the same class as my daughter. I was hoping I'd see her," said one woman.

The conversation faded into the background as Tucker recalled something Lois had done when she was little. Sylvia had gotten her hair cut short in a style that was popular. Lois was jealous and wanted her hair cut the same way, but was told, "no." She did it herself and accidentally cut off her bangs. Tucker laughed, but then he missed her. She had gone away, his own sister, and he knew not where. He remembered that her two front teeth were crooked, one slightly overlapping the other, which gave her voice a pinched, labored sound.

Reflecting on other things he had observed that day, Tucker noted something sad about families. Funerals exposed their stark and disparate frailties without mercy. His family was no exception. Unforeseen changes had taken place, deeply affecting him. So much so, he felt the loss of more than just his father. His entire childhood, the connections he had made, the lives in which he shared, taking every one of them for granted, merely because that is what children do, were all gone.

He had read something in a book recently and whispered the words as best he could remember them.

"Youth! Oh, selfish beings! They do live and love in the now. They think naught of others growing old and one day dying, never to be seen, for they are flighty creatures, more like hummingbirds and butterflies. They interest themselves but for a little while, when the nectar is sweet and feeds them richly, before they must fly. The very mention of old age and death is like a plague to youth. Oh, selfish ones! How I wish I were as blithely ignorant as thee!"

Resignedly, Tucker stood to go inside. However, before he turned to enter the house, he imagined Sylvia standing at the end of the front walkway, wearing a purple coat and carrying a handbag. On her head, was a purple hat he thought Jackie Kennedy might have worn, with a mesh veil drawn down to cover her face.

He imagined her saying, "Aren't you going to invite me in?"

Tucker pictured himself hurrying toward her, down the steps, to the end of the walk, and taking her in his arms. His eyes closed as he admitted to himself that, contrary to his better senses, he yet loved Sylvia. He wished he could hold her in a loving embrace, kissing her as he had so often imagined, as a man, not as the teen who had enjoyed one, brief experience with her in the woods. But she, like Lois, did not attend the funeral either. He needed Sylvia that day, but she did not come.

Sylvia lived too far away to have heard the news, but her Aunt Patty, with whom she remained in touch, had telephoned her, to let her know. All Sylvia said in reply was, "Oh, my." She was prevented from returning to Edenville. She was due to give birth and was advised not to travel. Her new boyfriend, Andrew, had married her, even though she was pregnant. He said he loved her, though it was not his child. Once Sylvia had started to show, she believed that everyone in Edenville would guess whose it was, so she stayed away.

Before the funeral mass had begun, Patty glanced at Howard and Mary Stewart. With a slight shake of her head Mary informed Patty that Sylvia would not be coming. Patty had not a clue as to why until Mary later whispered in her ear.

Patty and her daughter had parked their car at the beauty parlor, so they walked back into town after the service. When the time was right, Patty gathered her purse and gloves and called out to Dottie. She stepped out of the beauty parlor and began walking over to the Stewart's house. Dottie had little reason to object or complain. Her mother had caught her with a man in her room. Patty was furious and reminded Dottie she was "much too old to be carryin' on so" and, "what if you make a mistake?" Only to hear from Mary Stewart that her niece, Dottie's cousin, had done that very thing.

Obediently, Dottie trailed behind her mother while devising a plan to see her boyfriend again and again until—well, she was in her thirties and had been single long enough. She was secretly hoping to get pregnant, to force her boyfriend to marry her. Her best friend, Rosa Smith, was married and had a child. Dottie felt as though she was not only left behind, but left in the dust, matrimonially speaking. She would not be outdone nor would she ruin her chances waiting any longer. She had read in a magazine that the older she got the more dangerous it would be to have children. Her boyfriend had no idea what was soon to befall him, and neither did she.

Howard and Tucker greeted the two once they reached the house.

Patty said, "Hello, Howard. Tucker. I'm so sorry." Before heading into the house as Howard held the screen door open for them, she added, "It's a terrible thing to lose a father."

Dottie and Tucker exchanged hellos. Without thinking, Dottie hugged him and said, "sorry," leaving Tucker to briefly wonder if she was sorry for hugging him or for his loss.

Mary served them punch and began introducing them to some of the other guests. She was a gracious hostess and Tucker admired her, like Donna Reed. She was perfect. He was grateful to have her in the family. He put together a plate of food and sat in the backyard. He sipped lemonade and ate pork and beans with frankfurters, potato salad, some sort of jello confabulation, and a slice of cold roast beef wedged in a French roll with a slice of cheese and a dab of mustard. No one approached him. He was content to sit and eat in peace, imagining Sylvia again, wondering why she never showed.

He overheard Patty McGrew saying that she had telephoned Sylvia to give her the news, so he knew she was told. Disappointed, he sat alone at the picnic table, empty plate before him, muttering under his breath, "Why would she?" Reminding himself of his father and her mother in the house right next door, he recalled the words, "sins of the father," and wondered whose father? He feared whether anyone knew how his father had died. If Sylvia knew, would she care to attend, especially after Jim—

Howard came out with a plate of food and sat with him. Tucker spotted Freckles grabbing something off of someone else's plate when they went back into the house for some lemonade and a paper napkin. When they returned, they yelled at Freckles and ran to their plate. Tucker apologized to the man as the dog ran off with a piece of fried chicken between her teeth.

Turning to his brother, he tried to make conversation, by saying, "Well, Howard, I guess it's over, huh?"

"Yeah. It's pretty much over, little brother," said Howard.

Howard stared off into the distance, so Tucker took his leave. He patted his brother on the shoulder with his free hand and returned inside. Some of the guests had offered to clean afterward, so Tucker thanked them and his sister-in-law, his very own Marilyn Monroe and Donna Reed all in one.

"I'm gonna head home, Mary. Do you mind?" he asked her.

"Oh, no. You go ahead, Tucker. I think everyone that's going to come is either here or they've left already," she said.

"Except Sylvia," Tucker pouted.

Impatient, Mary shook her head and asked, "Are you sure you would have wanted her here, Tucker?" She drew her head back into herself with an expression on her face that asked, "really?" She walked away with a knowing smile. Truth was, Mary knew Sylvia was pregnant before she even left town, maybe even before Sylvia knew it herself. Mary would never tell. "Us women have to stick together," she muttered to herself.

Tucker rounded up his dog and set off for home. While walking, he reflected on his father's funeral. Many faces were absent, he recalled, not only his sister's and Sylvia's, but their old newspaper editor and two other men who once worked at the paper. No, he corrected himself, one of those men did attend the funeral, though it was not "that skinny beanpole," he whispered under his breath. Marjorie came alone, without her husband or the children Tucker learned she had. The other half of his observation was in the faces present that day neither he nor his brother had expected, like Patty and Dottie McGrew,

Sam Goodman from the hardware store, even an old high school buddy of his father's who had never lived in Edenville. The man had read about it in the newspaper. A few families of his father's siblings had attended, older cousins he could faintly remember coming to visit them in his childhood that was now dead and gone. Nothing was as he expected.

June's children, whom he figured must both be in their twenties, did not attend, he thought. However, when most everyone had left his brother's house, and the ladies who had offered to help were picking up plates and cups and napkins, talking amongst themselves as they did so, the doorbell rang. A woman and her husband were at the door and Howard told Tucker later it was none other than June's daughter, not-so-little Patricia Catherine, six-feet tall, give or take a half an inch. Her husband was a good six-foot-six and with hands his brother referred to as "mitts," they were as big as baseball mitts, recalling another term, "hams," then laughed.

Walking the dirt road back into Pine Way, Tucker was sadly disappointed that Sylvia had not attended his own father's funeral. Slightly perturbed at that, he said aloud, "I gave her everything I had to give, all my love and-and friendship. Why did she have to leave?" Recalling her note she had left under the doormat, which he had swiftly crumpled, he pondered, "I wonder what it says?"

Passing by the old post office in Pine Way, Tucker glanced in that direction. He recalled seeing Sylvia talking to Jim Hart behind the barn. Along with that remembrance, came another. Stopping in his tracks, he turned to look back toward Edenville. He recalled the look on Sylvia's face when she watched as Jim's coffin was being carried to his grave. That look on her face said it all, he believed. She appeared to be worried and sad. Tucker believed it was because she missed Jim, though he had failed to notice her palm lightly resting on her abdomen.

The note she left behind, which Tucker told himself to be sure and read, held the answer to all his questions. Yet, when he arrived at home, he forgot to read it. He would remember at some point and, once read, learn for himself the real reason why Sylvia Sumner left town.

CHAPTER TWENTY-FOUR

The following summer, Tucker stood in his garden, leaning on his hoe. He was completely unaware that Freckles was busy digging a hole where he had planted his lettuce seedlings. Her vigorous task complete, she plopped down and began to pant and whine. Yet oblivious, Tucker gazed into the treetops, noticing a new hawk in residence. He suspected it was hunting Harvey Six-Bits' laying hens. Turning to place the hoe with his other tools propped against the house, he caught Freckles.

"Freckles! No!" he shouted.

She dashed away. Instead of going after her, he used the hoe to repair the damage she had done. He gently replanted each of the seedlings, only to be shoved from behind by her when she jumped on him. Knocking him off-balance and into the dirt, he smashed the poor seedlings. Recovering himself, he stood and brushed off his clothes, watching the dog run down the road. He flung the hoe onto the ground and chased after her for nearly a mile and a half, which he later suspected Freckles had planned all along. She ran to the public library, where he spotted her scratching at the door and barking. The door opened and she slipped through the doorway, leaving Tucker face to face with Candelaria Hart. The dog's actions brought about an additional encounter with Katie Winters, who was petting and fussing over his misbehaving dog.

Since he last saw Candelaria, he was remembering more about her from when he was a boy. One incident that stood out was something so simple as bringing by some hot stew and bread one night when his father was late getting the paper out. With her and Rosa looking on, Tucker sat at his father's desk with his father's big coat on, savoring every drop of that stew. It had touched upon his loss, for that was something his own mother would have done if she were alive. Again, he wondered what happened over the years.

Candelaria busied herself, needlessly glancing through a stack of papers. Actively grieving her son the past several months, seeing Tucker served as a reminder of her own loss. Gathering her notebooks and shouldering her heavy purse she had lugged there for no good reason, she made an excuse about why she was leaving.

Surprised at her friend's sudden departure, Katie found herself alone in the library with Tucker. She secretly wished he would leave as well.

Feeling awkward, Tucker looked down toward Freckles. He could almost discern a wide, coyote-like grin on her furry face. The white tip on her tail swayed back and forth, mesmerizing his good senses, convincing him rather stealthily to ask, "Would you like to have dinner together sometime, Katie?"

"You know, Tucker, I've been hoping we could see one another," she answered.

"All right. How about tonight?" He winced, thinking, "Did I say that?"

Katie said, "Okay."

Taking Freckles by the collar, Tucker led her out the door, shouting behind, "Six-thirty? Your place?"

Before Katie could answer, he was gone. Unwilling to hide her annoyance with him, she gathered her own things before walking to the market. On her way, she planned their meal. "Hmm, let's see...I could cook lasagna. That would take a good long while, give us time to talk things over." Recalling their last date, she wondered why she was bothering with a man whose head was turned by a younger woman's pretty face. The fact reaffirmed the need to talk openly about it with him. Walking across the parking lot toward the market, she grew irritable over the prospect and sourly commented aloud, "I think I'll feed him some crow!"

In the meantime, Freckles ran off again. She followed Candelaria home along the woodland path that connected town with Villa Borracho. Candelaria stood by her front door, digging in her purse for her keys. Freckles snatched up one of Aurelia's future wood projects and began to gnaw on it like it was a prized bone.

"Oh, no!" said Candelaria. That minor outcry was soon followed by a string of oaths in Spanish. She tried grabbing the wood out of the dog's mouth, pointing her finger toward the road, and yelling, "Go home!"

Freckles would not leave. She scurried under the shack to hide, taking the piece of wood with her. Candelaria let it go and went into the house. She had more important things to do, like prepare for her next speaking engagement, one in which she would travel by airplane. While closing her door, she spotted Tucker out on the road, calling for his dog. Thankfully, Freckles left to join him.

Tucker told the dog, "All right, Freckles. You've made your point." His gait slowed to an uncomfortable, feet-dragging slowness, leastways for Freckles. She barked at him and ran off, stopping to look back at him as though to coax him along. "I've had enough of your mischief, young lady!" he said. Freckles barked again, but found an itch more urgent. She sat in the road to scratch.

Feeling his bachelorhood threatened, Tucker suspected there was a conspiracy afoot. He imagined the three women together, Candelaria, Katie, and Aurelia, including Freckles, all talking about him, plotting how to get him married off...to whom? He asked aloud, "What is it with women?" They could not stand a man wanting to stay single, he believed. He felt guilty, because he had promised his mother, over her grave, no less, that he would become a father to carry on the Stewart family name, which required him to marry. Tucker grit his teeth and dismissed that last thought.

He thought about his sisters, talking about marriage and having children, though Lois said the whole idea was revolting. That was the year June got married. Tucker laughed, remembering the women in their household, five, if he counted his grandmother. They were excited about the wedding. Aunts, female cousins, and friends had arrived, congregating in the kitchen or the girls' bedroom. He was outnumbered and outmaneuvered. He figured they liked to get together only so they could talk. No matter how personal the subject, he had observed, they would get louder and louder, as if everyone around them was deaf. He learned that was the worst time to walk into the room. One of his aunts commented, "Aw, look at little Tucker James blushing. Ain't he sweet?"

Where men were concerned, they typically got together to do something constructive, he believed, like work on a car or paint something. They might talk, usually about work or politics, involving a lot of joking and bragging. If it was about something serious, their voices would lower as if everyone around them could hear. Well, that's what he thought.

Almost to his house, he was about to let out a big sigh of relief, when he saw Aurelia sitting on his porch. They had not spoken to one another since the previous year, before Tucker's father had died. Freckles leaped and bounded toward her, whining and licking her face. Aurelia was laughing and nearly fell over. Tucker tried to get Freckles to calm down. Putting the dog out on her stake in the yard, he stalled talking to the young woman who was patiently waiting for him.

He was trying not to look at her, denying to himself that he felt nothing less than smitten, downright taken since the moment they had met at Harvey's house.

The last time she stopped by to visit, she had asked, "Do you ever think about us maybe having a spiritual connection?"

Attempting to avoid her, he said, "No, I don't think so."

Frustrated, before she left his house that day, Aurelia told him, "The Keeper of the Dream is my ally, Tucker Stewart, even if you don't see it."

Months had passed since then. He had no idea what she was going to say. But he was exhausted from chasing after Freckles, and being chased, now that he thought of it.

After saying hello, he sat with the young woman on his porch. He imagined saying, "Did you know that you and Johnny Henry are related? Jim Hart and Katie Winters are his parents and Candelaria Hart is his grandmother." He knew it was best not to say anything, not to her, or to anyone.

With that last thought, Tucker realized he felt cheated once again. He and Jim fought over every girl they liked. They were more like brothers, their sibling rivalry ever-present. The way Tucker saw it, his late nemesis had not only won Sylvia's heart, but Katie's, too.

Aurelia said, "I read your article on Char Lee Rosebud last year."

"You did?" asked Tucker.

"Yeah. Candelaria had a copy of the paper," she said.

"Char Lee was quite a character," commented Tucker.

"So, you've been to Laketon, huh?" asked Aurelia.

"Only once," he answered.

"Did you know Dreaming Man?" she inquired.

"Yes," said Tucker. "But I didn't know about that part of his life until I heard about it from Char Lee and Harvey."

Changing the subject, Aurelia asked, "So...what do have growing in your garden, here?"

Pleased she had asked, Tucker happily shared with her what he had planted that day. When he told her what Freckles had done, he acted it out, humorously showing Aurelia how Freckles dug the hole, then knocked him over and ran off.

When he showed her Candelaria's reaction to seeing him, Aurelia laughed out loud.

Their conversation continued. Tucker noticed Aurelia had a particular way of turning her head as she smiled at him, which made her short pony tail flip around. Listening to her and briefly commenting now and then, he thought, "I like her. In fact, I like her a lot. She reminds me of Natalie Wood." He wondered, "What's so wrong about liking her?"

His unspoken resolve to avoid getting involved with Aurelia was weakening. He caught himself admiring her curves, her face. When they looked at one another, he drew in a quick breath as the strangest sensation came over him, a feeling from a distant place, a remembrance of a time past that yet dwelled within himself. In that place, he already knew her, which somehow explained everything.

In the stillness of being with her, whom he knew, Tucker took a chance. He had not the words to explain what he understood regarding her last parting comment, so he asked, "What did you mean, that I'm your ally?"

"Oh." Aurelia hesitated a moment before answering, "Uh, I didn't mean you, literally. I meant the Keeper of the Dream."

"Isn't that the same thing?" he asked.

"No, not exactly," she said. "The Keeper of the Dream is who you really are, not—" She was about to say, "not this person you pretend to be."

Tucker wanted to know more and began to say, "Not..."

"Look." Aurelia had never needed to explain herself, or a way of looking at life, but it was important to try, she believed. She said, "Harvey said he told you about being the Keeper of the Dream and he said you understood what he meant." She looked at him, slightly irritated and added, "Why are you now pretending you don't know?"

Tucker lowered his voice as his tone softened and he said, "I just meant—how am I your ally? I just want to know what you meant."

Tucker felt like a different person, someone he had never been with anyone else, for he had unknowingly become the one who knew her and loved her. He was expressing deeper, heartfelt feelings he had shared with no one else, not even Sylvia. Never had there been anything so intimate between himself and a woman, as what Aurelia—

"Okay, okay," she said, interrupting his thoughts. Looking away from him, out into the darkening woods, she placed her clasped hands over her knees. She looked back at him, finding that she could not answer his question without experiencing her feelings of attraction toward him grow stronger. She said, "I've never had to put it into words before, so..." Struggling to speak dispassionately, and failing at it, she answered him through her tears. Her own tone of voice became gentler, kinder, as she continued, "I meant that you and I are connected in a very special way regarding Lucy Shoseegan's dream." What Aurelia knew about the dream, and how she felt about Tucker, was drawing them closer to one another. They shared the same space in her heart. She was asking him, needing him to honor that, to accept it, to—

Tucker knew he needed to let her speak, no matter how difficult, and said, "I'm listening."

"The way I feel about you," she said. Her tears were running freely, as she slowly continued, "My dreams, my visions. You can help me to-to make it real! Make it happen!" She looked away and then back at him. "Tucker! I can't explain it! I only know how I've felt ever since we met! I've never felt this way about anyone before!" She stopped talking then, rubbing her sleeve over her eyes to wipe her tears away, instead putting herself down. "Oh, jeez, I feel so stupid!" she said.

It was the dream, Lucy's dream, and it was fatherhood, and Tucker knew he needed to make his choice. However, he resisted how he felt about the woman sitting beside him.

Later that evening, he went to Katie's for dinner, but his date with her ended as badly as the last one had, with Katie telling him, "I had hoped we'd eventually marry, Tucker. But I'm not so sure anymore. Ever since—"

Katie looked away from him before saying, "I think you should leave. I hope we can stay friends, but I don't think we should date anymore."

After Tucker left Katie's, he wondered if she, or anyone else knew about Aurelia's impromptu visits to his house. Harvey had seen Aurelia go to Tucker's house, telling himself it had to be the dream awakening. He could do nothing to stop what was taking place, for it was drawing power from a seemingly different realm, between rational thought and emotion, dreaming and waking, restraint and desire. He had observed for himself that the dream was calling upon many others who lived in the valley and up in Laketon, too. Building community was his part of the dream, one ray of the Great Wheel, turning 'round until it reached the point, at last, where the dream would come to earth in Pine Valley. The following day, he got in his car and drove out of town, heading down into the great valley beyond. It was time for him to apply for a contractor's license. His construction crew, he told himself, needed to be ready.

CHAPTER TWENTY-FIVE

The soft, fiery look in Aurelia's eyes was on Tucker's mind. A sudden twinge of guilt struck hard the moment Harvey stepped out of his house to meet him.

Harvey was on guard for what Tucker might have to say. Pointing to the sofa on his porch, he said, "Have a seat."

Tucker sat, wishing he had not decided to speak with Harvey.

"So, what brings you here, Tucker? What did you want to talk to me about?" asked Harvey.

Tucker squirmed, unsure how to approach the delicate subject of his encounters with Aurelia. "Well, Harvey," he began.

Freckles dug furiously in Harvey's yard, going after a gopher in the overgrown, knee-high, weedy growth. Tucker paused with the derisive thought she was saving Harvey the trouble of digging a grave after he was gunned down for messing with Aurelia.

"Come on, Tucker. What is it?" Harvey asked.

Anyone who knew Tucker Stewart, was familiar with his straying imagination, the reason Harvey's people liked Tucker so well. He was a Dreamer. Harvey's faith and trust in his friend was renewed by the thought, and Harvey needed a friend. The people of Laketon were clamoring for their own homes in Pine Valley, wanting to return to their old village site, especially since the rough winter they had.

Tucker took the plunge and said, "Aurelia's been coming by my house, wanting to talk to me about something." He stopped, because the truth was he wanted to get to know her better and longed to reciprocate her attentions. He thought there was no easy way to say what was on his mind. His clasped hands drew apart and he spoke from his heart, "She's—I can't help but sense there's something—is Aurelia your girlfriend?"

"Ex," Harvey corrected Tucker, "ex-girlfriend."

Tucker's shoulders suddenly dropped as he relaxed, relieved, though puzzled. He was about to ask what happened, but decided against it. He could barely allow himself to think the words, that he was in love with Aurelia.

"I guess you know," he said.

"Yeah, I know," said Harvey.

Harvey had known Aurelia nearly all his life and knew her story, her history with men. It was time for Tucker to hear the story, too. Dirt flew from the tops of the weeds where Freckles was digging as Harvey shared Aurelia's tragic past.

"You know, in your culture," Harvey said, "when someone is sick or behaves strangely, they're sent to a doctor and given a label, diagnosing their condition. They get medicine and treatment and, when they stop having unwanted symptoms, they're considered cured or in remission or back to normal.

But, in my culture, it's different. When someone is sick, we look at their dreams and consider what Spirit is trying to tell them or teach them. They're given medicine, but only what our healers have heard Spirit tell them that person needs, never to get rid of or mask symptoms, but to restore balance."

Tucker was listening carefully, interested in what Harvey was telling him and eager to hear how Aurelia fit into the story. Harvey picked up a small stone and tossed it at Freckles. She leaped up and looked around for what happened. Tucker and Harvey laughed. She shook out her fur, snorted and sneezed from the dirt in her snout, and approached Tucker, who petted her. Harvey continued.

"I don't know if you've ever met her, but Ellie's great-grandparents lived in Laketon. Her great-grandfather died way before I, or Ellie, were born, but her great-grandmother was around a long time. Lucy. Lucy Shoseegan."

Harvey looked down as though considering what he further needed to say. His felt cowboy hat with the large feather in its brim reminded Tucker of Jim Hart. The feather would tip up into the air whenever Harvey looked downward. Tucker realized Jim Hart and Aurelia were cousins. They were both part native. Maybe that was why he thought of Jim.

Harvey went on to say, "Anyway, Lucy's son, Manny, lived with them, along with Manny's son, Leo. He was Ellie's dad. Ellie's mother took off."

Tucker was reminded of Char Lee Rosebud's story, how it seemed to be happening all around them. Harvey went back to the days of his childhood in Laketon, living in what the nice people of Edenville would call filth and squalor. He told Tucker about Ellie's seizures as a girl and Lucy trying to heal her, though failing.

Harvey cried, "Jeez! You people here have *no idea* what happened to my people. Our lives were ripped apart! We were nearly decimated by violence and disease. What was left, was broken and full of holes. We were lucky to have Lucy. She knew how to help us and she told us about Dreaming Man and then about you, the Keeper of the Dream."

Tucker noticed that Freckles, lying stretched out on the walkway, asleep, began wagging her tail, her legs twitching in a dream when Harvey said those words.

Harvey continued, "Her grandfather and her dad, plus some men from Edenville here, would get together, not just Dreaming Man, but Russ Walker and his low-life friends. They would meet up in Laketon. They ran a still off in the woods, called it 'Church,' sort of a code word, I guess. 'Goin' to church,' they'd say, like it was their religion." He shook his head as he said, "Ellie tagged along with them this one time and they sent her home. I saw them waving their hands at her to get on home. But she followed after them, just a little girl back then, maybe eight or so. They drove on up into the woods to their church, Ellie sneaking off behind them. But they weren't the only ones out there who followed the same religion. Those other men caught Ellie, angry she had found their still, thinking she would tell. So, they did things to her so she wouldn't."

Harvey grew quiet. The sun had gone down and the crickets were calling before he continued his story.

"I was about ten years old, I guess. She came running into our camp, her clothes torn, what was left of them, naked from the waist down, bloody and dirty, screaming and crying."

Harvey looked at Tucker when he said, "I was in shock! I was just a kid, too! What could our medicine do for that? What could herbs and burning sage do?"

Tucker was speechless, for he was there, hearing the girl's screams, seeing the people running to her, covering her, and carrying her home. She had gone into a seizure. The women told the men to stay away. They knew their little Ellie, the girl who had visions of animals, saying they came to her to tell their stories, had been raped, fearing it most likely had been done more than once to her.

"She was nearly destroyed! Those men almost killed her!" said Harvey. "She could have died and they would have left her there out in the woods somewhere, but she ran home. Her heart, her soul, her mind, it was all contaminated by what those men had done to her! Lucy did her best. But, Leo? When he came back and they all heard what had happened and saw Ellie staring like-like she was dead, or something, he took off. All of them did. They knew who'd done it and I'm pretty sure they killed them. There was all kinds of stuff going on after that, a big-time investigation, FBI men crawling all over the woods. They found the two stills. They found two bodies dumped elsewhere. It took them, I don't know, a few years, at least, to piece it all together. But they shut down the tavern, arrested Ellie's dad and Russ and his friends. Manny had already died by then. They cleaned up Laketon and, by the time I was a teenager, Ellie was gone. She was put in some kind of a home, but I heard she later took up with this one guy. Lucy had died.

"Me and Bear and Clay said, 'Hell! Look's like this is our town now!' The buildings were all abandoned, so we began to take up the construction trade and fixed them up and, hey, we did pretty good. Helped Char Lee with her place with our junkyard construction. We'd head over to the dump for some building materials. Found some pretty good stuff, too."

Tucker had visited the dump, himself, on more than one occasion, scavenging with his brothers, with Forty and Sylvia as well. But, Harvey was not done with his story.

"You wanna know the weirdest thing about it all?" he asked. "Did you know Jim Hart?"

Surprised, Tucker looked over at Harvey and answered, "What about him?"

"He used to come up to Laketon with that artist guy, Tommy McGrew," said Harvey. "They were drinking buddies with Bear and Barclay's big brother, Sampson. Everybody called him that, because of his long hair and because he was really strong, I mean, *really* strong. Back then, Jim Hart would come to see Lucy, until she died and, I guess about that time his dad had died, too. But Char Lee took care of Lucy and Ellie and invited Hart to come visit. Do you know, he was the only man Ellie would let near her back then? Whenever she would have a seizure or begin to get hysterical, he'd pick her up in his arms and hold her in his lap, rocking her back and forth. He'd sing this song I remember from when I was a little kid. It went something like," and Harvey sang it in his language. "It's a lullaby, kinda means, 'way up high in a tree, there's a bird for you and me, takes us flying on a stream, brings us home to live our dream.' He'd sing that over and over and she loved it."

Harvey looked at Tucker and said, "He was a good person. We were all sorry to hear that he died. Heard others say how messed up he was, but our people knew he was like a holy man."

Tucker found that shocking and asked in surprise, "A holy man? What-what do you mean?"

"He walked with Spirit, man." Harvey moved his fingers like a person walking. "He was in both worlds," his hand going out to show it, "walked in-between this world and that. It's not easy medicine to carry. You're never really a part of either worlds, never know where you belong, where you fit in. Home is nowhere and everywhere for people like that. Did you ever see his arms? All cut up. I saw them. That's the only way he could make it through the day, probably. A Wounded Healer. Sacred medicine." He paused, then blurted out, "Hell. I've got to let Ellie go. She's trying to find her path and I'm just in the way."

Harvey grew silent and Tucker knew it was time to go home. He was unsure whether the story was finished, but it was growing darker and he needed to get dinner and feed Freckles. So he invited Harvey to have dinner with him. They walked over to his place. He was exhausted from Harvey's story, completely in awe over what his friend had shared about Jim Hart. Also, he felt sad for Aurelia and had trouble thinking about what was done to her.

At home, he went all out on dinner, put a steak in the oven he was saving for the weekend. He baked potatoes, made a salad, and cooked up some carrots with broccoli and cauliflower. Harvey wanted some rice, too. Before Tucker knew what was happening, Bear and Barclay knocked at the door. They saw Harvey through the window. Grinning wide, Barclay held up a bucket containing their fried chicken dinner from The Chicken Ranch restaurant out on the highway. Freckles was barking and whining in glee at all the visitors. Tucker had ice cream, too, and they even baked cookies. The tv and the radio were both blaring and, in all of that, while Laugh-In was on, Barclay and Bear were smoking and giggling. Tucker knew all was well between them. He was once again grateful for his new friends, especially Aurelia. The long loneliness of his bachelorhood was urging him to let go of Sylvia and, instead, be thankful for Aurelia, plus a house full of laughter and good friends.

CHAPTER TWENTY-SIX

Nearly two years after her son's death, Candelaria Hart set pen to paper to write up her talk she was asked to give at a conference on peace, race, and politics. She was one of several authors invited as guest speakers. She saw the credentials of the others who had also been invited, PhD, MA, doctor of this and that, professor of this and that, and felt wholly unqualified. Yet they insisted, saying, "Your perspective on racial issues is unique and needs to be heard by others."

She noticed Johnny walking by on his way home from school, then directed her attention back to her writing. Soon, she was interrupted by the memory of her husband's voice. He was joking with Tucker Howard Stewart. Their boys were soon to be teenagers. She was standing with them, her arm draped across Tucker James's shoulders, having praised him for something, when her husband said, "You better keep an eye on that boy, Tuck!" That was what Jimmy Hart called Tucker Howard. "My wife's got her heart set on having another one to baby. She just might steal him away from you!" The two men had a good laugh over that. Embarrassed, Candelaria slid her arm down to her side. She knew she had to hide her feelings, accept the loss of her two baby boys, or face additional ridicule.

The wind brought Candelaria back to the present. It whirred above her through the pines. The sun-dappled shade flitted across the page before her. Yet the past lay hopelessly cast deep within her heart, where grief remained untouched by memory. It was a dark place she never wanted to see, for all her losses left her yearning. Losing the first baby was painful enough. But, the morning she discovered the second one, limp, like the little dead dog they had hit with their car, that she had to pick up to set off to the side of the road, she screamed.

Her husband ran into their bedroom, yelling, "What?! What's the matter?!"

"My baby! He's-he's *dead!*" she yelled.

She fell to the floor as her husband picked up the lifeless form that had been their child, held it close in his arms, and walked out of the house with it. He might as well have kept on walking, for he never really returned, not his heart, not his self, for he was truly not his self after that day. He was taken away by the shock of that loss, as though he was punished for daring to hope, having new life in their home once again.

Sitting on the porch of her Villa Borracho shanty, Candelaria knew that hope had also died that day long ago. It left her emptied out, her man whom God had given her, lost into a dream from which she had barely awakened.

"Yes," she cried into her open palms, held up to receive the mask of sorrow she had learned to wear so well, "he was only a dream." Yes, he was only a dream.

•   •   •

On the day of her speaking engagement, Candelaria held her purse and notebook close to her, with one small bag held in a tight grip. She appeared as if she might drop off the face of the earth at any minute and did not want to lose a thing. Waving goodbye to Katie Winters, Candelaria boarded the light aircraft, which held only eight passengers besides the pilot and co-pilot. Once the plane took off, she relaxed, discovering the experience of lifting away, as the ground fell beneath her, was thrilling. She could see Edenville in the hills, familiar roads, until they flew over places she never saw before, heading off in a wide arc, wider, wider still. The chugging motor was like a droning, vibrating hum, lulling her to sleep, until each time the aircraft dropped into an air pocket, suddenly jerking downward, side to side, upward. Feeling faint, as each passenger gripped their armrests, she prayed, "Dear God. I know you're up here in the clouds with us. Protect us. Hold us in your arms."

The flight would soon be over, so Candelaria bravely gazed out the window to see the enormous city below. Drawing downward, preparing to land, she saw hundreds, maybe thousands of automobiles on roads elevated above the ground. She had only seen freeways on television. Someone met her at the airport and they drove to a beautiful hotel with a swimming pool. It was near the building where she was to join the others who were invited. She placed her things in her room and returned to the hotel lobby, waiting beside the group gathered together.

The event was being held at the Victory Pavilion, which was built after World War II. She listened to the others chatting among themselves about their work. Standing quietly nearby, she wondered why she was there, believing she had nothing in common with them. She missed her shack of a house, its simplicity, and the comfort of all she knew, a small, yet important world. It was the world in which she was born and raised, as was the man she had loved, their children, and grandchildren. Rosa recently shared the news she was expecting another baby. Candelaria was happy.

She grew weary of the wait, but soon a few vans arrived to take them to the Pavilion. It was a grand building that was circular in structure, rather than square, with large windows all around, and white panels extending outward from the building's exterior walls at varying distances and heights, pointed as though reaching skyward in ascension. It lent an air of possibility and hope for the future. A wide stairway led up to the entrance where hundreds of people were entering the building. Dozens of others, off to the side, were shouting, protestors waving banners and signs.

Once indoors, she and the other speakers were taken to a small meeting room to await their cue, when they would be led by an armed escort to the stage. She noticed there were armed guards posted inside the building, as well as outside. Living in a small town had shielded her from the violence and upheaval of the times, a period in which she had stepped forward to add her voice to all those speaking on civil rights. Having heard the anti-war sentiments, women angry, this group or that group angry, it struck her that only a few rose to lead them and generate hope for peace to come, Candelaria felt in awe of the moment of which she was now a part.

While looking for a restroom, she spotted a familiar face. It was none other than Sylvia Sumner. Candelaria was amazed at the change in Sylvia, the way she wore her hair, in a cute pixie, and the way she dressed, in tight paisley-print pants with a tight sweater, and kitten-heeled shoes. She was with a man and was holding a child on her hip. Theirs? Candelaria wondered about that one and mentally did some quick math. Sylvia kissed the man and left the building as he entered the room where the speakers had assembled. He introduced himself to the group as Andrew Parker. Unfamiliar to Candelaria, she dismissed the light conversation he generated amongst the group. Anxious enough over being there, she was also distracted, fretting over the possibility that Sylvia had seen her.

She hurried along to the restroom, mostly to compose herself and splash some cold water on her face. Freely voicing her fears, she whispered, "Ay, Mamá. What have I gotten myself into? I don't belong here. I'm not like these people." Her confidence faltered as she panicked, wishing she had never agreed to come.

A toilet flushed and a woman exited the stall, surprising Candelaria. She later learned it was a professor of humanities from a nearby university, named Dorothy Johnson.

She told Candelaria, "I've never done anything like this before. I'm simply terrified." She bent over the sink to splash her own face with cold water.

Candelaria commiserated, "I thought I was the only one who was nervous."

"Oh, no. I am. Believe me." After patting her face dry, the woman dug into her purse for her lipstick and began putting some on and talking as she did so. "I saw your picture in a magazine," she said. "Candelaria Mendoza, right?"

"Yes, that's me," said Candelaria.

"Well, Candelaria Mendoza, if you speak as well as you write, you've got nothing to worry about." She rolled her lipstick closed and dumped it in her purse, continuing on, "Me? I've written nothing, talked only in front of my students. Yet, here I am," her hands slightly raised to question why.

Candelaria felt better listening to this woman, saying, "But, you're so confident, so—"

"Listen to me," Dorothy told her, "don't let all that PhD nonsense intimidate you. My father used to say that it stood for 'poor hungry devil.' You know, p-h-d?"

Candelaria liked Dorothy and grew confident herself. "I guess we better get back," she said.

"Yes, I guess we better," said Dorothy. They rejoined the group being herded backstage. Dorothy added one last comment, "If Doctor King were here, I'd feel a whole lot stronger."

"Doctor King?" Candelaria had seen him in the news on television. "Did you know him?" she further asked.

"I heard him speak one time. I was right up by the podium. Now, *he* was a powerful speaker. He knew how to inspire people."

Candelaria wondered if her words would inspire anyone. "Wouldn't that be something?" she whispered to herself.

Their cue came to step out onto the stage and seat themselves in chairs placed for them. The loud clattering roar of applause surprised Candelaria and, like her first airplane flight, thrilled her. She was glad she had come, proud to be a part of that important and thrilling day.

CHAPTER TWENTY-SEVEN

When Candelaria took the podium, she returned to that day when she sat on her porch, seeing Johnny Henry walk past her house. The breeze had caused light and shadow to play upon the pages of her notebook. The effect it had on her then, arose within her once again. She turned her head to look at Dorothy Johnson seated in the row of chairs behind. The woman nodded her head in encouragement, and it came to Candelaria, what she needed to say. It was so simple, yet so profound that it could not be ignored. Setting her typed speech to the side, she instead told a story.

"I once saw a boy walking past my house. I was sitting on my porch, as I so often do when I'm writing. I assumed he was walking home from school, but he was going so slow, like he was dawdling, not wanting to get there so fast. When I saw who it was, I wanted to call out his name, 'Hey, Johnny!' But, I didn't. Why? For the same reason I talk to practically none of the white people in the town where I live, because I am Mexican. Even though I know the boy, even though he seems like a nice person, someone who could use a friend, I held myself back from speaking to him. I have thought about this a lot, that my awareness of being Mexican can be so present, yet so unconscious at the same time, that it decides whom I meet and what I do, whom I associate with and what places I choose to go to or avoid. I ask myself again, why?"

Candelaria paused. She was aware the entire auditorium was silent, other than a cough now and then, someone clearing their throat, all eyes on her. She was pleased to find that she was unafraid. She continued speaking.

"Is it judgement? Am I judging they will see me as only 'that Mexican lady' who lives over in the poor farmworker shacks? Am I judging they are racist? I am judging them, seeing them as only white, so am I not being racially prejudiced? I want others to see me as just a person, as myself, but I cannot then exclude my brown skin, my ethnic heritage, my history, or my upbringing. Clearly, I need to accept all of myself if I wish others to accept all that I am. But I have yet to see myself through this dilemma. Where did I learn to be this way but on the playground in elementary school and in the corridors of high school? I didn't learn this at home. I wasn't taught to avoid white people by my parents. I married a white man. I was taught to avoid mean people, hateful people, people who look upon others with contempt. I have encountered people of all races express negative views, judging others for being different."

Candelaria knew how bold she was being, speaking on the topic being bold enough, but then to call out racial prejudice coming from all races—it was a leap of faith, for she believed in what she said, and it was her story, her voice, and her viewpoint that had been invited there, because it was unique. She kept talking.

"I have seen hatred for others, whether Mexican, Black, White, Jewish, Italian, Irish, Catholic, Christian, even what sports team someone supports, or which political party someone belongs to. Because of these observations, I have begun to ask the question, 'Why are *we* this way?' Where did we learn this? Is it competition? If so, why do we compete with one another? For supremacy? Why do we amass great wealth when we have more money than we could possibly spend in one lifetime? To see who has the most? Why do we berate those who care not for these things, the shy, the timid, the spiritual, the easy-going ones, as though they were something to pity, even to laugh at for not wising up and getting with it, or getting a job?"

Candelaria looked at her watch, one that Rosa and Buster had given her for Christmas the previous year. She had been talking a long time, she thought, but had only used up a small portion of her allotted time. A glass of water had been provided for her. She sipped a little before continuing on.

"I must take this question to a deeper place, for I know that it cannot exist within society unless it exists, first, within ourselves, within myself. I am all these things I have observed. I am prejudiced. I am judgmental. I am competitive. I am power-hungry. I am greedy. I am there in my ivory tower, feeling so smug about who I am and what I have, looking down on those who do not aspire to be like me. I am Catholic. Why aren't you? I don't assume Catholicism is the best, most righteous religion, but I do assume that many people I know who do not even attend church must be wanton in some way.

For, is it not at church every Sunday where I hear the priest tell me such and such type of people are sinners, that we must keep the sacraments holy? Do not do this. Do not do that. Or, you will go to hell. I tell you, Hell is not a place where I want to go. Do you? There's fire and eternal damnation, according to the priest. So I try to be a good Catholic and honor the sacraments, adhere to the Ten Commandments, go to confession, and sit there on my porch, judging a little boy on his way home from school, who had done nothing wrong, who had not harmed me in any way."

Candelaria needed to check her feelings. She only then realized how much Johnny Henry meant to her and how ashamed she felt for judging him, when it was really only love she had wanted to give the boy. Yet she also knew that others did the same as she and, so, continued speaking.

"I see his ragged clothes, because he is poor. I see the sad look in his eyes, knowing he was adopted. Yet I wouldn't speak to him, because of an old, old fear that had brought me to the opinion that not only are the ones who called me names or hurt me for being Mexican, people to avoid, but *all* white people, even little boys who did nothing wrong except to be born to white parents." She did not yet know that Johnny was her son, Jim's, child.

"I feel sorry for myself, but these fears that live within me, live within us all. They are what keep us locked in a cell of perpetual judgement, always in a purgatory of our own making, limiting ourselves, stunting our growth, and blocking our ability to expand our horizons. How can we say we are free or that we fight dictatorial or tyrannical regimes, in order to spread democracy and protect freedom, when we allow the greatest tyrant of all to reign unchallenged within our own minds, dictating to us who we shall say 'hello' to? This dictator, it is, who rules my ability to express love freely. It controls my body, telling me 'no, not that way, not that one, not that.' It constricts my very heart from opening up to the truth, that we are all One. I have read about this dictator."

Candelaria paused for a moment. People leaving the auditorium, did not go unnoticed. However, she was now speaking from that place of power within her as she had one day, years before at the state capitol and, so, went on.

"It is known as the ego. The ego decides who my heart shall love? No, but it controls my ability to share this love with others, to even be conscious of it. Beware the ego, for it is a very dangerous and vicious tyrant. I call for its overthrow! I call for a revolution! Free ourselves! Overthrow this domineering and cruel tyrant! Let ourselves love *all* people, just as we each wish to be loved! Set yourself free and wake up to the truth! *We are all equal!* We are all connected to one another! *We are all One!*"

After she said, "thank you," the audience applauded. Some were whistling and cheering. Had she inspired them? Or, had she started something she would later regret?

Turning to walk away from the podium, Candelaria was stopped by their host, who smiled at her and said, "No, Ms. Mendoza, they want you to stay standing. They loved what you said."

He began applauding her as she turned back toward the audience and smiled. Never in her life had she imagined such a reaction to her words. But it was more than words she had conveyed to them. It was the way she said them, fearlessly, from her heart, with courage and a willingness to look at herself and bare her private story with them. The other speakers gathered around as she laughed and cried.

Andrew threw his arms around her and hugged her. "You get it! You really get it!" he said.

He had spoken on his radical views of the war in Vietnam and the need for peace in the world. He spoke passionately and, like Candelaria, had taken chances by saying things to which most people closed their minds. He said that if they want to change the world, they must begin with themselves. If they want to bring peace to the world, they must bring peace to themselves. Finally, if they want there to be an end to racism, they must end it within themselves. All change, he said, begins within.

Afterward, he came up to her and praised her again, vigorously shaking her hand and smiling, eager to continue the conversation. He told her he had been reading her articles. However, she knew he was most likely married to Sylvia and wanted to avoid an encounter, even if Sylvia had changed. Thinking, at first, that she was being prejudiced, Candelaria admitted that she really wanted to see Dorothy Johnson again, who had invited her to dinner. Candelaria turned to Andrew and gave her apologies, telling him that she needed to accept Ms. Johnson's invitation. He nodded his head and thanked her before walking away.

People were filing out of the building as she and Dorothy walked together to Dorothy's car. Briefly, she saw Andrew meeting Sylvia by another car and simply ignored it. Whether

Sylvia had seen her, mattered little to Candelaria. The grief for her son was yet too new. She deemed it wise to protect herself from additional emotional strain. Nearly sixty years of age, she felt the need to pace herself. The day's experience was so new and exciting, but it was also exhausting. She trusted Dorothy and made a new friend in the process.

When Candelaria returned home the next day, after Katie Winters had dropped her off near her house, the first person she saw was Johnny, riding along with Walter Henry in his truck. Without hesitating, she smiled and happily waved to him. Johnny smiled and waved in return. She walked toward her house, her humble shack beneath the pine and oak trees, and laughed as she said, "Oh, how I missed you!" She went up the steps and into her house where Aurelia was waiting for her, having cooked them both dinner.

Aurelia was ready to change her ways and be cooperative and helpful. Candelaria would never know that her long time friend and neighbor, Esther Gutierrez, had a talk with Aurelia, who promised to stop being so irresponsible. Candelaria hugged her younger cousin and thanked her. She also praised her cooking skills.

Laying in bed that night, Candelaria was still riding high on the wave of her thrilling adventure. She recalled something Dorothy Johnson had told her the night before at dinner. Candelaria had confided in the African American professor, quietly telling her about all the losses she had experienced and something to the effect of how lonely and depressed she had become. She shared that she was yearning to love again, yet believed she was too old, that it was too late. Venting her worries, she added that she feared she could not even sustain a writing career for much longer.

The older woman said, "Oh, Candelaria, don't lose hope. Anything's possible."

They grew quiet, sitting there with crumpled napkins, the table needing to be cleared and dishes needing to be washed, when Dorothy dared to add, "Please, don't take this the wrong way, but, if you truly love to write and, if you really want to share it with others, maybe even share your life with another..." She paused, closing her eyes, then opened them and said, "Someone once told me, that a person who yearns for something they can't seem to find anywhere, needs to be willing to dig down into the depths of their soul and drag out every dead thing they've been holding on to. Until then, you can't say you're really living, can you?" She looked upon Candelaria as one who deeply cared, concluding, "It's no wonder you're depressed."

CHAPTER TWENTY-EIGHT

Walter Henry stood looking out the window of his woodworking shop. The old glass was rippled and cracked, but he could see Aurelia outside exploring the retreat center grounds. "Well," he muttered to himself, "I'm not teaching her woodworking." He knew he was being selfish, but, "doggone it, I'm getting too old to deal with a young woman with the kinds of problems she has." Returning to his latest project, he experienced a twinge of guilt.

Aurelia had discovered the retreat center after her elder cousin's speaking engagement. It was a peaceful place where she took the time to think about herself and her life, especially her relationships with men. She needed "to grow up," to "start being responsible," her neighbor, Esther Gutierrez, had told her.

Scolding Aurelia, Esther wagged her finger and said, "And, don't ever let me catch you fooling around with that-that welder, Tommy McGrew. I saw you go into that old store. Don't tell me you didn't!" Before Esther returned to her own shack at the edge of the woods, she left Aurelia with something to think about. "Laria was nice enough to let you live with her," she said. "The least you could do is help out around here and say 'thank you' once in a while."

Aurelia was trying to do better. She sat quietly beside the pond behind Lulabelle's old cabin, considering her options. She had neither the funds for college nor the desire to get married. What else was there? Work. She wondered, what was the point to having a creative gift if she could not pursue it?

"Some woodworker I'm turning out to be. I don't even own a knife," she said.

Setting the matter aside, she directed her attention to her surroundings. The area where she sat was shaded by a grove of sweetly scented conifers. Purple asters lay in withering masses encircling the small pool, which was fed by a small stream. It meandered and trickled along the mossy surface of stones and fallen leaves, its gentle pattering like the tinkling of bells. A sudden plunk sounded from the water's edge when a squirrel in the treetops dropped its prized cone.

The sounds of nature lulled Aurelia, bringing her a sense of calm. From out of that, rose the past she had daily strived to forget, a past that terrified her and drove her to seek out the very men she needed to avoid. Tears streamed down across her face to drip to the dusty earth below. Thoughts came and went, drifting from the past into the present, to other days, other experiences. Soon, she was surrounded by something remarkable, what she could feel but could not see. A mysterious, healing force surrounded her. Like a soft blanket, a calming sense of peace and safety enveloped her as the spirits of Lulabelle Henry, Lucy Shoseegan, and even Jim Hart, stood beside her. Though they were but spirit, they drew out the pain of that day long ago when she was assaulted by the moonshiners. Sobbing arose from within her soul deep down as though pulled from out of her being.

Walter Henry could hear Aurelia. He momentarily sanded the wood more vigorously, but stopped. Peering out the window, he spotted Tessie and Shep walking side by side up the hill. He smiled as Tessie nudged Aurelia's arm and licked her face, while Shep sniffed her hair and placed his forepaw on her leg. Walter Henry knew enough from Lulabelle's and Lucy's lives on the mountain to be thankful, especially when Aurelia hugged and petted Shep. At last, the old man was reassured.

"She's gonna be fine," he said.

Aurelia quieted and began recalling her dream from the night before. She was walking down a woodland path through lush greenery. Stepping into an open area, she saw a magnificent tiger. It turned and padded toward her and she awoke. There was an eagle in the dream, circling in the sky above, and a man was walking beside her.

Taking comfort from her dream, Aurelia reminded herself to consider Tucker's role in her life. Nearly a year had gone by since they had met. She was frustrated by his resistance to having a relationship with her, knowing in her heart that she loved him and that he loved her. The Keeper of the Dream. She knew the gift he held, had seen it in his eyes, and believed him to be the man in her dream who was walking beside her. It meant they shared the same path. Yet, aware of her pattern with men, dismissive, at best, eventually turning against them, she despaired, concluding that she was no good for Tucker.

"Sooner or later, I'll turn on him, too," she told herself.

Johnny Henry was curious about Aurelia's visits and spied on her whenever she visited the retreat center or went exploring in the woods. Since the old blacksmith shop and livery stable was rented out as storage space, Walter Henry kept the farrier's rig, the horse trailer, and their horse at a small stable he built on the retreat center grounds. Johnny went riding every chance he could get, lingering around the stable and riding the trails, hoping to see Aurelia.

He discovered she was on a search. While in the forest, she collected various pieces of wood, animal skulls, and feathers. Walter Henry's cabin was decorated with a variety of skulls. Johnny wanted to make gifts of them to Aurelia without her knowing he was spying on her.

The old man was concerned Johnny had developed a crush on Aurelia and told Millie so. They were both worried, since the two were cousins, however distant. They also knew Aurelia had serious problems.

"That girl needs to be left alone, Johnny," said Walter Henry. "She's troubled and no one you need to get involved with, you hear me?"

One evening, when Aurelia was visiting the retreat center, Walter Henry noted the fact to Millie. She got up to peek out the window beside him before returning to sit at the table.

Johnny overheard and stepped into the room, asking, "What are you talking about?" He had seen Aurelia, too, and had planned to approach her that evening.

Millie answered, "Oh! Gonna be getting' dark soon, don't you think?" Deflecting, she commented on Johnny's long hair. "Shouldn't you be getting a haircut, young man? You're looking like a shaggy sheepdog. Got your hair down in your eyes," she said.

Suspicious, Johnny sat at the table with them. He combed his straight blond hair behind his ears with his fingers. His adoptive father was sitting with his arms folded in front of his chest, one hand raised to pluck at the corner of his mustache. Millie busied herself with making a shopping list while humming to herself. Johnny fretted over how to meet Aurelia without their knowing about it.

Rising from his chair, he announced, "I guess I'll go check on my horse before it gets too dark." He went toward the door.

Walter Henry warned, "She's not the girl for you, Johnny."

Johnny turned his head and snapped, "What?! Oh, don't *worry!* It's not what you think!" He slammed the door on his way out, yelling back at Walter Henry and Millie, "I'm just trying to help her! That's all!"

He stormed off up the hill toward the horse stable. His horse was still standing in the corral, so he checked on her. He made sure she had enough feed and plenty of water before he led her into the stable and closed the doors for the night. Looking for Aurelia afterward, he realized she was gone. Disappointed, he sat at the campfire ring.

Above, the stars appeared in faint glimmers. The glow of a lantern shone at their cabin window. With the night, came thoughts about his real father. Johnny missed him. The ache in his heart seemed to never lessen or go away. He missed going to the blacksmith shop and livery stable every day, seeing his dad and working by his side. He often imagined the sound of Jim's voice. Yet, seeing Walter Henry walk past the window inside the cabin, Johnny felt ashamed. He could never tell his adoptive father that he wanted to help Aurelia because he knew that would have made his real father proud.

"I want to be like you, Dad," he said to the stars above. "I want to help others just like you helped me."

After Johnny graduated from high school, he decided to go away to college. Walter Henry and Millie agreed to help him become a certified farrier. Trying to hide his disappointment, the old man lamented that Johnny would never become a woodworker and take over the woodcrafting business. Once the graduation ceremony signified his adopted son's freedom, he watched as Johnny hitched the horse trailer to the used truck given as a graduation present. After loading up the horse, the young man drove down the hill and out of Walter Henry's and Millie's life. The old man sank into a gloomy period of regret.

Why he put off marrying and having children of his own, was his oft-repeated question to himself, the only answer being that he was tied to that barn, like a horse, himself. No matter which way he went in life, he always went back to the blacksmith shop and livery stable. He suspected it was his home. It was all he had left of his mother and father's memory, since the way station his father had built was long gone. He had not moved on since his father's death, not really, and grieved himself, the phantom of his own life.

Millie sympathized with Walter Henry. By the time they had married, she had been too old to give him children. Yet she also knew what truly grieved him. To her, he seemed to be stuck in Time, caught in an era long buried beneath the dust of a town that once was, but was no more. She tried, but could not reach him. Having learned from the doctors that her cancer had returned, she knew it would be a matter of a few weeks or months before she joined Lulabelle. Walter Henry would then be completely alone.

"Walt, please, listen to me," said Millie.

She was about to tell him the cancer had come back, but found it too hard to say. With her arm placed around him one day at the diner, she stood next to the booth where he sat and looked around the room. She had cut back on her hours, serving only lunch and sometimes dinner, but was forced to close entirely. Her lifelong passion for caring for others was about to be taken from her. The last time she drove away from the diner, she noticed the closed sign and the for sale sign at the front window, telling the whole world she was old and out of commission. All those hardworking years lay behind her. The only way she could face what lay ahead was to put all her time and energy into taking care of something that was very important to her. Aurelia, like Johnny, she told herself, needed her help.

CHAPTER TWENTY-NINE

Katie Winters was reading one of Andrew's articles that had appeared in a literary journal. Candelaria told her she preferred not to read it, saying it incited rioting and was full of "submersive" ideas, meaning "subversive." Katie knew what Candelaria meant, but encouraged her to read Andrew's article, with the added enticement, "he mentions you in it." She had a mischievous smile on her face and laughed when Candelaria grabbed the magazine out of her hand and said, "Let me see that!"

Katie was pleased to see her friend poring over the article, because there was an entire paragraph referencing something Candelaria had written months before.

Candelaria stopped reading and asked herself aloud, "Why hadn't I thought of that?"

Curious, Katie inquired, "Thought of what?"

"I never write about what everyone else is writing about," answered Candelaria.

"That's why people love your writing," said Katie, "because it's a unique perspective, a point of view no one ever considers."

"But I should read more, keep abreast of what's going on. Why aren't I following these things?" asked Candelaria.

"Because it's not who you are," said Katie. "People need to hear *your* point of view, because it's not mainstream, or subversive. You goof! They love the way you write. I love the way you write."

"But, why? It's so—"

"Don't do this. You're fine. Your work wouldn't be published, if you weren't. Someone referenced you! That's a big deal! Andrew Parker is a serious writer and was a professor at a prestigious university, no less, and he liked what you wrote." She grabbed the magazine back from Candelaria and pointed to something in the article. "Look. Look here," she said. "See what he says?"

Candelaria took the magazine back and read what Katie had pointed out. It was the paragraph she had not wanted to read.

Andrew wrote, "Ms. Mendoza fearlessly walks us through our home towns and shows us, quite plainly, the source and sustenance of our prejudices and our fears of letting them go. Yes, we are afraid of differences, as she mentions, but we are also invested in our fears, simply because we get something out of them. I urge everyone to return to their home towns. One has only to walk the Main Streets of America to find the rewards with which we laud upon one another, beginning with our children, teaching them that being different and standing out is only acceptable within the boundaries of the current societal rules and unspoken expectations. The rewards are many, blue ribbons and scholastic awards, bigger paychecks and beautiful homes in nice neighborhoods. Step outside the boundaries, however, and one will quickly see the rewards cease and turn to punishment, punishment for being different and, therefore, not fitting in, leading to ostracism. We are social animals. We need one another. We need community. Pushing people away who are too different for such a selectively narrow-minded view of society, forces them to band together in order to survive, forming tribe-like, sub-cultures with those who share their race, their religion, their politics, their values, even their very way of being in the world."

Candelaria's mind was swimming with the information, most of which was difficult for her to understand. She feared she had started something that others would find dangerous, a threat. Publishers had lately been urging her to write a book. However, she was becoming too frightened for such a big step, swiftly handing the magazine back to her friend.

"I don't know. I write how I write," she said. "I just write what I need to say, that's all."

"That's all you need to do." Katie was ready to go home and asked Candelaria, "Why not join me for dinner? We can talk some more. My treat!"

Pouting, Candelaria said, "The diner doesn't open for dinner anymore."

Katie shrugged and said, "We could go to the cafe up the hill."

Smiling, they walked together to the Hillview Apartments where Katie lived. Johnny was riding his horse along the side of the road, with Shep and Tessie following faithfully alongside.

Katie enthusiastically shouted out a hello to him and waved. "Hi, Johnny!" she said. He waved and said hello in return. After he rode past them, Katie commented, "That boy is getting to be such a handsome young man, isn't he?"

"Yes, he is." In all honesty, Candelaria added, "He's a fine young man."

Katie noted the tinge of sorrow in her friend's voice and wanted to tell her who Johnny was, but yet could not. Fortunately, Candelaria quickly changed the subject, insisting on leaving the tip and splurging on dessert, saying, "I've heard they have the best lemon meringue pie!" Laughing, they drove off in Katie's cream-colored Chrysler Valiant.

They were both forgetting, perhaps intentionally, the promises they had made to others. Katie had promised to join Tucker for dinner, but no longer saw the point. Nearing the cafe, she rationalized the relationship had simply run its course. She admitted to herself he had no intention of marrying her, probably never had. Still, she missed him. She enjoyed his company and valued his friendship. Candelaria had promised to babysit Betsy Marie and Rosa's newest, Robert James, whom they called, "Bobby."

Rosa and Buster had also planned to go to the same restaurant, the Mountain Mystery Cafe. They gave up waiting for Rosa's mother to show up at their house, so they brought the kids with them. Surprised when Katie and Candelaria showed up at the cafe, they all laughed. They ate together and chatted for awhile afterward. Once the kids became fussy, Candelaria took them to Rosa and Buster's house with her, all of them piling into Katie's car.

Contemplating her and Tucker's long-term, yet waning relationship, Katie found it interesting that she was both Candelaria's and Tucker's mutual friend for nearly fifteen years. She wondered why the three of them had never gotten together, and mentioned it on their drive home.

Candelaria said, "Hmm."

Katie had already mentioned it to Tucker, who smirked, as he muttered under his breath, "Why?" Unperturbed, Katie tried to think of the safest way to bring them together. She believed there was something in common between them, and knew them both equally well. They were her very best friends. The newly formed historical society meetings, attended by Rosa, Tucker, and herself, among several others, including the town veterinarian, was the perfect place to warm their cold feet, she thought. How could she get Candelaria to attend? She wondered. Tittering to herself, she pulled her car up to Rosa and Buster's house and parked.

Candelaria was suspicious and, before getting out of the car, asked, "What are you smiling about?"

Katie quickly replied, "Oh, nothing!" She felt like a matchmaker. While driving home, she was pleased with her idea and said aloud, "It's about time those two found out how much they have in common." By some mysterious, predetermined insight, she added, "Who knows? They could even write a book together." Getting out of her car in the apartment parking garage, she was delighted with her plan. However, if she knew what was yet transpiring between Tucker and Aurelia, she would not have bothered. Tucker and Candelaria had more in common than she knew.

•   •   •

It was nearing the end of the year. Candelaria was getting her writing materials together to walk to the school to use the typewriter, when Aurelia opened the front door and walked in, looking guilty. Candelaria reminded herself that Aurelia, while not timid, was an extremely intense young woman, quiet, but not shy, and led a very private life. She was an artist, Candelaria surmised, living in her creative fire and trying not to get burned.

Aurelia asked to discuss a worn-out subject. "Laria? Can we talk?" she asked.

Candelaria had heard enough about Tucker Stewart. Nevertheless, she asked, "What do you want to talk about?"

"I can't stand it anymore," said Aurelia. Her demeanor was one of such misery, tired and drawn, as she sat in a chair at the table and rested her head in her arms.

Candelaria asked, "What is it, Aurelia? Tell me. Is it Harvey?" Of course, it was not Harvey, but she hoped it was.

Aurelia said, "No. I wish it was that easy." She raised her head and sat back in the chair, looking blankly away from the table.

Candelaria ventured the dreaded guess, "Is it..." She knew darn well who it was and was exasperated with her younger cousin. "Oh, Aurelia!" she said. "You can't possibly still be—I told you to stay away from him! He's too old for you, for one thing. What is it with you? You've got to—"

Aurelia was crying by then, "I can't help it, Laria. I'm in love with him! He's all I think about day and night," and placed her head down again to cry, her shoulders shaking with each sob.

Feeling pity for the girl, Candelaria shook her head, stepping closer to rub Aurelia's back to comfort her. "There, there now," she said.

She wondered if Aurelia was seeing Tucker, or if the man was encouraging her in any way. Remembering again the scene of him and Sylvia Cadwallader as teenagers, it dawned on Candelaria that she needed to take action right away. She tried to think of someone to whom she could turn. Her daughter had said that some people in the community were meeting to create a historical society and Tucker Stewart was one of those people. That would work, so she called Rosa on the phone, asking her to come over right away.

The minute Rosa stepped in the kitchen and saw Aurelia, who had gotten up to sit on the sofa, she knew something was wrong.

"Aurelia? Are you okay, honey?" she asked. "Maybe you're coming down with something," she said. She sat next to Aurelia and felt her forehead. "I think you have a fever. It might be the flu. A lot of kids have been absent from school." She lightly ran her fingers along Aurelia's cheek, then held her chin. "You need to get some rest," she said. "Okay?"

While Aurelia took a lukewarm bath, they unfolded the sofa bed, so she could get into bed afterward. They noticed the sheets were spotted with blood.

"Mom! Look!" said Rosa.

Candelaria whispered emphatically, "Shh! Keep your voice down! She might hear you!" She gathered up the sheets and stuffed them in the laundry bag, getting an extra set out of the dresser drawer to put on the mattress.

"Mom. I think Aurelia is pregnant," said Rosa.

Candelaria flashed a look of surprise at her daughter, hurriedly tucking in the clean set of sheets. Still whispering, she asked, "Pregnant?! You told her she had the flu."

Rosa said, "I thought it was, but now...I'm not so sure."

"Mi hija. You don't realize what you're saying," said Candelaria. She was horrified with the thought. She sat on the bed in wide-eyed shock and said, "She just told me she's in love with Tucker Stewart. You don't think they've been—" She closed her eyes and covered her face with her hands, shaking her head back and forth.

Rosa was getting impatient, knowing she had been there long enough. "I don't know," she said. "We need to ask her, though." She went back into the kitchen, Candelaria following behind.

"I need to get home, Mom," said Rosa. "I promised Buster I'd only be a few minutes. I have to get his dinner."

Hands on her hips, Candelaria asked, "Why doesn't he ever fix you dinner? You work, too, you know."

Rosa breathed in deeply and let it go. "I know! I know!" she agreed. Opening the front door, she insisted, "Aurelia needs to see a doctor," and, with her index finger raised, emphasized, "Be sure she sees a doctor. Promise me."

"Yes, yes, I will. I'll see to it if I have to get the doctor to come here, myself," said Candelaria.

CHAPTER THIRTY

The doctor examined Aurelia, the same doctor she had seen all her life. He spoke frankly with her. "Before I prescribe you an anti-depressant, young lady," he said, "I need to ask if you knew you were pregnant."

"What?" asked Aurelia.

The doctor said, "You've had a miscarriage. You were pregnant, but not anymore."

Aurelia was in shock.

The doctor said, "I'm not going to lecture you, but you need to be careful." Handing her a prescription slip, he added, "Taking some classes would be a much healthier activity, don't you think?" With a serious expression, he looked at her through his horn-rimmed glasses, waiting for her response.

Aurelia looked down and nodded her head in agreement.

At the receptionist's desk, the doctor mentioned that his nurse was attending a class a couple of nights a week. He asked the nurse, "You wouldn't mind giving Aurelia a ride to a class there, would you, Eileen?"

Eileen said, "No, I don't mind."

The nurse was none other than Eileen Price, who once had a torch burning for Tucker Stewart, herself, but who had since become infatuated with Andrew Parker. She regularly attended his series of lectures held at the community college.

Eileen turned out to be exactly the person Aurelia needed to meet. First of all, she was not related and, secondly, she did not live in Edenville. They quickly became friends, oddly, because they were nothing alike. While Eileen was bubbly and vivacious and had an infectious way about her, Aurelia was moody, quiet, and had only begun to face her complex psychological problems. Eileen was not one to judge, nor was she one to linger in negative situations. She had a knack for finding what she needed in her life. Her only problem was the same as Aurelia's: men.

Driving her light-blue VW bug, chugging and puttering along its dependable way, Eileen darted from lane to lane, passing slower vehicles, and talking all the while. She was taking Aurelia to her first art class nearly an hour's drive away.

She knew Aurelia's history, unbeknownst to the younger woman. Besides what was on file at the doctor's office, her mother, Trudy Price, who owned Teapot full o' Whimsy, had mentioned it once. Aurelia had been working at the pet store. Seeing Aurelia outside, Trudy said, "Isn't it a shame what happened to that poor girl?" Eileen looked out the window at Aurelia walking by on her way home with a bag of laundry and swiftly disregarded what her mother said. She had learned from working at the local rest home, and losing her job there, that anyone could be in Aurelia's situation. Everyone had difficulties in life. It was unjust and unfair to treat them differently or to judge them, is what Eileen believed.

She asked Aurelia, "There's this lecture I've been *dying* to go to! You wouldn't mind staying late, would you? It's after our classes, over in the lecture hall."

"I don't mind," said Aurelia. She was very thankful that Eileen would give her a ride to her class and planned to stay out late so she could avoid Candelaria. Her elder cousin wanted to know what the doctor said. Aurelia was upset and humiliated enough as it was without Candelaria's prying.

After class, they hurriedly walked toward the hall. Needing some advice, Aurelia mentioned Tucker Stewart to Eileen, saying that he was her friend.

"Oh, Tucker? I know him!" said Eileen.

However, Eileen was not interested in him at the moment. She told Aurelia, "I am so in love with this professor lecturing here tonight." Her eyes rolled, she tsked, drew in her breath, and closed her eyes as though in a swoon, placing her hand on her chest, and said, "Pathetic, huh?"

Once Aurelia got a look at Andrew, in a sultry voice, she whispered to Eileen, "Not really. I see what you mean."

Eileen whispered back, "I saw him first."

They laughed quietly. Once the hall filled, his lecture began.

Aurelia barely heard a word of it. Mentioning Tucker drew her inward. She went over in her mind the last time they were together. The small lamp beside his bed lit the room as she cried in his arms and he held her close to him where they lay beneath the covers. Their eyes had met and she saw in his such loneliness, such deep longing for connection. That was when it came to her, that she had always loved him. It was not her usual attraction for a man, but something from her heart, something profound. Yet he would not share those deeper feelings with her.

Aurelia's awareness returned to Andrew's lecture, but she was not following it. She found herself bored and tried to stay awake. It went on until nine o'clock. Afterward, everyone stood and began filing out the door. She saw Andrew moving through the crowd to hail them, calling out, "Eileen!"

Eileen turned to see the object of her latest infatuation, smiling and approaching her. "Andrew!" she called out to him in return.

He was pleased to see her and said, "It's great to see you!" They hugged each other.

Aurelia grinned when, facing her, Eileen looked up toward the ceiling as though she had melted in Andrew's embrace.

Eileen said to Andrew, "I *loved* what you spoke about! I've been following all your lectures, I must confess." She introduced Aurelia, "This is my friend, Aurelia."

"Hello," said Aurelia. She shook hands with Andrew.

He asked them, "Say, you two wanna go get a coffee, or something?"

"Sure!" Eileen did not hesitate, but quickly looked at Aurelia to apologize, "Oh, I'm sorry! Did you want to get home? It's no problem."

"No! Let's go! I'm a bit of a night owl, myself," said Aurelia. After going over in her mind what had taken place between herself and Tucker, she was ready for a distraction and some enjoyable conversation.

They walked to the student lounge and, after ordering their drinks, sat together at a table. Andrew raised his hand, laying down one rule. He said, "Promise me we won't talk about the lecture."

Aurelia and Eileen promised and they all laughed.

They began the most interesting conversation Aurelia ever had. She felt she was invited into a new world. Eileen was several years older than she was, and Andrew was even older, but it was all right. They enjoyed good conversation, ideas, and topics she loved. She shared her creative ideas and how animals spoke to her. Eileen and Andrew were enraptured with what she was doing. For the first time, Aurelia felt she belonged somewhere, not in Laketon, not in Edenville, not in a man's bed, but amongst the thinkers and the artists, the lovers of good food and song, of poetry and cultural enlightenment. They all agreed it was a fantastic evening.

On their drive home, Aurelia was sure to thank Eileen for an amazing time. "I never knew there were such people in the world," she said.

Eileen assured her there were and promised her that, if she wanted, she could live the life of her dreams, but only if she had the courage to open up and take the first step. Aurelia's eyes teared up, knowing Eileen's words were true. Eileen turned on the radio and a song was playing that Aurelia had not heard before. The words touched her heart, so that she needed to keep from crying. They drove in silence up the highway, back into the mountains, in the late hour of that new day. Aurelia dared to gaze inwardly once again as the words from the song joined in with the words of her heart, words only she could hear.

"Out amidst the stars in night awakening, I flew into a dream, my soul a-shaking. There, I saw the presence of my beauty: A man I loved and lost, who said he knew me."

•   •   •

The night was cold when last Aurelia and Tucker had met. Sound played tricks on the mind as wind and rustling leaves blew down in the darkness outside. The moon rose nearly full and thus brought to life all animate things once stilled by day. Huddled together beneath the folds of night, they heard one coyote, then another, as each yapped and joined the raucous chorus.

Curtains open and the lamp turned off, Aurelia mused, her eyes glinting from the bright moonlight shining into the room. "Will they dance tonight?" she asked Tucker as she lightly swept her hand across his chest.

Tucker had never heard of such a thing as coyotes dancing. He held her close to him and ran his hands over her soft skin as he kissed her. When he did so, he sensed, in the inner reaches of his soul, an emerging hint of grace that revealed what was yet to come. He kissed her again, feeling her close to him and wanting her, nearly ready to surrender to what lay ahead for them both.

The dog stirred in the kitchen, whining and growling, also aware of the sounds in the night. Silent came the wings of an owl swooping down from its treetop roost to clutch a mouse skittering across the dusty road. A bobcat hidden beneath the porch, its kittens grown strong, stretched itself low to the ground to squeeze out from under the boards. The rasp of its fur pressed against the aged wood as it caught along the splintery edge, alerting Freckles. She growled again. In her dog's mind, she planned that, in the daytime, she would look for what had made that sound. Nose raised to catch its scent, she whined again before lowering her head to rest on her paws.

But, then, everything changed.

Aurelia likewise held Tucker close to her and kissed him. "I love you," she said.

Tucker made no reply, instead looking away, out the lighted window where played the shadowy forms of trees blown side to side in the windy and mysterious night. He felt unsure of what they were doing together, whether it was wrong, wondering if it was really love...or was it a sin? Again, he closed his eyes and felt a moment's remorse, asking, fearing, if he was like his father. Yet, too, he thought of Sylvia and his heart bled for her once more, recalling the moment's passion they had shared in the autumn woodland as youthful lovers.

"I'm sorry, but..." He glanced away from Aurelia.

Aurelia was stunned. She got out of the bed and quickly dressed.

Surprised by her actions, Tucker got out of bed and hurriedly dressed as well. He followed her out of the room, asking her, "Where are you going?"

"I can't do this anymore," she answered in her haste.

"Do what?!" asked Tucker.

Aurelia left the house. She was crying by then and furious. Hurrying off, she said through her screaming rage what she had believed all along and grew tired of believing, "You won't let me in! You know what I'm talking about, but you still act like you don't know. I'm sick of your games, Tucker! I'm through with you!"

Tucker pleaded with her, "I'm sorry! Ellie, don't go! Come back into the house!" It was only at that moment when he realized his mistake and yelled, "Aurelia!" His words were lost in the dark where the moon's light flickered across the imaginary figures he caught darting past him in the night. His desperate attempt at love was lost as well, for she was gone.

"Oh, my God! What have I done?!" he asked himself. The words rang in his mind as he ran a frenzied hand through his hair.

Aurelia had fled, arms wrapped tightly about her waist to hold a memory rapidly surfacing. It accompanied confused images that came with no sound, only feeling like murky water. Reliving a past that caught her in its grip, she experienced it as it came to life once again. It was happening again. She screamed within her mind and ran in terror of the darkness fast engulfing her.

Tucker sat on his porch steps where the bobcat had emerged from beneath with each of her kittens in tow. He buried his face in the same murky waters of his own mistakenness he dared not tell a soul he felt at all.

"What's the matter with me?" he asked himself. "Why couldn't I just say it?" He knew why, for his own fears had crept once more into his life, fear of loss, fear of rejection, fear of repeating his father's mistakes. He truly believed Aurelia would eventually leave, because, "they always leave," he asserted. His somber quiet tone expressed despair and signaled to him his defeat. Recalling something Jim Hart once told him about Sylvia, "Too bad her aunt hates you, Stewart. And your dad, too, for that matter," and Tucker hit bottom.

Aurelia finally reached the house she was seeking. She saw a light on and ran up the steps. Pounding on the wooden door, she yelled, "Harvey! Harvey, please! Open the door!"

Harvey knew that voice and what its insistent plea was truly saying. He flung the door open wide. His ex-girlfriend who fell for another, who was sleeping with another, ran to him and buried her face in his embrace. His own fear, his anger, his disbelief in all she said, yet held sway to her need to be held by him. The next morning, when he awoke and saw she had been true to her former deceitfulness, he swept a hand across the bedsheets where she had lay beside him. Or, was it a dream? He wondered.

Peering through the aged glass of his bedroom window, he saw it was not a dream. Aurelia, the girl he thought he loved, walked away from his house and out of his life, into the woman she had become, whom he knew he did not love anymore.

CHAPTER THIRTY-ONE

The creek was flowing high, splashing between stones and skimming beneath branches. Tucker lost his footing and stepped into the water, soaking his shoes. He climbed the embankment on the other side of the creek, crossed Pine Way Junction, then continued hiking the trail up the mountain. The bushes were so tall in places he was lucky if he saw the sky. But, eventually, the plant growth thinned, so he paused to appreciate the view of the valley. It was at the exact spot where Jim Hart and Katie Winters had met in the summer of 1951.

While Tucker admired the view, Freckles continued up the trail without him. When he turned around to continue on his way, he saw that he had lost track of her. He knew that Walter Henry's place was nearby, so he kept on walking, hoping Freckles might eventually appear.

Soon, the trail reached Lulabelle's boarded-up retreat center. Tucker had never seen it before, nor any of the buildings, except for the old miner's shack when he was a child. That was back when he would join his big brothers on one of their outdoor excursions around the valley. Walter Henry and Lulabelle were living there by themselves.

The miner's shack stood a couple hundred yards away. The roof of another, larger cabin could be seen beyond that. Tucker wanted to explore the buildings before him, the few rustic cabins past a small pond. He saw trellises and arbors, walkways, and the main cabin that had been Lulabelle's home.

Tucker was uneasy about trespassing onto someone else's property. He was also concerned about the noise he was making, stepping on and breaking scattered branches. He climbed over a fallen tree that came down during one storm. Freckles ran up to him with Shep and Tessie, whom Tucker recognized. Shep jumped on him, whining and barking in joy. Tucker shared in the family reunion, petting and praising the dogs whose tails were wagging as they licked his face.

The thought occurred to Tucker that Jim Hart's spirit might also be present. He sat on the fallen tree, taking the time to consider the possibility. Deciding to talk to Jim, he imagined the troubled young man was standing beside him. Sitting quietly, the peacefulness of that place was experienced. A woodpecker drummed in the heights of the trees above. Something stirred in the underbrush at the edges of the retreat center grounds, perhaps a bird or a small animal. Listening, it was not long before Tucker's mind wandered, remembering various things, nothing in particular, simply remembering. However, it drew him inward, connecting him to his heart. Without trying, without paying attention to where his thoughts wandered, images came and went, appearing within his mind as he gazed into the distance.

One image held his attention, that of Jim Hart when he was captain of the football team in their senior year of high school. Jim was the best player on their team and led them well. Everyone admired him and followed his leadership except Tucker.

Tucker frequently challenged Jim's decisions. At one game, he openly fought with Jim, which led to an altercation. The coach was forced to have team members pull Tucker aside. He was reprimanded and told to sit out the rest of the game. Humiliated, he sat on the sidelines, watching the team, his team, win the game and the glory that day.

Tucker remembered that, during half-time, Jim sat on the bench with him. Their teammates were nearby, guzzling water, spitting, talking amongst themselves, their spirits high. Jim said something that cut through the tension between them. It annoyed Tucker.

Jim sat there briefly, palms resting on his thighs. About to get up from the bench, he looked straight ahead and said, "Off the field, Stewart, we're rivals. But, on the field, we're a team. You'll never get anywhere in life until you see that. People have to work together. They have to cooperate with each other if they all want to succeed."

Tucker felt humiliated back then but, remembering it, was humbling. He knew it was time to work together with others, to be thankful for friendship, love, and companionship, the connection and sense of community that was missing from his life. Community was the playing field upon which his fellow townspeople strived toward a goal through working together. Katie, Candelaria, Rosa, Aurelia, Harvey, Barclay, Bear, and the people of Laketon were counting on him to work with them as a team. He knew it was time to stop fighting it and learn to cooperate. He needed to grow up, the awareness of which was most humbling of all.

Setting his mind to task, he thanked Jim for the lesson and added, "A lot has gone on since you died. I know about your son, Johnny. He's a good man. Reminds me of you." He continued to ramble on about Katie, saying that he figured they were nothing more than friends, though he appreciated her and cared about her very much. He mentioned Sylvia and his dad.

Aurelia was also at the retreat center, her first visit since overhearing Johnny's argument with Walter Henry and Millie. The dogs ran off to greet her. She spotted Tucker, so she remained in the shadows of the denser growth of trees, circling around to see him without him seeing her. Luckily, the dogs ran off again, so she could hear Tucker talking. She sat still and listened.

He said, "I've heard that the people of Laketon think of you as a holy man, Jim. I never thought of you that way, but they would know. I'm sorry you suffered. I'm sorry for a lot of things." His voice trailed off as he mumbled softly, "Thank you, for helping Aurelia."

He lowered his head and closed his eyes, thinking of Aurelia and remembering when she looked into his eyes that awful night when she had left. No one had ever seen him so clearly, so deeply as she had. It both liberated and terrified him. In that brief moment they shared, he felt his soul meet with hers. He saw in her eyes the love she was waiting to give to him, searching for a sign that he loved her, too. Sitting at Lulabelle's old retreat center, Tucker relented, admitting that he loved Aurelia and that he yet grieved. His shoulders wracked with sobbing the losses of family and friends, lovers that never materialized into fully-fledged relationships. He asked himself what was the matter with him that he would turn away a beautiful, loving, and kind woman like Aurelia? The answer, which came to him upon a light breeze, simply said, "Good things shall rise above." Love would always win out over fear. He knew that to be true.

Aurelia hurried off into the woods, branches cracking and snapping in her swift departure. The dogs roused Tucker, nudging him to get up and get going. He stood and continued exploring the property, when something caught his eye. It was a red sweatshirt jacket Aurelia had held in her lap, but had dropped on the ground when she left in her haste. Recognizing it, Tucker picked it up and, without thinking, held it close, smelling her within the cloth as he had smelled her that night, a scent of soap and pine trees, plus something sweet and flowery. Looking out and around at the woods, he wondered if she was also visiting the retreat center. After searching the area, he realized she was gone. Unsure whether he should leave the jacket or take it with him, he decided to leave it. He draped it over the railing on the main cabin's deck and went home, Freckles by his side. Shep and Tessie ran back to Walter Henry's cabin to lap up some water from a bucket by the front door.

Walter Henry witnessed it all from inside his woodworking shop, saw Tucker show up and the dogs walking together. He saw Aurelia arrive, hiding from Tucker, then flee, her red sweatshirt falling from her lap as she did so. He witnessed Tucker finding the jacket and draping it over the railing.

He said, "I ain't never seen a more star-crossed pair in all my days." He shook his head in sympathy and went back to work.

His work, at that stage in his life, was sorting through his wood projects according to their progress. Having fallen behind, the work piled up to where he had lost track. Too old to buy and haul lumber anymore, he was glad he had plenty to do to keep him occupied and employed. He was too old to drive his truck into the mountains, so he found it necessary to make arrangements for someone to deliver for him. That person was due to come by, but Walter Henry was forgetful, wondering if they had already done so or if they were coming that day, later in the week, or the following month. So he engaged himself with his sorting, to be on the safe side, placing finished items to be boxed in one area by the door. Not too much in the way of toys, though. They required greater skill and steadier hands, which he no longer possessed, hence the furthest pile to be chucked out the window. It contained unfinished, hopeless causes for the burn pile, proving to himself that he could no longer work the wood.

Peering through the ancient, rippled window panes, out across the valley of his youth, he saw his memories clearly, as if flowing through clean water. When he was a boy, he used to come up to the miner's shack and visit with Berto Mendoza. Berto would tell him about things in the world, things that were unjust, that were unfair. He could remember the man's face, his black hair and brown weathered skin, his bony body, and his hair in long braids like the Indians, fashioning a pair of sandals or a hat out of shredded bark. It was Berto who showed him the bark houses where Hector Shoseegan and Dexter had lived. Lucy had come to live with Berto, to be his wife, but Walter Henry rarely talked to her. They would share with him whatever they had cooking over the fire, sometimes a rabbit on a skewer or a tea made for some special purpose. He loved the view and was proud to be able to point out every house, who lived in it, who their children were, what they were like, and what their father did for a living. He would walk back to the blacksmith shop and livery stable, maybe see his dad with a team of horses, and scarcely notice he had left one world and entered another.

Walter Henry realized he yet dwelled in those two worlds. He came to live in Berto's old mining shack beside Lucy's healing place on the mountain. He also continued to be at the barn in Pine Way, once a thriving blacksmith shop and livery stable. He never found it difficult, stepping from one world into another, from the peaceful ways of his life on the mountain into the activities of the town. On the mountain, he could hear the soughing of the wind in the pines, witness it softly lifting a bough to pass beneath as though it were something living. Going down the mountain into Edenville, mingling with the townsfolk, he entered another world. It was a world where the sounds were of machinery and engines chugging out in the fields, people shouting and laughing, doors slamming, radios blaring. It was all one world to him, not two. He flowed between them like the wind, because they were really the varied aspects of one world, and he had unknowingly made his home amidst it all.

CHAPTER THIRTY-TWO

The Big Storm began late one day, its presence announced in loud drops of rain. They smacked the dust, raising it up until the air smelled like mud. The lightening struck in jagged streaks of flaming, golden light, its sound cracking down the quiet, penetrating the earthen core. Trees were toppled by gusty winds. Branches were torn from stalwart oaks and flung aside like twigs. People ran with newspapers in hand, purses, bags, or boxes to shield themselves from the pounding waters that flooded the streets in minutes. Hours later, the creek was overflowing its banks and, still, the rain came pouring down.

The following day, the weatherman said the storm had brought nearly twenty inches of rain to some places. In Pine Way, its passing was known when the back road to Edenville was closed due to flooding and one of the great old elm trees fell on the Jones's place. It was a single-story house built by Bartholomew Jones in the 1800s, the house in which Tucker's mother was raised. It sat opposite the back alleyway from his house. He went out first thing in the morning, having heard the loud crash and boom of the massive tree hitting the ground during the night. The fence behind the house was reduced to smashed splinters while the house itself was covered in branches. Tucker telephoned his brother, Howard, who soon stopped by on his way to work to survey the damage.

"Mom's house," said Tucker.

"It's done for," said Howard.

"What should we do?" Tucker asked.

Thinking about it for a moment, Howard replied, "We've got the weekend coming up in a couple of days. We'll have to clean it up."

"Can we afford it?" Tucker queried.

"We can do it ourselves," Howard reassured him.

"This tree?! Look at the size of the trunk! We'll have to pay somebody!" argued Tucker.

"Now, now, Tucker." Howard's hand gently patted the air to tell his younger brother to settle down. "We'll pay someone to move the tree, but you and I are going to have to deal with the house. Maybe someone'll help us. We can offer the scrap lumber for free to—"

"This was Mom's house!" said Tucker. "We can't just—"

"Just what?" asked Howard. "Look at it! It's destroyed!"

Tucker calmed himself and said, "Okay, okay. I'll ask Harvey if he wants the lumber. He'll help us."

Howard perked up, inquiring, "Harvey? Oh, you mean that Indian fella?"

"That 'Indian fella' is my friend," said Tucker.

"I didn't mean anything by it," countered Howard. "Well, I've got to get to work. Got a client coming in right at nine."

Before Howard left, Tucker made sure it was all right to ask Harvey to demolish the house. He also confirmed the day to get the tree removed. "So, we'll meet here Saturday morning? Say, seven?" he asked.

Not wanting to start so early, Howard replied, "Seven? How about eight, and I'll have Mary pack us a nice big lunch, thermos and everything. Like the old days, huh?" Howard was grinning, hopeful.

Tucker remembered when he was a kid, heading out with his big brothers on a pretend reconnaissance mission, exploring and climbing trees. His mother would pack them a big lunch they would load into army surplus knapsacks. Of course, they had to have walking sticks, a compass, and a snake bite kit. Their mother was thankful it was never needed. Yet, if she knew how rusty the blades had become, she would have taken it away from them. The last time they went was before the war started.

Grinning along with his brother, Tucker said, "Yeah, just like the old days. So, Saturday morning at eight."

Before Howard got in his car, he asked Tucker, "Is anything going on, little brother? I mean, anything you'd want to talk about?"

Tucker froze, saying, "No...why?"

"You look a sight, like you slept in your clothes," answered Howard. He reached into his car and drew out a yellow envelope. "That, uh, Mexican girl, used to work at the pet store, came by the other day, left this on our porch. Here."

Almost gingerly, as though hesitating giving it to him, Howard reached forward to hand the envelope to Tucker, whose face could not hide the damning shame he felt within himself.

Tucker quietly responded, "Thanks." He half-heartedly waved to his brother as the car drove away.

The rain came down again. Tucker dashed back to his house, splashing through a low spot where the rain had collected. It poured down and the rest of him was soon drenched as he clambered over another, smaller tree that had fallen behind his house. Freckles ran up to the porch and shook herself out. The garden was another victim of the storm, branches strewn across it and areas washed out.

"Well, I guess the garden's done. Huh, Freckles?" Tucker commented.

They went into the house as he held on to her collar, drying her off with a towel, neglecting the fact they both had muddy feet. When he turned around, he saw the muddy prints, human's and dog's side by side, and groaned, wondering when it would end.

"Is it possible that things could just go back to normal?" he beseeched the heavens with arms upraised.

Freckles looked up at him, the way she did that made the whites of her eyes show, whining and pretending to sneeze. Before Tucker wiped her feet, she bounded across the living room, leaped onto the couch, and lay there, muddy paws and all, grinning and satisfied. Tucker took her off the couch and pointed to her bed. She circled before finally settling in with a great sigh.

Tucker cleaned up the mud on the floor and on the dog, thanking his good judgement in covering the couch with an old blanket. He changed out of his wet clothes and got ready for work. He needed to leave right away, but sat down by the lamp and opened the envelope, realizing at that moment that he had never read the note Sylvia left for him when she "skipped town," which made him laugh and groan. He read Aurelia's words and was hurt by her admission. He felt worse about what he had done.

"Dear Tucker," wrote Aurelia, "I went to see Harvey that night we argued. I stayed the night with him. I'm sorry. It was a mistake. He told me that he told you about what happened to me when I was a girl. I'm scared what you think of me now. Is that why you don't want to see me anymore? I guess I'm damaged goods. I hope that's not what you think of me. I hope you can forgive me. I won't bother you anymore. Yours truly, Ellie."

Tucker's heart swelled with an ache and a need that had no other way to be relieved except to answer her letter right away. He thought of men he had seen in the movies. They would be taunting him, men who found nothing more satisfying than pounding their fist through a wall. John Wayne would grab a woman gruffly and yank her toward him. Planting a heavy kiss on her lips, in her overcome state, the woman's wild mop of hair would fling back, and she would become putty in his hands. But Tucker was not that kind of man.

He dug out his clipboard and notepad from his newspaper-magazine-and-unopened-mail-pile growing behind the lamp. He plopped onto the couch, wondering what to say to Aurelia. Nothing came to him, except to shake his head and say, "Every woman I've ever loved has either left me or I've rejected them. What am I supposed to do?"

The dog momentarily looked at Tucker, then lowered her head to rest on her paws, sighing deeply as she closed her eyes, giving out an unmistakable whine.

Despite his anxiety, Tucker needed to do the right thing, even if it turned out to be wrong.

The rain settled in for the long haul and the clouds sank down and darkened the day like it was nearly nightfall. He wrote to Aurelia as he wished he could have spoken before he said those regrettable words, "I'm sorry, but—" It was not that long ago, but it felt to him like one of life's crucial moments that would pass him by and never return if he did not act.

"Now or never," he whispered.

He wrote, "Dear Ellie, I love you. I've been so worried about being just another man who would use you or hurt you, that I haven't even allowed myself to tell you that. There is so much I wish I could say, but it seems you already know. You have seen me as I am, just a man, and you have seen into me as I know I am, which is the best that I can be. I love you and I think I'm ready now to be the Keeper of the Dream. Tucker."

He read it over and, reaching over the arm of the couch, dug out an envelope from the pile, folded the paper, and stuck it in the envelope and sealed it. The rain was letting up as he drove to Aurelia's house to deliver the note, splashing in and out of puddles on the way. He parked the car in front of the farmworkers shack, climbed the steps to the porch, and slipped the note under the doormat. With Candelaria indoors, forbidding her younger cousin to go to him, when he turned away to go back to his car, Aurelia drew the kitchen curtain aside. Her sweet, teary-eyed face showed Tucker the truth, right as he looked back at the house before opening his car door. About to go to her, he instead willed himself to get into the car and drive to work, hating himself.

Perhaps it was not Aurelia, but Fate, Itself, with whom he had drawn the line in the sand. He had resolved not to be like his father and do to Aurelia what his father had done to young Charity Walker. Tucker believed that his longing to be with Aurelia was something the Keeper of the Dream was never meant to pursue, what his role as her ally was never called upon to involve. Recalling his father's words, "Don't do what I did. Do what I should have done," Tucker drove onto the highway, finally understanding the full meaning of those wise words.

No matter what Tucker believed was the right thing to do, Lucy's dream would have its way in the end, for it did not follow convention and it was not aligned with Fate, but with the stars. It drew down the moon to rest upon the earth and mingle with the seasons of all things beautiful, all things not made by man, but by a force, a vision unseen, except by those who believed in it and knew it to be so.

CHAPTER THIRTY-THREE

The Big Storm had passed. Tucker stood outside his home surveying the damage. He noticed the sound of hammers and the metallic squeak of nails getting yanked out of wood, followed by lumber smacking as it was stacked. Looking behind his house, he saw Harvey and his crew busy tearing down the ruined homestead where his mother had lived as a child.

The tree was cleaned up and hauled away the weekend before, leaving a gaping hole in the sky where its branches had once spread to immense proportions. He and his brother took only a few minutes afterward to check inside the house before they called it quits. Little appealed to either of them in the old place. Most of what remained of their mother's family home were the remnants of a life no one wanted anymore, like a worn-out brass bed, an armoire with doors that creaked, and a musty, claw-foot sofa.

Howard kept an old photograph he had found. It was of their mother's parents, standing in the apple orchard during harvest time. People in the background were standing beside horses hitched to wagons filled with bushels of apples. A note on the back of the photo read, "Two bums in love. Bart and—" The other name, that of the much-younger woman in the picture, their grandmother, was smeared.

Staking out the dog with a length of rope, Tucker began to clear his garden area. Tossing branches and dragging limbs to the back of his house, a pile steadily grew. The sun came out by late afternoon. The heavy, stake-side truck Harvey's crew had loaded with lumber and furniture, strained its gears. It trudged and rocked its way along the back alley. Tucker welcomed the returning silence. He was not a loner by nature, but he appreciated the quiet.

He sat on his porch to rest, noticing the state of his shoes, the soles flapping loose and his holey socks soaked through to the skin. A cat-like snarling arose from under the porch, which Freckles missed. She was alerted to the sound of someone walking down the road. The snarl arose once more, so Tucker stepped off the wooden porch and peered underneath. It was too dark to see. He needed a flashlight and was about to go indoors to hunt for one, when he saw Aurelia.

Freckles was barking and whining and wagging her tail, straining on the rope to greet their visitor, so Tucker set her loose. She ran to Aurelia, greeting the young woman without holding back.

Hands in his front pockets and smiling, Tucker slowly approached Aurelia.

Aurelia asked, "Walk with me?"

"Sure," he said.

They went down the road as the sun neared setting. The last light of evening shone on each raindrop clinging to the leaves of trees and bushes. The light dimmed as the sun's final rays withdrew behind the hills to the west. Dusk settled into the chilled air.

Passing before Harvey's house, Tucker noted the man's car. He glanced at Aurelia, but she appeared unconcerned. She thanked Tucker for his letter. Remembering the words, he nodded, but was yet anxious as to what would come of it. He felt unusually awkward, like a helpless, lovesick high-schooler. Worse, he felt real.

Aurelia asked, "Have you ever seen the cemetery down here?"

"A couple times," he answered. "I tried to clean it up once, but, it's pretty overgrown. Why?"

"Oh, I thought of what I could do to help my people, you know? I want to give back, in a good way. I thought I'd start—" She became frustrated and blurted out, "Oh, I don't know what I'm trying to say!"

"No, no." Tucker tried reassuring her. "I think it's a good idea," he said. "They need to be honored. It's a special place that ought to be protected before it's forgotten and somebody bulldozes it."

"Exactly! That's what I was thinking. Can you help?" Aurelia asked.

Tucker again smiled as he answered, "Sure. I'll help."

They were walking toward the old picnic grounds. Tucker assumed they would approach the abandoned cemetery from that direction. However, Aurelia turned down Ev Mendoza's old driveway and said, "Come this way." From there, she led him onto a pathway he figured was the same one Candelaria used to visit the two little graves. A feeling of dread overcame him. He hesitated going any further. Placing his hand on Aurelia's shoulder, he said, "Wait."

She turned toward him and asked, "Why? What's wrong?" She was genuinely concerned, sensing Tucker uneasiness.

"Oh, it's-it's nothing," he said. "I just have a weird feeling about this place, like there's something about it I don't want to face. I've—it's strange, that's all."

"You wanna talk about it?" she asked.

"I just feel too sad here," said Tucker, "like I'll be so sad, I won't be able to bear it."

Aurelia was looking up at him with such kindness. He knew why he loved her, why they met, why they were there, approaching something sacred, terrible, and hallowed...hallowed ground. He sensed something about the place asked, no, it demanded reverence of the sacred. His whole countenance shifted in response, liked he filled out a larger self, his senses sharper. It surprised him, but it also felt empowering, as if the town's skin was sloughed off, revealing who he was, the Keeper of the Dream.

Aurelia saw the change in Tucker, knowing and loving that they, as two souls, knew one another before they, as people, were even born. In the nearing darkness, she said, "I love you."

"I know," Tucker responded before gently kissing her. "I love you, too," he said.

They walked onward down the path into increasing darkness that fell eerily silent. When they reached the native cemetery, Tucker was surprised to see that someone had already cleared the entire burial ground. A wooden staff with feathers and colored ribbon tied to it was planted in the center.

Despite previous misgivings about going there, Tucker stood in place, looking all around and listening. Soon, what he had feared began to unfold. It came upon a cold draft of air. He placed his arms around Aurelia, drawing her near to him to keep her warm and to protect her. What he had experienced when he and Katie first attempted to clear the weeds and grass from the white quartz headstones, swiftly returned once nightfall arrived. It was something heavy he was not prepared to face back then. It drew him downward, as if into death, as if the blood in his body was sinking downward and pooling at his feet. A strange howling or whooping sound emanated from the trees surrounding them.

"What's that?" Aurelia asked him. She looked around for what might have made that sound.

"It's the ghosts of the massacre," said Tucker.

Tucker had known of it since he was a boy, out in the woods with his big brothers on one of their explorations. One time, they built a campfire and the sounds of the dead approached, their forms like upright wisps of smoke, their native dress visible. Others were mere shadowy forms blending, reaching, merging into the woodland's shadows. Then came the moaning, the crying of babies, heard but not heard, sensed within the mind's perception of what was real, or, was it? His brothers quieted and looked around in darting glances, until Howard said, "We better get Tucker James home," and the chorus ended. All disappeared until the night returned to how it was before the memory of horror struck upon the very earth had begun.

Tucker's brothers talked about it after they had arrived at home. They sat on the front porch, swapping hearsay about what they had witnessed. Others had warned, "Don't go out to the picnic grounds at night." Clarence McGrew stopped by, having stayed late at Forbush's Market to clean, and joined the other young men on the Stewart's front porch. Tucker was supposed to be in bed. He listened to the deep seriousness of their conversation from his bedroom window, their lowered voices in the dark, discussing something awful, something horrifying. He felt like he had been through some kind of initiation. He would not have called it that as a child, but he felt older, somehow, and wiser, knowing a great secret that was to be carried with great responsibility. He never told anyone about it until he and Aurelia stood in that place, hearing it again as he had that night long ago.

Tucker knew why he was told Char Lee Rosebud's account of the massacre. It was a furthering of his initiation into his sacred task as the Keeper of the Dream. Char Lee's ancestors had gone through a slaughtering of their flesh, dozens of them murdered outright, their lives destroyed. He and Aurelia were summoned to that place, he believed, for some purpose yet unknown to them.

Tucker had played innocent long enough, he realized in that moment, for he was no longer able to deny the experience that rose from out of the earth. He felt himself being pulled into the fleeing melee of brown-skinned people running for their lives. He watched the soldiers on horseback charging through the village, shooting as they went. Immersed in the confusion, he bore witness to the inexplicable and unpardonable nightmare as it was being relived. His arms were yet around Aurelia, who was sharing in the experience with him. After all, they were allies, the ones whose task it was to behold the atrocity, so the nightmare could be transformed into something beautiful.

Tucker saw a man, a soldier in blue, acting quickly, as though the only reason for his being there was to help save as many as he could. Other soldiers were rushing past on horseback. Tucker saw a native girl, maybe only three years of age. She was looking directly at him and Aurelia as though seeing them, and he saw Lucy as a grown woman in native dress, also looking their way. Once he acknowledged her, she raised her head toward the heavens and began to sing.

Freckles ran for home, frightened by the sounds, only to find she was alone, so ran toward Katie's. It was too far for her to go at night, so she ended up at Candelaria's, whining frantically and scratching at the door. Candelaria opened it to learn that her younger cousin, who had mentioned she was visiting the native cemetery, was most likely there with Tucker Stewart, in that place that made the Grandmothers weep in remembrance. Tucker was a kind man, she thought. She loved him like her own son, but she yet worried regarding their intentions.

Whispering, "Dear God, watch over them," Candelaria closed the door. She wrapped her robe more snug around her and went back to the sofa. Freckles settled at her feet and worried, too. She let out an occasional whine until Candelaria petted the dog and welcomed her onto the sofa, reassuring them both as she laid her hand on the dog's fur, gently smoothing it.

Tucker held Aurelia close before taking her hand and walking back to his house in the dark. They went indoors and began dreaming their love into the terrible tragedy that had befallen a tribe of peace-loving people long ago. No one knew they were together except Harvey and Candelaria.

Harvey was clearing brush at the old picnic grounds earlier that evening and had returned before dark to retrieve a hand tool he had forgotten. He spotted a black bear with cinnamon-brown fur lumbering into the cleared area at one end of it as Tucker and Aurelia walked toward the cemetery from the other end. Candelaria kept Freckles in her house all night, having snuck onto her bed with her, not the first time. Once morning came, she opened the door and let the dog run home. Stepping outside onto her porch, her arms wrapped around herself, she looked toward the houses in Pine Way, knowing that Aurelia had been with Tucker all night.

"Well, Aurelia," she began, "I guess you finally got what you wanted. At least, now, you can move on." Chilled, she wrapped her robe closer around her and turned to go back into her little house.

CHAPTER THIRTY-FOUR

Eileen Price looked across the tea shop at the yellow flyer she had taped to the front window. She recalled Andrew's previous lecture. The Vietnam War was a controversial topic, yet the lecture hall filled with young people eager to hear what Andrew had to say. She had tried to listen to every word, but was concerned about Aurelia. Recalling her young friend mentioning Tucker Stewart, Eileen realized nothing more was said about him and wondered why.

Dismissing that last thought, her own desires once again stepped into the foreground. She wanted to take part in political activism to be near Andrew. However, her plans to leave town were thwarted when her mother became very ill, necessitating a return to "boring old Edenville," she said. Dividing her time taking care of her mother and running the shop, she grew frustrated knowing that fellow students were dropping out of school and leaving home to join marches across the country. Some were staying to help organize rallies and protests in nearby communities. Through watching the news on television,

Eileen learned that things were turning violent in some areas, even escalating into outright urban warfare. The community college, where she and Aurelia were taking classes, was "closed until further notice," according to school officials.

Realizing there would be very little opportunity to see Andrew for a while, Eileen resignedly stepped around the counter and yanked the flyer from the glass. Balling it up and tossing it into the trash can, she stood with her arms folded in front of her, gazing out the front window as though foretelling her dismal future.

"Well, Eileen," she began, "looks like you won't be seeing Andrew any time soon. You're stuck here in Small Town, USA with no hope for marriage *or* romance." With that last word, she reminded herself to call Aurelia about Tucker Stewart. Now, if he was free...

What Eileen did not know was that Andrew was planning to join all those eager young people taking part in anti-war protests and demonstrations. His activist friends were traveling the country together. He argued with Sylvia over his need to go with them. Frustrated, he paced the floor at home, heatedly and passionately beseeching Sylvia's support.

"I've got to go, Syl!" he said. "I can't stand it! I feel like I'm going to go crazy if I don't get out there and fight alongside others who know this war has to end!" His entire being was crying out to her. "Don't you see?! We've got to stand up to the president's campaign to regain support for the war!"

"All right! All right!" Sylvia yelled. "But, I'm going with you."

Ecstatic, Andrew cried, "You are?! Oh, Syl! This is *tremendous!* You don't know how much this means to me!"

"We're going to take the bus, though," she said. "I'm not hitchhiking."

They left Sylvia's two-year-old daughter, Rebecca, with Aunt Patty in Edenville. Patty had informed them that Dottie needed practice taking care of someone other than herself, seeing as how she was expecting, and unmarried. Her plan to hook her boyfriend had backfired. He had married someone else and left town.

Andrew and Sylvia planned to be gone for two weeks. He was scheduled to attend rallies, speaking at many of them, and to help organize marches. Sylvia dreaded it. Andrew was immediately swept up in the surge of angry voices and the equally angry forces that sought to silence them.

Sylvia hated hearing the dissent, the harsh words against the president, against the government she had never questioned before then. She felt her views were not only being challenged, but were under attack. She loved the president, what he stood for, the idea of "one nation under God." It frightened her seeing Andrew alongside those in opposition, seeing him yelling and shaking a sign. They were all so hateful, she thought, until one scene took place that opened her eyes.

It was when the police squads came marching up the street, armed with rifles. Water cannons were spraying people, toppling them over. The protestors were in agony, some were running away and screaming. Police dogs were barking and lunging at them. Smoke from tear gas was everywhere. One woman's face, contorted in fear, terrified Sylvia. The people, she realized, were no longer human, but things that needed to be knocked down and pushed aside, their ideas and what they cared about rejected and retaliated against. What had happened to democracy? Her childhood innocence was gone and so was that of an entire nation. One nation under God was being torn apart in an uprising for change, for what they believed. They were fighting against what they knew was wrong. That woman's face was her own, aghast, traumatized by the reality of their government turning against the people, lying to them, attempting to squelch their dissent, to destroy the truth. She understood that to be true. Andrew always talked about democracy, but it was silenced that day.

Fleeing the scene for her life and for her sanity, Sylvia bumped into others running for safety. Unaware of the consequences of her impulsive actions, she was instead consumed by the devastation and shock over what the government was doing. She wanted to make it unseen so she would not have to face what she felt about her once-beloved, yet sadly flawed president. She ran across the campus to the other side where the bus station was located, where they had left their belongings in a locker. Grabbing only her shoulder bag full of clothing and personal items, Sylvia bought a ticket and sat in the bus. She wanted to become part of the masses who were oblivious and, therefore, innocent. It never occurred to her she should have told Andrew, that she should have turned to him, her husband. She was in flight, knowing only that she had to get away, vaguely aware of others on the bus who were fleeing as well.

•   •   •

After a couple of day's rest at her aunt and uncle's house on Spring Hill, Sylvia was ready to return home. Noting that she needed some things from the drugstore, like an emery board and a new hairbrush, she finished packing, tucking Rebecca's things amongst her own. Her cousin, Dottie, had offered to drive them.

They stopped at the drugstore first. To Sylvia's surprise, Rosa Smith was approaching the store with Betsy Marie toddling behind and Bobby James in her arms.

"Rosa! It's so good to see you!" Sylvia said. Unnoticed, her daughter followed Dottie into the store.

Startled by Sylvia's changed appearance, Rosa said, "Sylvia! I'm surprised to see you. Didn't you move away?"

They hugged one another and stood out front on the sidewalk to talk. Rosa's children were fussing too much, so they went inside the store. Soon afterward, Rosa excused herself. While holding Bobby James in one arm, she dug into her purse for some money with her free hand and quickly paid for a box of tissues on sale for twenty cents and a can of soup on sale for a dime, plus a small box of cookies for her daughter. Taking the bag and her change from the clerk, she called her daughter.

"Betsy! Time to go," she said.

Glancing once more at Sylvia, Rosa noted that Sylvia's looks had not dimmed. She felt jealous of her. Telling herself to be happy for Sylvia, she walked toward the door to leave.

Dottie said, "We were on our way to the bakery for some tea, Rosa. Why don't you join us?"

"With these two?" Rosa asked. "No, I've got to get home and get ready for work." She said to Sylvia, "It's good seeing you," and left the store.

Dottie scooped up Rebecca and, after attending to their own purchases, they drove to Teapot full o' Whimsy. Sylvia was no longer in the mood for tea and pastries. She told Dottie, "I'll join you in a minute." Dottie took Rebecca with her into the tea shop while Sylvia remained in the car.

Sylvia had given little thought to what it would be like to return to Edenville. Seeing Rosa had reminded her of Jim. She felt shaky, even scared. Thinking of her daughter, she mumbled, "What a mess I've made of my life."

She casually watched the townspeople, busy going about their day. One woman tried to enter the bookstore, Read 'Em & Weep, which was next to the tea shop, and found it was yet closed. Past the bookstore, people entered the market. Others were placing bags of groceries into the trunks of their cars or pushing wobbly-wheeled shopping carts across the parking lot. Cars came and went. It was a familiar scene, so much so, it was like no time had gone by since she had left Edenville.

Beneath her awareness, the past had made its way into the present. She had hoped to see Tucker while in Edenville, but Jim's memory had unexpectedly shadowed all thoughts of her old friend. She felt the cloud of Jim's attentions pressing in on her. Recalling the night he was demanding an answer from her, his angry voice arose. "Sylvia, answer me!" he said. "Would you leave your husband for me?"

Meanwhile, Rosa's mother, Candelaria, came walking from across the parking lot toward the market. Sylvia saw her and anxiously looked over at Dottie, who was sitting in the tea shop at one of the wrought-iron tables with Rebecca. Sylvia realized it was best to join them inside, whispering to herself, "I can't let her know I'm here."

Once Sylvia entered the bakery, Eileen immediately recognized her as Andrew's wife and Tucker's old flame. She was glad she had taken the flyer down before Sylvia spotted it. Making a casual exit, she pretended she had something to do in the back room, hoping the two ladies were leaving soon.

Dottie excitedly chattered on about getting out of town. Sylvia, a little too eagerly, agreed it was time to go. Soon, they were on the highway, making their way across the valley. The radio played and, shifting to a lighter mood, they laughed in hysterics over anything and everything. Like a forgotten child, the brown-skinned, spindly waif Sylvia had brought into the world, slept soundly on the back seat.

It was a long drive to Sylvia's house. Eventually, she and Dottie were quiet. Sylvia looked out the window, remembering something about Jim Hart when they were children. A wistful sort of memory, he had said that he wished he was an angel, so he could put an end to the war, which was the Second World War. Piecing together events that took place after his death and her father's death, she could honestly say that an angel had a hand in all of that. It seemed as though she was carried away on angel's wings into a new life that was made for her. Smiling over the name of the dress shop, "From the Heart," she believed that was so and marveled at it. However, her thoughts wandered again onto Tucker, wanting to see him. Going over the past week and a half in her mind, traveling the country with Andrew, she recalled the people she had met, hearing the chanting as the protestors shook their signs to the beat of their pleas to end the war. She realized what had appealed to her about Andrew. He had reminded her of that better side of Jim, wanting to help put an end to the Vietnam War. What did Tucker want? Sylvia had never thought to ask.

CHAPTER THIRTY-FIVE

It was late in the day when Andrew arrived at home, flinging the front door wide open to bang against the wall. Distraught and frantic, he began shouting at Sylvia, "What are you doing here?! How could you just leave like that?! I thought you had gotten lost or hurt or arrested or something! Sylvia? Answer me!"

While her cousin picked up Rebecca and hurried outside, Sylvia yelled at Andrew, "I panicked, all right?!"

She turned her back on him and went into their bedroom, slamming the door behind. Crawling onto the bed, she laid herself down and drew in her arms and legs. With the many mistakes she had made in life piling up like so much dead wood, made apparent by seeing Jim's sister and his mother again, Sylvia felt disappointed in herself. How could she ever return to Edenville?

"I don't care," she whispered. "I need to see Tucker."

Andrew slowly opened the bedroom door, carefully closing it behind. He joined her on the bed and gently placed his arm around her. Softly, he said, "Sweetie...honey...Sylvia...I'm sorry." He drew her into his arms and kissed her. He said, "I was scared. You should have told me. Why did you leave? Why didn't you tell me anything? I was so worried."

Andrew said no more regarding his experience of that awful day. It had terrified him, leaving a wound of cynicism and distrust. He needed Sylvia by his side when things turned horrible and ugly. Finding her gone, nowhere to be found, made him realize how much he loved her, how much he wanted her in his life and to be a part of hers.

When the violence began, their group was moving as one body, in solidarity for the cause. But the opposition squashed their voices, turning their passions to fear, their outrage to terror, and their higher ground for hiding places. Andrew forgot the sign in his hand as it dropped to the ground, seeing the water cannons knocking people over, sweeping them off the streets. He was too stunned to move. In a brief moment that seemed like the end of the world, he stepped far away into another state of mind, seeing the chaos of thousands as through a lens. He scanned the area all around him, suddenly alerted that Sylvia was gone.

Mobilized by worry, he searched everywhere for her, checking the crowds, the ambulances that were taking away those who were getting hurt, and the police cars. He was frantic, not knowing where she was nor how to find her. Asking those who knew her, if they had seen where she went, they would say, "no," and suggest where to look. He went to the hospital, the police station, wherever she might have gone. By the end of the day, he was in anguish, not knowing what had happened to her.

That night, he had nowhere to sleep. He joined a group of others going to a house that offered to house protestors. They warned not to spread the word, because there was only so much room for people to stay. Walking hurriedly with the others, they arrived at an old, two-story house down a tree-lined street. The streetlights shone dimly through the damp mist wetting the pavement. Earthy odors filled his nostrils and a police siren could be heard in the distance. Up the steps, they filed in silence, looking behind and all around to be sure no one saw them as they went inside. People were laying everywhere, all over the floors, in the stairwell, and in the bathtub. He found a corner and sat leaning against the wall, exhausted, grief-stricken, and overwhelmed. The fumes of cigarette smoke and opened beer cans reeking with cigarette ash sickened him. The sight of cardboard boxes from eateries spread on tables, hearing strangers coughing, their mumblings in the dark, somehow made him feel alone. But it grew faint and he slept.

The next morning, when the telephone was finally free, he called Sylvia's Aunt Patty. Learning what his wife had done, he hurriedly boarded a bus for home. Over the next couple of days, he called from towns where the bus had stopped. Finally, he reached Sylvia's cousin. All he could think of was returning home to Sylvia. Holding her in his arms as they lay in bed together, he realized how much she meant to him. However, it was not yet over. Sylvia pulled away from him and announced that she could not continue the life he had carved out for himself.

"What do you mean?" asked Andrew.

"I need to go home," said Sylvia.

"This is your home!" argued Andrew.

"No, it's not!" she yelled. "This is *your* home, Andrew. I belong in Edenville."

"What are you saying?" he asked. "You told me you never wanted to go back there."

"I changed my mind, okay?" she said.

Andrew considered what she said, then told her, "He's dead, Sylvia. Remember? Jim's gone."

"Don't say that!" she yelled at him.

Andrew became impatient with her, trying not to get angry as he said, "Sylvia, you're just upset. Calm down and we'll talk it over."

Sylvia flashed back to the memory of Jim, when he aggressively grabbed her by the arm and said, "You're mine! Got that?!" Infuriated, she yelled at Andrew, "You don't own me! I can go wherever I please!"

Shocked at what Sylvia said, Andrew grew concerned, saying, "Sylvia. Let's talk this over rationally."

"I don't want to talk it over! I want to go home," she said.

Meanwhile, upon entering the house, Dottie could hear them arguing in the bedroom. She hurried back out the door with Rebecca. While pushing the stroller down the street toward the park, she thought about what she should do. Thinking aloud, she said, "I don't think it's a good idea to stay."

After an hour had gone by with the child complaining, Dottie returned to her cousin's house and carefully opened the door. Noting how quiet it was, she entered the living room. Rebecca had fallen asleep, so Dottie collected her things and placed them in the trunk of her car.

Eventually, Sylvia came out of the bedroom and went into the bathroom. She was there for what felt like a long time. When she finally came out to the living room, it was evident she was still very much upset.

Dottie needed to inform Sylvia of her plans. "Uh, I wanted to tell you," she began, "I'm gonna go ahead and drive home, okay?"

"Okay," answered Sylvia in an I-could-care-less manner. Sitting on the sofa, she had an emery board in one hand and was busily filing her nails. Sharpening them, is what Andrew would say if he saw her. She acted as though she was seemingly unconcerned about what was going on, yet, within herself, she was seething.

Dottie was concerned, at least for Sylvia's daughter, and asked, "Why don't I take Rebecca with me? That way you and Andrew can...get caught up."

It was agreed. Sylvia told her she had to be back to work on Monday, so they would pick up Rebecca that weekend. Dottie could not leave fast enough. Had she paid attention, she would have noticed something had changed in her cousin's demeanor. There was a look to her gray eyes that seemed almost animal-like. It was a look that her ex-husband, Fortuitous Sumner, would have advised Andrew to pay heed.

CHAPTER THIRTY-SIX

Patty McGrew was busy sweeping hair off the floor, complaining all the while about how many times she had swept that floor and it was never finished. How many times had she done Eunice Chapman's hair and it was yet as gray as ever? It refused to hold any color. Only minutes before, she told the woman, "You need to give up already and let it go gray once and for all."

Eunice Chapman, whose mother was also a Walker before she had married, stormed out of Patty's Beautique with a pout on her quivering lower lip, saying, "What has gotten into you to say something so heartless to me, Patty McGrew?"

Patty wondered until she spotted her unmarried pregnant daughter squirting solution on a perm customer's hair. Dottie was starting to show. Patty figured that was what had gotten into her.

"Dottie," she said.

"Hmm?" Dottie asked.

"You've got to do something, girl," said her mother.

"What do you mean?" asked Dottie.

"You know what I mean," Patty told her.

"*Mother!*" Dottie glared in anger at her mother, directing her eyes and head in the customer's direction to give her mother the hint to watch what she said.

Patty was adamant, saying, "You can't just let this go on."

"I'll handle it," said Dottie.

When she bumped her growing belly against the customer's shoulder, the woman, whose eyes had been closed, popped open her eyes, then re-closed them real quick, which Patty saw.

Knowing that shop as well as that customer did, and its proprietors as well as she did, the woman hardly needed eyes to know what had taken place. Sitting there until her perm was complete was unbearable. She was dying to tell everybody. No matter how many magazines she thumbed through, not a one would hold her interest. Finally, the wait was over and she was out the door, paying as she went.

"Thank you, girls! See you later!" The bell on the door jangled as she flung it open.

"What was that all about?" Patty asked her daughter.

Dottie lit in to her mother, saying, "You know damn well what that was about, Mother! She *heard* you! That was *terrible!* I'm so embarrassed! And, now, she's on her way to blab it all over town!" Her hand was thrown out in the air toward all the awful places in her imagination.

Patty noticed something outside and muttered, "What's she doin' back here?"

Dottie joined her mother at the window. "That's Sylvia!" she said. "What's she doing at the cemetery?" She turned away from the window and hastily cleared her station, grabbed her purse, and was out the door.

At the cemetery, Sylvia was holding her daughter on her hip, telling her about the person buried in that spot. Startled, she turned at the sound of Dottie's car parking by the road. Feeling awkward at first, because she had neglected to tell anyone she was coming, Sylvia felt reassured once they greeted and hugged each other.

Months had passed since Sylvia last saw her cousin. It was close to noon, so they went to her aunt and uncle's house to have lunch. Afterward, they sat in the sunken living room with the shag carpeting and stereo console, listening to records. Rebecca played in another room.

With Elvis crooning in the background, Sylvia told Dottie why she came to Edenville. "I miss living here," she said. "I've been thinking about moving back."

Surprised, Dottie blurted out, "Why?!"

"I don't know. I just miss it, that's all," Sylvia explained.

Still concerned, Dottie said, as she played with strands of her blond hair, "But it's so, you know, everybody knows you and talks about you behind your back and, well, look at me." She raised her blouse to reveal her pregnant belly to Sylvia. They laughed, but Dottie was serious. She said, "Maybe you just need...a little break." It was then that Dottie recalled Sylvia and Andrew's argument, catching on to what Sylvia was up to.

"You're not thinking of leaving your husband, are you?" she asked.

"No!" answered Sylvia. While straightening the edge of her blouse where it lay against her capris, she sighed and said, "It's like I left in a hurry. I ran away, Dottie. I ran away from this town, the gossip, the staring...and the whispering. But it's still my home. I miss it!"

Feeling bad, Dottie told Sylvia, "I'm so ashamed. I was one of those people who were gossiping about you. Now, look at me! I was at work and that old bat, Mrs. *Frump,* could hardly wait to run out the door and down the street, shouting, 'Dottie's pregnant! Dottie's pregnant! And, guess what? She's not married!' Oh, I've been a fool," referring to her plot to snag a husband. Laying her palm on her belly, she said, "I'm nearly six months along. I'll have to stay living with my parents." Lowering her voice, she said, "Mrs. Frum and all her kind, be damned."

Quiet for a moment, Dottie thought there was more to Sylvia's visit and ventured a query. "Sylvia," she began, "why are you really here? You work at that darling dress shop, managed to catch yourself a handsome husband probably every woman's in love with, and you live in the cutest house in Old Town. Tell me. What is it?"

Sylvia asked her, "Do you remember Tucker Stewart?"

Dottie answered, "Oh, him. What about him?"

"I feel like I need to talk to him," Sylvia explained. "I left town without saying goodbye to him and he was my very best friend." She tugged a tissue loose from a box on the coffee table and then lay back to recline on the sofa. Resting her head against a large pillow, she dabbed her eyes and blew her nose.

Perplexed, Dottie looked at her cousin, not knowing whether to hug her or get mad at her. She shook her head and tsked in disgust, not realizing she had done that. She was baffled as to why that woman could not appreciate all she had in life, crying over every other good-looking man in town, while Dottie, herself, could not find a one that would—

"Sylvia! Tucker is such a—"

She stopped herself, because whenever she saw Tucker she wished he would ask her to marry him. He was considered, among Edenville's singletons, the most eligible and, therefore, the most sought-after bachelor in town. But, rolling her eyes at the thought of it, he was currently involved with a much younger woman, about which Dottie refrained from telling Sylvia.

Eager for Dottie to say what was on her mind, Sylvia asked, "What?"

"Well, first of all, he was a big flirt in high school. I went over to their house all the time, Rosa and I, to see Lois and Marjorie. He was pretty cute when he was a little boy, but once he got into the ninth grade, oh, boy! He was so full of himself!"

"Tucker?!" asked Sylvia.

"Yes!" answered Dottie. She weighed whether she should say any more, but went ahead. "Do you know what he did?" she asked.

"What?" answered Sylvia.

"Remember that one girl? She was a cheerleader. Saw her at the football games. Used to walk like she was a—well, you know. *Her* and *Tucker.*"

"What?!" Sylvia was aghast.

"Yes, her and Tucker," Dottie said before going on, "saw them in person, cross my heart and hope to die. So did Rosa."

Sylvia found it unbelievable, inquiring, "You don't mean..."

"Yes! They were in the back seat of her father's convertible up at The Hill, doing you-know-what!"

"Dottie, you can't be serious!" After a pause, Sylvia asked, "What were you doing up at The Hill?"

"Rosa and I double-dated once with a couple of as—"

No longer paying attention to Dottie, Sylvia's voice changed to a wistful whisper. "Tucker?" she asked.

However, Dottie was still worked up about her confession, what she saw and had told no one about ever since she saw it. "Rosa made me promise not to tell anybody," she began, "because we had sneaked out that night. And, do you know what? What's-her-name didn't only spend time in the back seat of her daddy's convertible with Tucker!" Her loose lips halted right there in their tracks, because she knew that to mention Jim Hart's name would be cruel. Yet, she was ignorant of the fact that Sylvia was another one of Tucker's—

"Oh, Dottie," Sylvia lamented.

They looked at one another and, in that very moment, burst out laughing. They laughed and laughed some more, going on about the old days, other memories and other scandals.

However, Dottie sensed the real reason Sylvia had come back to Edenville, without her husband, skipping out on work. Plainly and clearly, she asked, "This isn't really about Tucker, though, is it?"

"What? What do you mean?" asked Sylvia.

Dottie became impatient and said, "Sylvia. He may be dead, but I saw whose grave you were standing over."

Sylvia froze as Dottie went on, inspecting her nails as she did so. "You know...I can see why you ran away, like you said, about leaving town so soon after your father's funeral. But, maybe it wasn't only Edenville you were running away from. Maybe it was Jim Hart."

Sylvia remained silent as Dottie continued on the subject. She said, "I mean, you had just lost your father. How could you face Jim's death, too? It would have been too hard for anyone! And, then, there's your daughter. Doesn't look a bit like Forty Sumner. Anyone who knows math can figure out she's not Andrew's child." She finally stopped, knowing how right she was, once she saw Sylvia close her eyes and cover them with her hand.

•   •   •

Transported into the past by Dottie's words, Sylvia recounted the memory of meeting Jim one day behind the barn. He was washing up at the outdoor sink. She joined him, nervously looking around to see if anyone had spotted her. When he was done drying his hands, he tossed the towel back at the sink. Peering at her from beneath the brim of his cowboy hat, he approached her with a look on his face, something like a smile, and something else. Every time Sylvia recalled that look, she would ask herself, why? Why him? Why me? Why *us*?

Since her last argument with Andrew, it gradually dawned on Sylvia that something within herself and within Jim had risen to the surface that day long ago. Jim's countenance had registered it within her own gaze as she watched him drawing near. Sylvia had seen it in her mother's eyes once, when her mother stood in the kitchen wearing only her undergarments as Tucker's father closed the door.

Sylvia felt it rise up once again, and she knew the truth. She had prized Jim Hart. Her mother's cunning ways lived on in her, ensuring she did not lose him, hers, her man. All the years they had known one another, being his first love, sharing in their first sexual experience at his parent's house, and continuing to fool around long after they were both married...and then he was dead. It dawned on Sylvia that she and Jim had been more than lovers. They were drawn to one another at the level of a deep-water well. They sank into its depths every time as though falling down and down and—

"What is it, Sylvia?" Dottie had returned to sit in the living room, having put Rebecca down for a nap.

A great, wrenching darkness sheared away from deep within as Sylvia cried, "Aunt Justice spoiled everything for me! I couldn't even enjoy just loving somebody! She kept me from Tucker! It was horrible what she did to me! And, now—I'll never—"

Sylvia cried, grieving too many losses, mostly the innocence of childhood. She held her bent arms drawn in close to her heart, feeling it breaking open, like a sharp fissure tearing.

Dottie leapt from her chair and hurried to Sylvia. She tried holding her cousin, but her arms were not strong enough. Sylvia's awakening and emerging self needed the strength of someone much larger than she, someone—recalling her Uncle Robert Cadwallader's funeral, sitting next to Granny Walker when Tucker entered the church with Sylvia, Dottie remembered watching how he held on to Sylvia as they walked down the aisle. He held her close to him should she falter, whispering in her ear after they were seated. Dottie was mesmerized by the tender look on his face, his love and devotion for Sylvia clearly evident. He adored her. Dottie remembered thinking that was the kind of man she wanted to marry, a kind man, a caring person, and was sorry she had spoken so harshly about him earlier, wanting to take it all back.

"I'm sorry, Sylvia," she said. "I'm so, so sorry. I shouldn't have said those things about Tucker. He's a good man. He loves you. He's always loved you."

Sylvia was thankful to her cousin for standing by her. However, she needed to rest, so she joined Rebecca in the guest room for a nap. While she slept, she dreamed she was walking up to a house that was painted white with green shutters and a green roof. Rose vines clambered up trellises alongside the house and a lawn grew with a white picket fence around it. Approaching the front door, it opened wide and, as she walked in, the house disappeared. She was in the sky among the clouds. It was a pink and golden sky with white clouds edged in golden light. She was made of sunlight as golden as the bright sky. When she awoke, it was morning. Someone had covered her with a blanket. She rose from the bed and went out to the kitchen where Dottie and Aunt Patty were talking to someone. It was Andrew. He was telling them about moving to Edenville. He had gotten a job teaching at the high school. All they needed to do was find a house.

Sylvia timidly stepped into the kitchen. "Do you really mean it, Andrew?" she asked.

He looked her way, then hugged her. "Yes, I really mean it," he said.

CHAPTER THIRTY-SEVEN

When Walter Henry was a young man, he walked to work at the blacksmith shop and livery stable. In the evening hours, he would walk home, up on the mountain where Berto and Lucy welcomed him and his sister to live. The elm trees that lined the road were growing tall enough to provide much-needed shade. One time, he saw an old woman sitting on her porch in a wicker rocking chair, shawl wrapped around her shoulders. She lived in the house on the corner, across from the post office. Her white hair was but a wild spray of loose, wiry strands blowing with each passing breeze. She beckoned him to come over, which he did. He opened the gate and walked up the dirt pathway to her porch.

"Have you seen my poor dog, Walter?" she asked him. "It's run off. Never come back since my boy went off to war and got himself killed."

"No, ma'am. I haven't seen him," Walter Henry replied.

The young man who had gone to war, the First World War, was named Isaac Chapman. His brother, Phineas, was prevented from going, because his father said he was needed to help run the orchards for the upcoming harvest. They grew several varieties of apples. The Chapman's also grew peaches, but apples were their specialty. Apple cider was plentiful, as was applesauce, apple pie, apple cobbler, and the fermented stuff out behind the fruit packer's shed. Even Walter Henry got a taste of that. He remembered the laughter as the jug of home-concocted brew was passed around. He had never been so sick in his life. His partner, Timothy Hart, would have none of it, the hard stuff or Walter Henry's nonsense, telling him to get to work anyway.

Jiminy Walker and his brother, Joseph, cousins to Phineas and Isaac, were in charge of the orchards back then, once their father, Jebediah, had died. They had buried their father off in a corner of the orchard, too lazy to make any sort of arrangements for a proper burial. No one knew about it, at least until plowing time came around. They had conveniently forgotten their rotten deed, "to treat their father in such an ill-begotten manner," one woman later commented. The tractor came around the corner, the disc blades plowing deep into the loamy earth. Being off in a dry part of the orchard, over by the berry thickets, the body had yet to decompose, but it had lain there long enough to ripen, giving off a horrible, noxious odor. The smell assailed the plowman as the disc blades tore at and twisted the then-unearthed form. It stalled the tractor's forward momentum, hanging up the plow, yet he kept on lurching ahead, dragging the wretched sight behind. Wondering what held him up, the driver stopped the tractor, hopped down and went back to see. He expected maybe a large tree root, since he drove too close to the alder trees. He spotted some blue cloth and something brown. They were Jebediah's denim jacket and his brown hair. The tractor driver, covering his nose and mouth with his bandanna, lest he gag and spew his lunch, got close enough to see it was a man he had exhumed.

Jiminy and Joseph "about hit the ceiling in God's house," someone later said. The young scalawags were so terrified about what had happened, they feared the sheriff would think they had done in their own father. They hid in the woods for a while, but their uncle went looking for them. He told them there was nothing to fear if they made it right and gave their father, Jebediah Walker, a founding citizen of Pine Valley, the burial such a prominent citizen deserved. After that, Jebediah's misbehaving sons went back to their enterprise behind the fruit packer's shed. Apple wine and hard-cider eventually led into the real hard stuff.

It was in that house on the corner, the Chapman's house, where Phineas and Isaac's sister, Eunice, yet lived. Walter Henry wondered why Eunice never left that forlorn house. Some said she was waiting on a beau, a young man she once loved, but whom Phineas had chased away. Phineas wound up marrying, but not poor Eunice.

Walter Henry always liked her, younger than he was, and very dainty, with tiny feet. He never got enough of looking at Eunice Chapman. She wore her long hair up, shining in a radiant, golden-brown, auburn hue. However, she would have none of him and spent her life waiting, quietly residing in that corner house, so quietly, people forgot about her.

She went to Patty's Beautique regularly to get her hair done, dyed and set for years. One day, Patty, in a sour mood on account of her daughter's unmarried and pregnant state, gave

Eunice a sharp dose of the truth. When the wounded old bird arrived home that day, she looked in the mirror and saw that she was no longer a young woman, no longer anything, except old.

With her lower lip a-quivering, Eunice beseeched her mirror, "Why'd you have to say something so mean to me, Patty McGrew?"

It was the summer of 1970, a new decade, and Walter Henry was alone. Johnny was away at college and Millie had died. Feeling lonely and useless, he tired of sitting in front of the barn and walked home. Every house he walked past had a story to tell, like the Chapman's old place. He had lived in Pine Way for so many years that the long memory of the past flowed in constant partnership with the present. Passing by Tucker's house, he remembered when the young man's father, Tucker Howard Stewart, was a boy. Walter Henry had stopped going to school once he became an orphan. Young Tucker Howard would wander over to the blacksmith shop and livery stable from the newspaper office whenever he was tired of being yelled at by his father. He would pester Walter Henry to make him something out of metal. One time, to get rid of him, then thirteen-year-old Walter Henry gave the younger boy a wheelbarrow, sending him on an errand, scrounging up all the scrap iron he could find. Walter Henry promised that not only would he make the boy something, he would give him a lucky, Indian head penny he had saved.

The boy searched every roadside ditch, every alleyway and old shed no one was minding. By late afternoon, he had that wheelbarrow so full of junk, heaped so high, it about fell over every bump or rock he hit with the front wheel. Timothy Hart suspected Walter Henry had played a trick on the boy, sending him on his own errand and giving him nothing for it. So, when the boy rounded the corner and parked the wheelbarrow, took off his cap to wipe his brow with a dusty swipe of his shirt sleeve, Timothy stood by. Walter Henry, looking sheepish out the corner of his eye, dug into his pocket for that penny, and slapped it into Tucker Howard's open and waiting, be-blistered palm. The younger boy let out a yelp of pain everyone in Pine Way could hear.

Hardly remorseful, Walter Henry had rather wished he never promised that penny. "Some lucky penny!" he complained. It was in his father's pocket the day Josiah Hart shot him dead. Begrudgingly, he set to work making a length of chain for the boy, who marveled at how that was at all possible.

On his walk homeward, Walter Henry returned to the present once he approached the end of the row of houses in Pine Way. His legs were about to give out when Harvey Six-Bits spotted him from his yard and hurried over to catch him before he dropped.

"Let me help you, Walter," Harvey said. Holding on to the old man, he added, "I was just about to head over to the hardware store. Can I give you a lift anywhere?"

"Well, tell you the truth," answered Walter Henry, "not many places left I need to go to anymore. Can't remember if I drove my truck to work or if I even drive it anymore! Maybe I better stop driving. Don't know how I'll get around, though."

"Why don't I take you over to the barn and we'll see if your truck's there. How's that sound?" asked Harvey.

"Sounds okay," replied the old man.

Without a fuss, he settled in the front seat of Harvey's gold Chevy Camaro. They drove off as the old man fell into his usual tired and befuddled look he had acquired since Millie passed away. At the blacksmith shop, he dug into his pockets for his car keys and opened the truck cab door, managing to climb in. He said, "There's so much I can remember, but so little of it left anymore, you know? Almost everybody I knew is gone. Kinda makes me wonder why I stick around."

"Maybe you have something important you still need to do," said Harvey.

Harvey moved his head in such a way that gave Walter Henry a start. The cowboy hat and the feather, the sight of him, reminded the old man of Jim Hart.

"Are you okay, Walter?" asked Harvey.

"I-I thought you looked like someone I used to know," the old man said.

He turned the key in the ignition, but nothing happened. "Well, now I know why I was walking down the road," he said. "I was walking home. This truck's been sitting here and won't start, since...don't know when."

Harvey gave Walter Henry a ride home, seeing the cabin, the mining shack, and retreat center for the first time. Enthralled, he asked, "Did you build all this, Walter?"

"Sort of," said Walter Henry. "That shack back over there," pointing to the old mining shack, "Berto Mendoza built that way back in the old, old days."

Harvey was amazed. "Berto? Really?" he asked.

They wandered around. Harvey was looking at everything, peeking in windows and examining the woodworking details on railings and doors. Walter Henry tried to keep up, but kept stopping to catch his breath.

"Yep," he said. "This is all Indian rancheria land."

He was getting tired and needed to take a nap, but merely set himself down on a round of wood near the old fire pit. "Berto made this fire pit, too," he said. "We used to sit around it and listen to him tell stories."

"Yeah, I heard he loved telling stories," said Harvey. "Never got to meet him, though." He paused for a moment, as though considering something, before asking Walter Henry, "Hey, do you know he was my grandfather's brother-in-law?"

"Your grandfather? Who was that?" asked Walter Henry.

"Dexter Shoseegan," answered Harvey. Harvey was a smiling man, but his smile grew even larger when he said that name.

Walter Henry was surprised and asked, "Dexter? You mean to tell me—well, how did he come to be your granddad?"

"His daughter was my mother, Cassandra Shoseegan," answered Harvey.

Walter Henry was quiet, letting the information settle in, wondering how that bit of news escaped his observant eyes and eavesdropping ears. "Cassandra Shoseegan. Hmm," he said, then quickly asked, "So, who was your papa, your-your dad?"

Harvey's mood changed and became somber as he said, "My dad? Oh. I don't like to talk about him. He didn't use to be a very nice man. He's done a lot of bad things."

Walter Henry, still struck with how much Harvey resembled Jim Hart, took some time recollecting all of Jefferson and Jimmy Hart's children, then ventured, "He wouldn't happen to have been Jackson Hart, would he?" He looked in fear at Harvey, lest it be true.

"Jackson Hart." Harvey nodded his head and said, "Yeah, that's my father. My mother never told anyone, except me, far as I know. She wasn't the purest woman in Laketon, mind you, but she was good to me. She asked me one day if I wanted to take his name or keep hers. I had heard all about Jackson Hart, making enemies out of anyone and everyone, except my mother. She said he loved her, treated her real nice. He took care of us." Harvey's arms were folded tightly in front of him, but he relaxed, realizing it was all right to tell.

"That Jackson was a mean s-o-b," said Walter Henry. "I'm glad you told me about him having loved somebody and treating them nice, cuz I honestly never knew he was capable of such feelings for other people."

Harvey added, "We call him 'Pappy Jack' now. Aurelia Mendoza told me, not that long ago, that he was the one who killed the men who hurt her. You know, back when the Big Bust happened? Did you ever hear about that?"

Walter Henry was shocked, not because of what Harvey said, but because Tommy McGrew had told him the very same thing once, not long after Jim Hart had died. Walter Henry had doubted the story.

The men Jackson Hart had killed were his moonshining partners, working the still together out in the woods when Aurelia stumbled upon them. The other two men began roughing her up, with Jackson yelling at them to stop. He never forgot what he had done to Jim Hart and regretted it, hating himself for it, wishing he could undo it somehow. He was drunk and easily knocked aside as the other two men took turns assaulting Aurelia. It was unbearable seeing another child get hurt because of him, so he shot the other men, killing them. The girl's loud cries could be heard as she ran off for home in a panicked state of terror.

Jackson staggered over to the bodies, knowing he would go to prison if he was caught, so he switched clothes with one of them, making sure his wallet was in their pocket before he stumbled into the woods. A few Laketon residents discovered Aurelia was taking him food and clothes, along with the only spare blankets they had. Once the winter got too cold, Harvey's mom brought him to live with her and Harvey. That was when she told her son that Jackson was his father, leaving the boy with a terrible sense of awe.

Aurelia believed she was the only one who knew the truth, that Jackson Hart had saved her life. But Jackson had confessed to Tommy McGrew. Shortly afterward, Jackson had a stroke and was no longer able to walk, and had difficulty speaking.

Walter Henry and Harvey continued to sit by the fire pit. The evening quieted and Harvey relaxed, his arms growing limp and his legs stretching out away from the round of wood he sat on. His words drifted on the wind as he told Walter Henry some more things he had told no one before, which did not surprise the old man. He was used to people coming to that place on the mountain and unburdening themselves. It was Lulabelle's spirit, he imagined, present in that quiet place on the mountain, maybe Lucy's, too, he thought. Although, whether it was grief or remembrance, Walter Henry sensed Jim Hart's presence in that moment as well.

Harvey needed to say one last thing, something that was on his mind ever since he came to live in Pine Way.

"You know," he began, "Lucy told me there's a curse on the Hart family." He grew sad and wistful, looking out over Pine Valley. "That's another reason why I didn't want to take that name." He perked up in hopefulness, asking Walter Henry, "Do you think I did the right thing, Walter? Maybe I ought to have taken my father's name. I'd be Harvey Hart, though. Sounds kinda funny. I've always liked thinking of myself as Harvard Shoseegan."

Walter Henry was aggrieved at the remarkable resemblance between Harvey and Jim Hart. They were first cousins. His eyes closed and he wished he would never have to open them again, remembering the sage bundle Lucy had given him. Lulabelle's spirit haunted his every step.

"Walter, you need to do this one thing," her spirit would say. "Walter."

"I'm sorry, Son, but I'm real tired. I need to go lay down." Walter Henry got up, but reassured Harvey, "You can stay if you want. Walk around the place. Come back anytime. You'll be welcome here. This all belongs to your people, anyway."

The old man went inside his cabin to lay down and sleep, or try to. His sorrow ran too deep for peace, though. His end was coming too soon to put off any longer what Lucy had asked him to do, to help clear the curse placed on the Hart family long ago. He thought he would rather die than have to clear some curse, dance around in the middle of the road, waving a moldy old sage bundle.

"People'd lock me up if they saw me doin' that!" he said aloud.

Too tired to worry anymore, he slept instead, saying as he drifted off, "It's all just a story, anyhow. Every bit of it, just a story." His eyes closed as he settled into his thoughts, the words streaming through his consciousness. "One more day, Lord," he said. "Just let me live one more day."

CHAPTER THIRTY-EIGHT

Sylvia was stunned when Andrew parked at her childhood home, the house on Fig Tree Lane that no one would buy. He was so excited, he practically leapt from the car, while Sylvia merely got out and stood on the walkway.

"Come on, Syl! Let's look inside!" he said. He waited by the front door holding Rebecca in his arms.

Sylvia was in a daze, not wanting to look at the house, and was annoyed with Andrew. He was so insistent, though, she had to listen to him. Turning to look over her shoulder, she saw him by the door. In that moment, she realized that was the one thing she had stubbornly refused to do back in '46, when Aunt Justice took her away. Her father had said, "Goodbye, my wee girl," but nine-year-old Sylvia ignored him, telling herself, "I'm not sad and I'm not sorry."

If she had looked over her shoulder that day, she would have seen her father's desperate cry for help written on the lines of his pale and beard-stubbled face. She would have seen him hanging on to the door jamb as though to hold himself up, before turning to go back into the house.

Sylvia was sad her mother had died and that her father could not take care of her. She was very sorry for their tragic fate in life. Her pretending to not care, may have helped her to cope as a child, but it failed to stave off the grief she felt ever since that day.

Trying not to show how bereft she was in that moment, Sylvia expressed it when she fully turned and said through her tears, "Andrew! I used to live here!"

· · ·

The unloved and unwanted little house was a bungalow, painted white, with a few, nondescript shrubs alongside and a fading lawn. The reason everyone gave for not wanting to buy it, was that it was too small. Robert Cadwallader knew the main reason no one wanted it, so gave up and took it off the market. He asked Howard and Mary Stewart to look after the place. They promised they would as Robert handed them the keys. They aired it out and watered the yard when needed. But, as the years went by, they could only hope it would sell. After Robert Cadwallader's death, they assumed the banks would take it over, take it off their hands, which is what Howard wanted.

His wife argued, "Dear! You know that house is special."

"Special?" Howard was impatient. "What's so special about an old house nobody wants to buy?" he asked. "Personally, if you ask me, I think it's haunted. Place gives me the spooks."

"Oh, *Howard!* It just needs a little love, that's all."

Howard noted his wife was taking a tone with him. What happened to his complacent, demure, and sweet little wife? He knew. It was her friend, Rosa Smith, putting ideas in her head about getting a full-time job and making a contribution. She was already making a contribution, taking care of her husband. That's what he thought. Deep down he was pleased, though he would never admit it. If she was happy, then he was happy, and that was that.

Robert Cadwallader. Now there was an un-happy man, Howard thought. Taking out a small loan and buying the house themselves, Howard and Mary often reminisced about the man whose wife left behind a wake of ruined lives, hers included. They agreed to sell the house to the first taker, no matter what. When Andrew approached them, they accepted his offer. Mary was pleased and Howard was relieved for a few days.

"You know what, Mary?" He asked her this at the dinner table, where they were eating pork chops and applesauce, green beans, and apple pie for dessert. She looked up, chewing her food like an impatient doe, waiting for him to continue. He asked, "What are we going to tell Tucker? He's going to find out sooner or later." Grinning wide, he said, "His old flame's back in town!" He let out a guffaw.

"Oh, Howard!" she said again. "*Really!*"

He looked at her and asked, "Must you keep speaking to me that way? I'm only bringing it up, because, well, I think there's a few women in town chasing after him already." He chewed and sucked on a tough and fatty piece of pork, then pulled the grizzled chunk out of his mouth to set on his plate.

Mary sat across from him, horrified at the man, baffled she was actually married to him. She wanted to know what happened to the dapper young man with whom she had fallen in love? He looked old enough to be her father. However, she had seen the lines in the mirror, herself, the gray hairs she had Patty carefully conceal, and the sagging, flabby skin daring to appear on her upper arms.

Howard saw her looking disturbed, maybe indigestion, he thought, but had to ask, "Dear, are you listening to me?"

The issue was revived one night when they had invited Tucker over for dinner. They tried to keep secret that none other than Sylvia She's-Got-Your-Number-Tucker was moving in next door. Every time he went by a window, they pulled the shade down and made some excuse. When he decided to go home, Howard offered to drive him. Wanting to go out back, Mary said they had fertilized the lawn.

Tucker suspected something was going on, but was too tired from work to bother. No one had told him Sylvia was back in town. Absorbed in his own misery, regarding Aurelia, he had missed that bit of gossip.

Attempting to move on, he looked up Eileen over at the bakery, hoping she was still available, which she was. He asked her out on a date and they stopped by Howard and Mary's afterward for dessert. Tucker wore his only suit, minus the jacket, and Eileen was wearing a blue dress that showed off her figure. The evening wound down, so they collected their things, his suit jacket, her black clutch purse and, with the porch light illuminating their way, proceeded to leave.

Tucker opened the car door for Eileen, when a familiar voice shouted, "Tucker!"

Tucker looked around as Freckles ran to the neighbor's yard, barking and whining in excitement. At Sylvia's parents' old house, he saw a man pick up a little girl so Freckles wouldn't knock her down. A woman was standing beside the man, waving and jumping up and down. She was smiling and shouting his name. "Tucker! It's me! *Sylvia!*"

CHAPTER THIRTY-NINE

It was dark outside, so Tucker offered to walk Candelaria home after the historical society meeting, where it was decided they would write a book together on the history of Pine Valley. He was hoping to see Aurelia, but Candelaria told him she was at school. Millie, from the diner, she said, left Aurelia enough money to go to college to learn to be an artist.

"I'm so proud of my cousin," she said. "But I-I feel bad, Tucker. I know you loved her."

They sat together on her porch steps for a few minutes before she said, "You know, I don't think I ever told anyone what happened to Jim...when he was a little boy." She was unsure whether to share the awful story with the man sitting beside her, but she had held on to its memory for too long and needed to tell it to someone. Tucker's calm voice reassured her.

"What happened?" he asked. "I've often wondered."

In the dark places of Candelaria's soul, there surfaced that day, so many years past it made her heart ache with remembrance. Tucker sat patiently and listened as she peered through the lens at a scene which took place in 1938. When she was finished, they sat in silence.

Tucker was horrified by what he had heard, as well as deeply affected. He hugged Candelaria, thanking her for sharing the memory with her. They each said good night. Candelaria went into her little house and Tucker walked to his own home in Pine Way.

Arriving at home, he sat on the couch to write what was on his mind. Hearing what had happened to Jim as a boy, reminded Tucker that the people of Laketon thought of Jim as a holy man, which he wanted to understand.

He wrote, "To say that a man is holy, is to set him apart as sacred, someone to be revered, a hallowed being. When I think of Jim Hart now, I am given a glimpse into this place, a sense of place that is Pine Valley. I see it as it once was, ages ago, the native people peacefully tending to their life on the valley floor amongst the oak and the pine, the fir and the maple. It was a wild land, a natural place, a vision that is holy. If I am the Keeper of the Dream, then Jim was the Dream, Itself, that vision of peace. His wounding was an initiation into the sacredness of his task, to hold the wild within his heart, to carry the dream of the wilderness once here and the possibility of its return upon this wounded landscape, this hallowed ground.

"Jim Hart was no saint, but he was wise. As a friend once told me, Jim walked between the worlds, never truly a part of either. He didn't leave for college, because all he ever wanted was to be a part of *this* world, here in Pine Valley, to be welcomed here, to belong. That was the essence of the dream dwelling within his soul, its longing and waiting to be welcomed in this valley. I have, with great pain, learned of my mistake. By rejecting Jim, I rejected the dream. In rejecting the dream, I fought against myself, my own task to protect and to honor something sacred.

"I have often felt that Jim and I were more like brothers. Now, I know that to be true. In the Dream, in this valley of dreams, he was and still is, my brother. I will miss him always, and yet, I know in my heart that he never died. He simply went home."

Tucker continued to sit in the quiet of his house. Freckles was snoozing on her blanket in the kitchen. The hours grew late. Thoughts and ideas of the day faded into the coming moonlight, when other thoughts returned and found little resistance. He thought of his time with Aurelia, their friendship, their conflict, his surrender, and her departure. It still hurt. He needed to move on, though. He yearned to share his home with another, his life with someone who wanted to stay. Wondering about Eileen, he was yet unsure. Hopeless, things seemed, believing his life's journey had become nothing more than a confused struggle. Yet, he had something new to uncover.

Looking over the edge of the couch, he thought he should at least straighten up the pile of papers he had gotten in the habit of simply flinging in that direction. Climbing over the arm of the couch, all he did was slip and nearly fall over. He tried to stack the newspapers, growing frustrated and disgusted with the mess, when he spotted a crumpled envelope. It was Sylvia's farewell note. He picked it up and climbed back over the couch to sit and read it. Giving a deep sigh as though to bolster his courage, he smoothed the paper and began to read.

"Dear Tucker: I need to tell you something. I'm pregnant. It's Jim's baby. You might as well know. You'll find out soon enough. I just wanted you to be the first to know, except I told your sister-in-law, Mary. I hope you'll understand why I have to leave town. I recently met a man, Andrew Parker, who loves me and we plan to marry right away. We're giving the baby his name. I found a place to work, so I will stay busy. Please, be happy for me, and forgive me. Never forget that I love you. I have always loved you. I was not able to show it. I pray that, if we see each other again, we will meet as friends. Your sister-in-law advised me to accept my Aunt Patty's offer to help me leave town and to marry Andrew. He's a very good person. I know you would like him. Sincerely, your friend, Sylvia."

That was it. Stunned, he merely sat, one palm to the side of his face, mouth slightly agape, staring. However, something within himself began to brew. Before he could discern what it was, out it came. Without giving it a thought, he pulled the sofa away from the wall. Grabbing an armload of papers, he carried it out the back door and dumped it by the incinerator. He returned inside the house and gathered more of it. Several more trips were made before he cleared away the pile. After building a fire, he fed the paper into the flames, regardless of any bills or other important items.

Tucker had never gotten drunk, but he knew why people did, to render unconscious what was known, to obliterate all knowledge and feeling of something they did not want to know or to feel. It gave them the courage of fools to do that which anyone would be called a fool for doing. Men may cry and sing when drunk and women may lose their fear of speaking their minds, but Tucker's anger was enough to destroy that which needed to end. His feelings regarding the women in his life, his pain, his hanging on, were holding him back. Sylvia's shocking revelation—what he could only call a betrayal—had freed him. It liberated him.

Grown, as a man, he was, yet in his heart, he remained that boy who had lost his mother too soon and felt to blame. No more would he blame himself. No more would he carry the guilt he had no reason to carry. No more would he fear the dark.

Flames flew out the grate of the crumbling incinerator and upwardly swirled and danced among the fleeing sparks of red-hot lights. Stoking the fire, Tucker became a free man, a man who could go and do whatever he pleased, to create, to dream, to live, and love anew.

Having seen him by the fire, Harvey came over and stood beside him, talking low. Bear and Barclay soon joined them. They stood and watched as Tucker fed the fire, no questions asked. The feelings Tucker had, the guilt and rage, the anger, the sadness, disgust, and shame, all of it drifted up to the stars, leaving him very thankful, for friends, for community, for truth. Letting go was painful and uncomfortable, but he was thankful. For Sylvia's letter, he was thankful most of all, because it opened his eyes and changed him. Only a few years ago, what seemed like a generation past, he would not have stood by a fire with the young men of Laketon, burning paper and looking up at the stars.

EPILOGUE

Standing alone before the barn, Candelaria Hart recalled a day that encapsulated for her the peacefulness of Pine Way. Warm and dry, she recalled, it had heralded the need for rain. Lowering in the west, the culprit sun that had abetted that year of drought, was slowly settling behind the mountain ridge. Long, slanting rays of light angled onto faces and squinting eyes. Buzzing flies circled in the late afternoon dusty haze. Horses' brushy tails swiftly flicked them away. Candelaria savored the memory.

The Edenville Historical Society was meeting in Pine Way to present their case to state representatives arriving later that morning. Tucker walked from his house with Freckles. After greeting Candelaria, he began setting up a visual display of archival photographs and family pictures. Some were found stored in the newspaper office, others were collected from the community. Johnny drove up in his truck with his mother, Katie Winters. The town's veterinarian, Joseph Cadwallader, brought a booklet on the history of Pine Way. Compiled by the historical society, it not only chronicled its history but contained memories collected in interviews with local residents. Soon, other members arrived. Rosa brought her children with her, Betsy, Bobby, and her newest, Buster Jr. She was leading the presentation.

The historical society planned to save Pine Way and restore it to its heyday in the late 19th century. Their first order of business was to have the town designated a historical landmark. The grander vision, however, was to create a living history park, providing educational opportunities for school children and a peaceful byway for tourists to explore.

Change had come to Pine Way. Several of its historic homes were added to the Pine Valley Rancheria as housing for local tribe members. A clinic was under construction, as well as a tribal office. Discussion over the plight of the valley's native population convinced the historical society to play their part and officially recognize the Pine Valley Massacre of 1855. Two commemorative plaques, mounted on stone historical markers were installed, one in Pine Way, the other in Laketon. They would stand as silent witnesses, which neither time nor obscurity could ever diminish or render unseen. The story of native people decimated throughout the state was finally being told. The Pine Valley Massacre was but one among many tragedies in the state's overall history.

At the Pine Way picnic grounds, the story emerged from the shadows as the first historical marker was unveiled. No longer could the valley's deep dark past be denied. However, like the Pine Valley natives returning from exile, the marker, and the truth it conveyed, stood at the forest's edge awaiting acceptance.

Amidst ceremony conducted by Harvey Six-Bits, the people who lost their lives in the massacre, and the one man who strived to aid them to safety, were finally acknowledged. Everyone in attendance gathered in a circle, joining hands. Standing side by side, Aurelia looked at Tucker and smiled, then bowed her head. Taking her hand in his, Tucker bowed his head and smiled, too. Harvey stood within the circle and called upon the spirit of healing, praying blessings onto the land. A wind came up through the trees, softly, gently sighing and he said:

"There is a dream that longs to live in this valley. It yearns to bring peace and bless all people with its gift of community and connection to the land and its history. It offers the wild heart freedom to soar. It offers acceptance to all those who live in fear and persecution. The dream is a promise of healing and renewal. It was Lucy Shoseegan's dream, but now it is ours."

When Harvey finished speaking, everyone stood in place for a moment of silence. The sun's rays filtered down through the shadows as the memory of a time long gone, an age and all its changes, came to rest in that special place. Some were in tears, others rejoicing in their hearts, knowing that the people of Laketon, whose ancestors had once fled the valley for their lives, were being welcomed home to Pine Valley.

After the ceremony, Candelaria walked home, eager to write about that beautiful experience. Mostly, she wished to honor the Grandmothers. To the north, she directed her gaze, standing in what was once an alleyway. Unused by cars, the dirt road had become overgrown. Like all things returning to their origins, it was becoming reclaimed by the fields and the woodlands. She likened it to the old ways, lived close to the source, without which people would lose touch with their beginnings and have no way to find them again. That was the vision and dream which Candelaria held, a pathway to the ancestors, connection to the old ways yet living and breathing in her heart and in the quiet places of Pine Valley.

Once inside her little shack in Villa Borracho, she took her notebook and pen and sat outside on her porch steps.

She wrote, "All things come in circles, our lives and our very reason for being. At the ceremony today, I saw the completion of one circle with the honoring of my ancestors, and I saw the beginning of another, seeing Aurelia and Tucker smile. Aurelia's life as an artist has begun to flower with her first woodcarving. We are all very thankful to Johnny for inviting her to use Walter Henry's old woodworking shop and for offering to teach her how to work the wood."

Candelaria set her notebook aside and gazed at the trees in their shady woodland. She saw cars leaving the picnic grounds where the ceremony was held. Startled by the disturbance, a coyote dashed across the dirt road and ran past her house on stilts. Surprised, she thrilled in joy at the sight and said, "Yes, Coyote, I will not forget you. I will tell your story, too, because I am a Storyteller."

That night, when she sat on her porch, she said goodnight to her grandparents, her parents, her sister, her husband, and her son. She thought of her two baby boys that she had lost, and whispered, "We'll meet again." She also thought of Johnny, her grandson, and included him in her conversation with the heavens.

"Watch over Johnny," she asked, "He's yet young and I worry about him. He's so angry."

She was alluding to the curse she suspected was placed on her family. Although, she recalled something Tucker had said when the historical society had gathered in Pine Way. They were waiting for the state representatives to arrive. Eunice Chapman shared concerns she had about the town's history involving Josiah Hart and Henry Henry.

Patting her pink-tinted white hair, she asked, "Should we even mention it?"

Tucker said, "We don't need to worry about that anymore. Walter Henry took care of it."

Candelaria felt reassured. Healing had at last come to Pine Valley. She was thankful and knew that Lucy's dream, like all dreams borne of the heart and nurtured in the soul, had finally come home to stay.

THE END

ACKNOWLEDGEMENTS

I would like to thank my family and friends for their support of my writing career and, most especially, my recent odyssey into fiction. I would like to thank my husband, Dan Ardoin, for his assistance in reading and discussing my books-in-progress. He created my website and maintains it beautifully. Thank you!

I am also thankful for the generous time given me in interviewing blacksmiths and museum volunteers at La Purisima Mission State Historic Park, Mariposa Museum & History Center, Columbia State Historic Park, Marshall Gold Discovery State Historic Park, and the Empire Mine State Historic Park. Their time and insights into California's history is an invaluable resource. I urge everyone to visit their state parks and local museums.

I would also like to acknowledge and show my gratitude to the local independent bookshops and businesses on the Central Coast of California that have welcomed me and my books, Chapter 2 in Lompoc, The Book Loft in Solvang, Chaucer's Books in Santa Barbara, Gavin's in Santa Maria, and the Dana Adobe & Cultural Center in Nipomo.

My gratitude also goes to the Santa Maria Valley Genealogical Society and the Santa Maria Family Search Center for inviting me to share my Pine Valley series with them.

Many thanks to three, terrific, local journalists, Caleb Wiseblood from the Santa Maria Sun newspaper, Brian Reynolds with KCBX Central Coast Public Radio, and Juliann Hemphill from the Orcutt Pioneer newspaper for their time interviewing me and for doing such a great job.

I am also thankful for my local libraries for letting me spend hours and hours writing in an out-of-the-way corner of the library and for carrying my books over the years. You have been very kind to me.

I also appreciate all those who gave of their time to read excerpts from my manuscripts for feedback and reviewing. It is so appreciated!

Thank you, to my fellow authors for providing me with an online community of writers. Let's keep supporting one another! I am truly indebted to the online support I received from, not just other authors, but all the many resources I found invaluable for research, marketing, and promotional efforts. This cannot be overstated that, during the covid-19 pandemic, everything was online. I am truly grateful we have had that to rely upon as well.

Also, last but not least, my appreciation is extended to the good folks at Black Rose Writing, Reagan Rothe and his awesome staff. Thank you, everyone!

Sincerely,
Corrine Ardoin

ABOUT THE AUTHOR

Corrine Ardoin lives with her husband on the Central Coast of California where she pursues many interests, such as hiking, nature study, and gardening. A deep love and understanding of the natural world is evident in all her writing, drawing readers into the worlds she creates. Having lived and worked in isolated mountain regions and rural areas throughout California, she brings firsthand knowledge of small town people and history. Her life experiences and a background in trailwork, firefighting, genealogy, and shamanism, lend a unique sense of realism to her *Pine Valley* series.

In addition to awards for poetry, in 2022, Corrine received a Literary Titan Silver Book Award for her novel, *A Place Called The Way*.

Check out where the story began!

"If you love a good story written with loving detail, *Fathers of Edenville* is for you."
–Matthew J. Pallamary, author of *Land Without Evil*

FATHERS

OF

EDENVILLE

CORRINE ARDOIN

NOTE FROM CORRINE ARDOIN

Word-of-mouth is crucial for any author to succeed. If you enjoyed *Dreamer on the Mountain*, please leave a review online—anywhere you are able. Even if it's just a sentence or two. It would make all the difference and would be very much appreciated.

Thanks!
Corrine Ardoin

We hope you enjoyed reading this title from:

Subscribe to our mailing list – *The Rosevine* – and receive
FREE books, daily deals, and stay current with news about
upcoming releases and our hottest authors.
Scan the QR code below to sign up.

Already a subscriber? Please accept a sincere thank you for
being a fan of Black Rose Writing authors.

View other Black Rose Writing titles at
www.blackrosewriting.com/books and use promo
code
PRINT to receive a **20% discount** when purchasing.